SLIPKNOT

INSIDE • THE • SICKNESS
BEHIND • THE • MASKS

JASON ARNOPP

EBURY
PRESS

First published in UK in 2001

Copyright © Jason Arnopp 2001

1 3 5 7 9 10 8 6 4 2

First published in UK in 2001 by
Ebury Press
Random House, 20 Vauxhall Bridge Road, London SW1V 2SA

Random House Australia Pty Limited
20 Alfred Street, Milsons Point, Sydney, New South Wales 2061, Australia

Random House New Zealand Limited
18 Poland Road, Glenfield, Auckland 10, New Zealand

Random House South Africa (Pty) Limited
Endulini, 5A Jubilee Road, Parktown 2193, South Africa

Random House UK Limited Reg. No. 954009

A CIP catalogue record for this book is available from the British Library

ISBN 0 09 1879337

Designed by seagulls

Jacket Photographs © Paul Harries and Lisa Johnson

Printed and bound in Great Britain by Biddles

Papers used by Ebury Press are natural, recyclable products
made from wood grown in sustainable forests.

Contents

vii   Acknowledgements

ix   Preface

xi   Introduction by Ozzy Osbourne

1   0 – Zeroes to heroes

17   1 – Breeding ground

39   2 – Surfacing

69   3 – Resurrection

101   4 – How to make a monster

125   5 – Summer of hate

157   6 – The firing line

191   7 – Tattooed and torn

213   8 – Future war

239   Afterword by Gene Simmons

Acknowledgments

This one goes out to ...

Slipknot (most notably Joey Jordison, who required aspirin after one bout of hyperactive recollections).

Kiss's Gene Simmons (one of the biggest rock stars ever, yet a delight to deal with ... smaller bands take note).

Ozzy and Sharon Osbourne and their amiable assistant Michael Guarracino.

Jack Osbourne.

Ross Robinson (a ridiculously cool gentleman who spoke on his cellphone until it started melting in his hand).

Todd McFarlane; SR Studios' Mike Lawyer and Sean McMahon; Trent Reznor; Rob Zombie; Amen's Casey Chaos; Nadja Peulen; Kittie's Morgan Lander; Robb Flynn of Machine Head; Kas Mercer and Lisa McNamee at Mercenary PR; Michelle Kerr, Monte Conner, Maria Gonzales and Mark 'Eternal Devastation' Palmer at Roadrunner; Steve Browning at Excess Press; Emma Lyne and Mary-Anne Hobbs at the Radio 1 Rock Show; Phil Alexander, Paul Rees, Caroline Fish, Paul Brannigan, Ben Myers, Josh Sindell, Mörat, Birgit Martinussen, Lisa Johnson and everyone at *Kerrang!*; Ross 'Make It Ring' Halfin and William Nash at Genesis; Paul 'Slider' Harries; Dante Banutto and John Robb; Ill Literature; Altrockworld.com; Loud & Heavy; IGN For Men; MTV.

Ray Zell, for Jack Daniels and ideas, always simultaneously.

My fine editor Natalie Jerome and everyone at Ebury Press.

Ma, Pa, Uncle John, Uncle George and all the family.

I wish I could break with authorly tradition and label my girl-friend a viciously unsupportive hellspawn, but that's sadly not possible. Dijana Capan, prepare the thimbles.

Preface

Fittingly, it was Halloween in 1998 when I first laid ears on Slipknot.

It was always fun, visiting the Manhattan offices of Roadrunner Records. Their A&R guv'nor Monte Conner would always take some pleasure in playing me the latest – and allegedly greatest – signings to the label. This afternoon, Conner had a particularly confident gleam in his eye as he played me rough cuts from a new work-in-progress album by a little known Des Moines act.

The first Slipknot song I heard was 'Spit It Out' – all crazed raps and massive guitar riffs which squealed like pigs, *Deliverance*-style. Next came the truly warped marriage of thumping techno and raging metal that was 'Surfacing'. I was hooked, and not even the subsequent blast of Amen's new demo recordings could outshine the memory. Then Monte showed me a picture of Slipknot.

Oh.

My.

God.

These people looked like characters from the finest slasher movie there never was. And they actually had the music to back it up. Could this be – whisper it – the perfect band? Indeed it could. In ten years of working at *Kerrang!*, the UK's weekly rock Bible, I had rarely been so heavily bowled over by a new outfit.

Today, when I tell people that Slipknot are my favourite band, they tend to look at me as if I had said, 'I derive intense enjoyment from dancing on hot coals.' While Slipknot are loved by a few million people worldwide, they have at least as many detractors. These people take great pleasure in sneering at the band, writing them off as a mere gimmicky flash in the pan. My stock response is that, even if Slipknot turn out to be one or two-album wonders, being an incendiary band of the moment never did the Sex Pistols any harm. This is the brightest, fiercest flash in the pan you could ever hope for.

Slipknot are all about today, and they are a thousand times more exciting right here, right now, than any number of generation-spanning rock behemoths who stumble onwards, despite having cut their best material decades back. Even if the individual members of 'Knot lose the plot or end up plugging solo projects which suck the big one, they can always tell the grandchildren that they shook the world with a mighty band who made countless draws drop.

This book is not only about cataloguing Slipknot's rise to fame, but tugging back those masks and taking a look at the people behind them. For nine grown men who jump around stages for a living, the 'Knot men are remarkably complex characters and I've tried to capture that, while examining the slings and arrows which have been thrown in their general direction.

In January 2001, I experienced first-hand how far the band's sickness had spread. Leaving Japan's Narita Airport, I dropped some pocket items in a tray which went through the X-Ray machine. On the other side, a female security officer spied my Slipknot key-ring and eagerly exclaimed: 'Ah, Slipknot! I love them!'

This band clearly have friends in high places. Here's to them making many more with their second album. Dust, I think it's fair to say, will be eaten.

Jason Arnopp
London
January 2001

Introduction by Ozzy Osbourne

On January 20th 1982, I bit the head off a bat onstage in Des Moines, Iowa. At the time I was pissed out of my mind. I don't drink any more, and if you think I'd put a fucking creature in my mouth today, you'd be crazy. When you're drunk you think you can do anything.

These days I don't go to many rock 'n' roll gigs as everyone seems to be smoking weed and getting stoned which is not my scene. But when I do go you'll probably find me hiding in the corner like a lemon, while everyone's expecting me to leap onstage and do something outrageous like rip the singer's head off!

It seems that the situation with the bat and me caught Slipknot's attention when they were kids. It probably made them go, 'I want to be in a band and I want to be crazier than *that* fucker!'

I know the feeling. When I was about 14, this mad Texan called PJ Proby really inspired me. He was banned from playing a load of halls in the UK. Back then, everyone in bands were fucking idiots in suits, with short hair, playing guitars up by their chins and all doing the same thing. But then along came PJ Proby. At one gig his arse accidentally came out

of his trousers and his bollocks flopped out onto the audience.
I thought, 'Fucking A!' I loved it, because PJ had the balls to
carry on after such an embarrassment. He *had* to be a good
frontman!

I first heard rumblings about Slipknot when they played on
the Ozzfest in the summer of 1999. My wife and manager
Sharon and the kids kept telling me about this really cool band
on the Second Stage. Sharon's very tuned in to everything
that's going on – I've got the *easy* job, to be honest with you. I
just go down to the venue, get onstage, do a gig and go home.
I listen to my son Jack too, because he wakes up every day and
plays new music that makes me afraid the house is gonna cave
in. That summer, he really got off on Slipknot and said they
were really cool.

The exciting thing about the Ozzfest is that there's always a
rumble about who's happening that year. Before you even
hear the word, you get the feeling from the crowd. In 1999,
that band was Slipknot. I'm really happy that the Ozzfest
helped break them. It proves that the idea Sharon and I had
years ago wasn't all that wrong. When we first put the Ozzfest
on in 1996, no-one was playing our music anymore. We
thought, 'Fuck you – we'll show you there's an audience!'

We started off small, doing a few of them to see how it
went. I don't know anything about promotion, but I knew
we'd either have a giant turd on our hands or a fucking great
Woodwork. We booked four shows and it grew from there, by
word of mouth.

On the surface, Slipknot deal in shock value, but I'm not
about to put them down for that. They've got a really good
visual approach to what they're doing, and their interviews are
out there. A band like this comes along once in every generation. In the Seventies it was The Sex Pistols, whilst — like it or
not — in the Eighties everybody wanted to look like Bon Jovi.
Someone has to stand out from the pack and Slipknot have got
that edge over other bands. Maybe I've been around too long,
or I'm showing my age, but to me a lot of newer bands sound
very samey. It's all growly, 'You will die tomorrow!' stuff.

The band's masks are great. It's like when Gene Simmons had all that make-up on. People used to wonder what he'd look like without it. It creates a mystique. Slipknot can go off stage, get dressed in normal clothes and stand in the audience. People wouldn't know it was one of the band. It's like Adam West and Batman!

The fact that a success story like Slipknot are a by-product of the Ozzfest makes me so proud. They're a great inspiration and they've put a bit of fucking jelly-juice back into the business. They've now gone on and done their own thing, which is tremendous.

It's all proof that when I handed the torch over to them, it wasn't such a bad idea. And in future, Slipknot will hand the torch over yet again. Long may they live!

Ozzy Osbourne
October 2000

P.S. I wonder where that bat is now? Maybe he's sitting in Bat Heaven somewhere, with his own bat roadies...

0
Zeroes to heroes

You come into this world a zero, and you leave a zero.
Shawn Crahan, #6

DOMINATION

'Jump the fuck up!'

The adrenaline rush could have powered Disneyland for a year. Most of the 40,000 people in this field had spent the last 30 seconds crouching down, at the request of a masked humanoid figure on the huge stage before them. This was the calmer mid-section of a gargantuan song named 'Surfacing' which brutally mashed metal and techno together. Now, as the dreadlock-faced frontman roared this order, we leapt to our feet as the song's chorus slammed back in.

'Fuck it all, fuck this world, fuck everything that you stand for!' raged the singer, and you'd swear the sky was about to crack and rain down in shards.

The video screens on either side of the stage made the nine angry men in this band appear all the more larger-than-life. All wearing individually customised masks, and numbers from zero to eight, they presented a formidable array of characters. Among their number were an evil clown, a demonic pig and a towering six-foot-plus behemoth who banged his head like he was attempting to crack the stage with his skull.

When Slipknot were onstage, the air was thick with noise, blood, sweat, urine and weighty metallic objects. This evening, they stormed through a 40-minute jackhammer set, leaving a whole ocean of new converts bruised and agog.

This was August 2000, and Slipknot had not merely taken over England's Reading Festival. They were sinking their teeth into the world.

Rock 'n' roll was perennially expected to churn out freaks, extroverts and characters who were dangerous to know. Yet we had never seen anything like this.

SIGNS OF SICKNESS

After the summer 1999 release of their self-titled debut album, Slipknot proceeded to stomp all over the world, beating the living shit out of themselves and each other.

Incredibly, for an album on an independent record label, *Slipknot* would sell over two million copies worldwide, fashioning a bright new prong on the crown of the fledgling nu-metal genre. The album hit platinum status in America, sailing way over the million mark. It also struck gold in various territories, including Australia, Canada and the UK.

Given the fact that Slipknot were nine boiler-suited characters from Des Moines, Iowa, who wouldn't understand the word 'compromise' if it stomped up to them and pummelled their masks with both fists, this was the unthinkable.

As their success dawned, drummer Joey Jordison told me: 'We never even expected to sell 30,000 copies, let alone this. Maybe the world needs us, in a weird way. We filled a void and we're glad to be that band. We were just doing something we felt was normal – even if it may be sick and completely disgusting to other people.'

In the year 2000, Slipknot's website www.slipknot1.com (one of the two which they themselves ran) received well over 10 million hits. Fan sites sprung up so quickly, it was difficult to keep track of them. When the band finally approved a range of Slipknot boiler suits for commercial sale, they were eagerly snapped up at $120 a pop. For the first time in years, this was a convincing band who you didn't just have to love – you could *become* them. Fans made their own versions of the band's masks and turned up to shows in full 'Knot regalia.

People had been crying out for Slipknot – even if some of them didn't realise it. By the late '90s, even punk had lost its ability to shock. It was now an acceptable commodity. Sanitised pop-punk bands like Blink 182 rotated on MTV like a shop window kebab skewer. The Sex Pistols had re-formed for a swift cash injection, caused a minor stir in worldwide terms, then shelved their great swindle once again. Even The Prodigy, who had digitally reinvented punk, had reached the end of a mammoth world tour and launched an indefinite hiatus, in order to catch up on the latest instalments of *Tomb Raider*.

Slipknot, then, were truly the new punk – a vital shot in the arm for this worryingly comfortable status quo. Even better, in musical terms they were the best thing to hit the world in some time.

They were the ultimate nu-metal band.

Why? Let's start with a definition of nu-metal itself. To understand this genre, you have to understand how it was born – and thus, how 'old' metal was buried.

By the time the '90s kicked off, the likes of Mudhoney, Soundgarden and Nirvana had already started to exert a stranglehold on America's generation X.

A new age of guitar music, which had yet to even be labelled grunge, was easing its way under the spotlight.

While grunge popularised rock once again, it did little to help extreme metal's ailing cause. Hard-edged metal bands were facing a long, cold winter, which many of them would not survive. Not that most of these acts had produced anything incredible for some time. Fans of hard music might not have admitted it at the time, but the genre had yet to better Slayer's barnstorming *Reign In Blood* album or Metallica's viciously progressive *Master Of Puppets*, which had both been released back in 1986.

The even more subterranean death metal movement – a musical genre founded on mega-fast snare hits, gory lyrics and evil gurgles – had also become complacent and was already starting to repeat itself. Another year brought another Cannibal Corpse album, with yet another list of ways to slaughter the innocent. All perfectly good fun in its own right, but where was the next real buzz going to come from?

In many ways, grunge provided all these bands with a richly deserved kick in the guts.

Texan cowboys Pantera were doing a sterling job of keeping ugly music alive. Sadly, their landmark 1992 album *A Vulgar Display Of Power* had to compete with the sleeper success of Nirvana's 'Smells Like Teen Spirit' single. It was a thankless task. Mainstream press, TV and radio couldn't care less about the likes of metal crusaders like Pantera or Anthrax. Of far more interest to them was getting the scoop on Nirvana frontman Kurt Cobain's February marriage to Hole's Courtney Love.

Nirvana undeniably delivered their own breed of catharsis, even if was generally self-pitying as opposed to self-empowering. They also dragged a whole new audience into the rock arena. A fair proportion of these new grunge fans weren't dyed-in-the-wool rock fans – they were kids who identified with this loose movement's sentiments, or lack of them.

Slackers didn't especially want to have a good time if they didn't have to, and the likes of Nirvana and Mudhoney basically reassured them that it was okay to do very little. Rock clubs became infested with grunge and its attendant anti-fashion codes. Almost overnight, fans went into 'Seattle lumberjack' mode, growing their hair long and modelling flannel shirts. The who-gives-a-fuck look was well and truly in vogue.

Grungers made it their business to be as down-to-earth as possible. They didn't introduce their individual members onstage and they most definitely didn't split the audience into two halves and launch a competition for both sides to yell louder than the other.

None of which was a bad thing, in its own right. Yet if you wanted straight-down-the-line, hard-edged bands who didn't wear overly long cardigan sleeves, you would have to search pretty hard. Metal bands started feeling the pinch, both in terms of record sales and the size of venues they could play. Glam rock in particular all but perished – a casualty which many music fans would describe as a laudable example of natural selection.

NU MODEL ARMIES

Grunge died tragically with Kurt Cobain's suicide in April 1994. Something new and more intense had already started to rise from the ashes, as rock's cyclical evolution continued. Nu-metal was coming.

In early 1993, Rage Against The Machine sowed the seeds. These four LA agitators were a godsend for those who preferred their knuckles white. Coming on strong with a hard-line political manifesto, Rage had a musical strategy to match. Combining rap and rock like they had never been combined before, the band would take their songs way down low, then build them up again ever so slowly, letting the anger gradually uncoil ... until it *exploded* like a thousand mortar bombs. At that time, Rage seemed like the most incendiary band on the planet. Seen in smaller venues, they were a truly amazing experience. Their 'Killing In The Name' hit also introduced a lyrical catchphrase, which would be embraced by rebellion-hungry fans and condemned by critics for its playground chant mentality: *'Fuck you, won't do what you tell me!'*

Up and coming musicians took careful notes of Rage's modus operandi – and few more studiously than Korn. This Bakersfield, California posse hit the rock scene two years after Rage – by which time the latter's creative stagnation had arguably already begun. If Rage had paved the way for nu-metal, Korn defined it. Their self-titled 1995 debut album was produced by nu-metal's sonic godfather Ross Robinson, who was destined to work with Slipknot four years later. It saw the band assimilating some of the best sounds of the last seven years. Here was a killer cocktail of Rage's powder-keg dynamics; the schizo vocals and big, tribal beats of Faith No More; and a dose of grunge's bleak introspection and rumbling bottom-end. All of these elements were sucked in and spat out in one fantastic, resentful eruption.

Musically and philosophically, *Korn* was one gnarled, bloody raw album. This band positively encouraged America's formerly introverted, apathetic misfits to thrust a livid middle finger in the face of the high-school jocks who would traditionally bundle them into a locker and brand them 'faggots' for sporting hair longer than an Army buzz-cut.

Korn were also about getting shit out of your system, as opposed to wallowing in it. They swiftly came to attract and represent kids who had suffered any form of abuse – mental, emotional, physical, sexual ... the list goes on. Their shows became euphoric self-help sessions, as increasing numbers banded together to yell, 'You can suck my dick and fucking like it!' along with singer Jonathan Davis. Being a freak was now fun. It was okay. In fact, it was absolutely the thing to do.

Korn was the album which taught Robinson how to produce – and made him as much a celebrity as some nu-metal musicians. During the recording process in 1994 at Malibu's Indigo Ranch studio, Robinson wrenched some incredible performances from Jonathan Davis. The album climaxed with the hair-prickling 'Daddy', which saw the frontman descending into his own personal hell, breaking down in a flood of very real tears. Not a tune to file under Easy Listening.

Davis subsequently said: 'People think "Daddy" was written because my father abused me, but that's not what the song's about. When I was a kid, I was being abused by someone else. I don't really like to talk about that song.'

You can only imagine what it must have been like to watch Davis implode in that vocal booth.

'He had been in a frenzy of tears all night,' Ross Robinson recalled. 'All he could think about was what his mom and dad would think when they heard the song. He didn't go to sleep. The next day, we set up and I told him, "You know what to do on this one".'

The outcome surprised even the producer.

'Personally, I don't think I've ever done anything better,' Robinson told me in October 2000. 'That's God's record that right there brother!'

Robinson's passion for capturing ragged emotion on tape subsequently helped lend nu-metal its shape. This was a movement based on catharsis – provided the purveyors were for real.

Korn's influence on '90s rock is as vital and far-reaching as that of Metallica, Faith No More or indeed Nirvana. Davis and co spawned countless nu-metal bands – the best of whom lent the basic formula some new spin.

LA's Coal Chamber fed on Korn's churning rage, emphasising similar grooves and song structures. So did Limp Bizkit, who focused more on the sound's hip-hop elements and eventually found considerable success in doing so. Even established bands like Machine Head and Sepultura took note of what Korn were doing and weren't too proud to pick up a few tips themselves. New bands seemed to spring up every five minutes, generally with unusual hair, customised names, bizarre fashion statements and obligatory clip-on personal traumas. Spineshank, Orgy, Disturbed, (hed)PE and Mudvayne were just a few of the second-generation acts inadvertently spawned by the Bakersfield five. Then, of course, came Slipknot. Korn's influence was undeniably present in some aspects of the band's sound – a fact which the Des Moines posse would never refute, while qualifying that they only liked the band's first two albums.

Korn laid down a template which Slipknot twisted, expanded upon and ultimately outshined. This, the Des Moines maulers achieved by virtue of the following ...

VISION THINGS

Slipknot looked incredible from the moment their record label Roadrunner began circulating promotional photographs in early 1999. Their red boiler suits and strikingly twisted masks immediately grabbed your attention and provoked a reaction, whether it be horror from parents or exclamations of 'Cool!' from their offspring.

Immediately, you could picture US comic book guru Todd McFarlane designing dolls of the band, as he had with Alice Cooper and Rob Zombie. Dolls of all nine members, to boot. That was another fantastic thing about Slipknot – the fact that they were literally the size of two nuclear families combined. They were not so much a band as a swarm. Did they multiply when they came into contact with water?

Early in 2001, McFarlane told me: 'I'd love to make action figures out of Slipknot. The only problem is, if I do it, I'll have to make all nine. There's not one guy in that band who doesn't look cool enough to be made into a doll.'

The *Spawn* creator had always been into horror, and Slipknot reminded him of the film *Halloween*. 'There's something about masks,' he said. 'You can't get a reaction from the person's face. When you can only see someone's eyes through slits and you can't tell whether they're sad, happy or angry – that's quite haunting.'

McFarlane confessed that Slipknot were far more appealing to him aesthetically than sonically. 'I'm a child of the seventies,' he laughed. 'But if Slipknot are packing halls and juicing up the kids, then as far as I'm concerned it's no different from The Beatles.'

Until Slipknot sprang up like a rash, modern rock had been lacking visual excitement: over-the-top stuff to look at. In nu-metal, Coal Chamber were one of the few bands who brought with them their own distinct sense of style – multi-coloured hair, insectoid braids, facial tattoos and numerous piercings. They played an often under-valued role in the evolution of rock fashion.

Adidas provided Korn's hip-hop-style street gear, although the band's company of choice would later become Puma. It's debatable whether this brand mentality was preferable to grunge's thrift-store chic. Either way, hard music lacked eye-candy punch. Again, this was partly due to the post-grunge depression: slacker bands had stripped away what they perceived to be rock's glitzy bullshit and phoney stage personalities.

While Korn and Coal Chamber made more of a sartorial effort, they tended to wear their gear onstage and off – a fact which admittedly proved their integrity. Nevertheless, the decades-old Alice Cooper concept, of the rock star becoming uncontrollably consumed by a Dr Hyde-style personality before striding maniacally onstage, remained seriously outmoded. Grunge had sadly thrust a stake through the heart of larger-than-life alter egos, and pyro-packed stageshows were similarly forbidden. Kiss, those all-American originators of The Rock Star As Super Hero, had scrubbed off their make-up long ago, in 1983. Trent Reznor, the frontman of industrial gods Nine Inch Nails, may have been an enigmatic, dark miserabilist, but he was hardly transforming himself into a bat-lord up there every night. Even good old mad Al Jourgensen of cyber-rockers Ministry simply threw on a hat and cool shades, and placed a skull on his microphone stand. It was scarcely high theatre.

Slipknot, on the other hand, turned themselves into a different lifeform every night – and proudly wore a uniform of their own devising.

Throughout the '90s, a handful of bands had attempted this brave metamorphosis, but failed to advance beyond limited cult status. US metallers GWAR dressed up like chunky, cartoon aliens and squirted green gism over their bewildered audiences. Starting out as Richmond, Virginia art students hungry for laughs, they certainly achieved their goal. Giving themselves ludicrous names like Balsac The Jaws Of Death, Beefcake The Mighty and Nippleus Erectus, they stomped around the world sexually assaulting stooge priests with crucifixes and generally acting the goat. They were good fun, but the problem was their music. It was, in a word, rubbish.

Comedy-rockers Green Jelly sounded and looked terrible, dying a swift death after releasing 1993's lousy *Cereal Killer* album. Sure, we wanted entertainment, but we weren't about to buy any old tat. An image alone didn't make you reach for your wallet.

White Zombie were one of the few bands who found success through excess. One of the biggest metal acts in America circa 1995, their US tour in support of their *Astro-Creep: 2000...* album saw them cram explosions and neon red gravestones into arenas the length and breadth of the nation. Even better, this band were causing offence and getting into trouble with various principled institutions – the hallmark of any proper rock band. The Zombie's Say You Love Satan T-shirts certainly weren't going down a storm in the country's Bible Belt. Death threats and bomb scares – some of which possibly came from religious types – followed the Zombie-mobile around America, only serving to amplify their profile and momentum. The band ultimately burnt themselves out, however, leaving mainman Rob Zombie to form a new self-titled solo band and don more undead make-up and milky-white contact lenses than ever before.

In October 2000, he told me: 'Slipknot's music is pretty crazy and I always hear how great they are live. I think their whole look is pretty cool. When bands do anything like that, it always gets my attention. Dark, scary and fucked up is always good. Every couple of years, there's the new extreme band. One time it was Slayer, then it was Pantera and now it's Slipknot.'

Even Slayer's own Kerry King – who initially dismissed the 'Knot out of hand – readily concurred that this band were the new flag-bearers for filth. 'It's the new age of Slayer, in my eyes,' he said. 'They get the same reaction. There's chaos onstage and offstage.'

When it came to Alice Cooper-isms, no-one knew the score much better than Marilyn Manson. This man was fundamentally Alice reborn for a modern-day audience. Manson's early band The Spooky Kids went all-out to grab the attention of Floridian kids with such OTT antics as throwing meat into the crowd and performing oral sex on each other.

Manson, the band, may have taken a few years to find a place in the hearts of rock's faithful, but when they did, it was clear that Marilyn himself was the new messiah. The concept of the rock star had been reborn – albeit courtesy of a gangly hedonist.

Manson and his band backed up their headline-grabbing controversy with an intelligent and painfully heavy album in 1996's *Antichrist Superstar*. The Bowie-esque frontman may have looked great and his band rocked hard, but most importantly he had something to say. Rob Zombie was always entertaining, but Manson's brain made him more dangerous than any spookshow. In 'The Beautiful People', Manson perfectly lampooned a world which ranked surface over feeling. He was truly the people's fiend, opening audience's minds up to accepting potential comic book characters as heroes once again. Slipknot? They had enough OTT characters in their ranks for a whole rack of graphic novels.

Nine Inch Nails frontman Trent Reznor originally signed Marilyn Manson to his own Nothing Records label, and believes his protégé opened the floodgates for a beast like Slipknot.

'You have to give Manson a degree of credit for heralding the way,' he told me. 'It's fun to dress up and offend people, and it's fun to be ridiculous and outrageous. That's a healthy bit of rock 'n' roll that disappeared for a while. It's probably good that it did disappear, because when it came back, you realised you missed it. I don't think there's anything wrong with grunge or the do-it-yourself punk movement it sprung out of – or the Washington DC hardcore movement. But there's also nothing wrong with some fucking good entertainment and outlandishness. Extremities have always been what attracted me to anything in music, books, movies, art, film or whatever.'

Reznor recalled rock's lingering anti-showbiz mood when he signed Manson, post-grunge. 'If you had any kind of show, you were full of shit. It was all about being real, "man", wearing your gas station attendant outfit onstage and being just like everybody else. But you know what? Fuck that. I wanted my rock stars four-dimensional and giant. I wanted Gene Simmons' boots biting my dick off. Excitement, blood, gore! Even with someone like David Bowie, there's a charisma and a larger-than-life aspect. It's a hero. If the effect can be pulled off right, there's nothing at all wrong with that.

'I'm not taking credit for this,' he continued, 'but I encouraged Manson, back in the day. Yeah – of *course* piss people off! Yeah – don't be afraid to do any of that type of shit! He wasn't afraid, but I tried to nurture him in that department. Whereas maybe a big label might say, "Hey, maybe if we tone it down a little bit, the record can get sold in K-Mart." Fuck that. Don't be afraid of the politically correct grunge movement. What happened? They're gone.

'Slipknot win my approval,' said Reznor. 'I'd much rather see them than a fucking Creed or a disposable, hip rap-rock crew going, "Look how mad we are – we're fat kids from California!"'

Kiss bassist Gene Simmons added: 'When people say of your band, "Gee, I hate their music but their show was the best ever", that's grand praise. Because if everything depends on whether or not people like the songs, you're dead.'

THE X-MEN

While Slipknot might like to play down this factor's importance, one of the joys of the band is that so few people know what their real faces look like. Many fans work it out, and hunt down their heroes after shows. But if they want a souvenir snap of themselves with their heroes, the band conceal their features. This makes for some awkwardness when some people get a little snap-happy without permission.

Slipknot percussionist Shawn 'Clown' Crahan: 'When I

bust someone for taking a picture, I never take the camera from them. I just ask them, "Please, for me and for you and for what we're both trying to do, don't put that photo out anywhere." There are a couple of photos of me out there, but that's okay. Onstage, I'm a masked man. Anywhere else, I don't like my picture taken.'

Laughed the band's frontman Corey Taylor: 'I'd love to spread this sick rumour that we were all chicks. It'd rule to keep that rumour going for about six or seven months, and really work the shit out of it. People would be going, "But I *met* them!"'

Few rock bands besides Kiss had tried concealing their true identities. If groups did, they were generally laughable.

As far back as 1979, British metal band Samson had a masked drummer named Thunderstick. US punk sickos The Mentors wore executioner-style hoods, but turned off audiences at large with their misogynist babbling.

Big-haired Floridian rockers Crimson Glory came out with stylish-looking metallic masks which appeared moulded to their faces. This caught the imagination of a limited audience during the campaign for their first album. Come their second LP, however, the band modified their masks to reveal half their faces. On the third, they ditched the masks altogether – and inadvertently threw their careers away, too. The fundamental problem here, was that no-one cared what Crimson Glory really looked like.

One of the more entertaining attempts at maskery came from The Dwarves' guitarist Hewhocannotbenamed, who often appeared on stage with the now-defunct San Francisco punks wearing nothing but his gimp head-piece. Rap-rocking duo Insane Clown Posse kicked up a storm in the clubs of Detroit during the mid-'90s, acquiring a cult following with their Kiss-esque evil clown make-up, ultra-violent lyrics and the riotous nature of their gigs. The latter involved Violent J and Shaggy 2 Dope squirting their audience with a local soda pop named Faygo. By the new millennium, however, their musically blinkered antics had acquired a more 'selective' appeal.

Also on a clown tip were The Prodigy, whose frontman
Keith Flint didn't exactly conceal his wild-eyed fizzog while
performing, but nevertheless adopted a character which was
equal parts Bobo, Satan and Johnny Rotten. Similarly, the
band's MC Maxim Reality developed his own onstage persona
and look, marrying a kilt with those increasingly popular cat's
eye contact lenses.

Over in Scandinavia, a new breed of anti-Christian
metallers were stirring. Dubbed the 'Satanic terrorists' by the
UK press, bands like Burzum, Mayhem, Darkthrone, and
Emperor were daubing corpse-paint on their faces and award-
ing themselves such grand titles as The Lord Of Silence
(Emperor guitarist Samoth) and Count Grishnacht (Burzum
mainman Varg Vikernes).

On the whole, masks were far more likely to be seen on the
faces of superheroes than bands. Batman and Spiderman
concealed their identities with iconic secondary faces, while
Superman and Wonder Woman managed to remain anonymous simply by donning spectacles.

Then there were the slasher film slayers. Jason Voorhees of
the *Friday The 13th* series famously sported a hockey mask
from the second sequel onwards; *Halloween's* Michael Myers
modelled a rubbery creation with hair, reportedly moulded
from the face of *Star Trek* legend William Shatner; and the
ghostface killers of the *Scream* trilogy rocked the Edvard
Munch look.

Slipknot liked superheroes and horror movies. They
wanted to get away from the whole concept of image, by
dehumanising themselves.

Masks were cool. It was amazing that no-one had done this
before ...

NO-ONE GETS OUT OF HERE ALIVE

It was a rare live artist who gave you that frission of wondering whether everybody present would survive their performance. In the midst of a Slipknot gig, though, you couldn't help

pondering exactly when one of Shawn 'Clown' Crahan's airborne oil drums was going to stave in the skull of some innocent bystander. When the band's DJ Sid Wilson hesitated for that agonising split-second before diving from a high balcony, it could quite conceivably be the last moment you'd see him alive.

Slipknot were also, at any given moment, likely to cause a riot or be dragged offstage on stretchers with blood pissing out of their masks. This, needless to say, gave them an edge.

There were, of course, a few precedents for this kind of danger in rock 'n' roll. The Dwarves were notorious for cutting their sets short, due to fighting with members of the audience, or simply among themselves. This tended to make their shows the equivalent of a double espresso – short, but delivering a major buzz. Legendary maniac GG Allin developed an underground name for himself by cutting himself to ribbons, defecating onstage, frolicking naked and generally causing utter havoc against a sonic backdrop of frenzied punk.

So few bands even have a discernible presence, let alone manage to intimidate. Ironically, while most people poked fun at the aforementioned Satanic Terrorists of Norway, some members of their collective transpired to be quite literally the most dangerous metal 'stars' ever. Besides the genre's despicable racist overtones, various bands burnt down churches, which in one instance led to the death of a fireman fighting the blaze. The genre's most incredible event saw Burzum frontman Varg Vikernes jailed for life, after stabbing Mayhem leader Euronymous to death.

At that point, it seemed that extreme music could hardly become more radical. And thankfully, it didn't. What it was about to do, upon Slipknot's arrival, was rise to a whole new level and become a great deal more fun.

All the best rock 'n' roll frontmen were out of control, or at least gave you that impression. In Slipknot, you had nine of these frontmen to look at, all at once.

This was the most exciting band in the world. Which, by 2001, would put them under no small degree of pressure. Still, when you learn exactly what it took to drag themselves under this microscope, and how long they fought to get there, you won't expect them to throw in their masks any time soon.

Just as with metal itself, the story starts with Ozzy Osbourne. The Double-O not only helped Slipknot out with the Ozzfest: he provided them with one of their first life-shaping events...

1
Breeding ground

People ask me, 'Why Des Moines?'
I say, 'Why *not*, you ignorant motherfucker!'
Shawn Crahan, #6

THE OZZ-MAN COMETH

If you believed in destiny, as Joey Jordison assuredly did, then it was no mere coincidence that in January 1982 Ozzy Osbourne chose to wreak havoc in the hometown of kids who would go on to form Slipknot. Judging by the fuss Joey Jordison's parents made, you'd swear that their native Des Moines was under attack.

That morning in the Jordison household, a six-year-old Joey could tell that something major was going down. The unmistakable buzz of outrage streamed from the living room. Joey walked through the door, still half-asleep, to see his parents sitting in front of the television, engaged in shocked discussion.

'I can't believe what the world's coming to!' his mother told her husband.

Gazing at the local TV news report, Joey soon gathered

that a heavy metal musician named Ozzy Osbourne had bitten the head off a bat, live onstage in Des Moines.

This had been viewed dimly by the townsfolk and the press.

'I immediately thought that Ozzy ruled,' Joey would recall. 'I knew something was going on with that music, and I had to get my hands on it. I bought his *Blizzard Of Oz* album soon after.'

Osbourne himself spent that morning comatose on his tour bus, which was parked outside his hotel. 'I remember waking up on that bus, as pissed as a wheel,' he told me. 'When you're drinking on tour as much as I did, you go to bed in one world and wake up in a completely different one, but you don't realise what you did the night before. That day, when I peeled my tongue from the pillow, got off the bus and went into the hotel's reception, everybody was looking at me and whispering to each other: "It's him!" I thought, "Have I shit my pants or something?!" My wife Sharon thought it was my usual paranoia, but it turned out I'd been on the television all morning.'

Ozzy eventually discovered this for himself. 'I went up to my room and turned on the TV. I nearly crapped my fucking bed! It hit me like a ton of bricks when I realised what I'd done.'

'The Ozzy story was huge here,' Joey recalled, 'because nothing happens in Des Moines. He was banned forever. Ozzy's had concerts scheduled here since and they always get cancelled.'

Osbourne insisted that the bat was not a publicity stunt. 'Believe me, I could think of something far easier on my system than ripping a fucking bat's head off,' he said. 'I had to go around with this syringe and a bottle of rabies vaccine. It wasn't funny, man!'

Clearly, however, it was. And for Joey Jordison and his eight future comrades, highly significant. 'It was one of those things which is permanently burned into your mind,' said Joey. 'It hasn't left me, to this day. It was meant to be. It was almost like Ozzy bit the head off that bat to pass the torch, way early on, to another sick band.'

THE BEAUTIFUL PEOPLE

On the bare face of it, there is little by which to recommend Des Moines, Iowa. Despite being subtitled The Beautiful Land, it is generally depicted as miles of dying cornfields and barren farmlands. As far as most folk are concerned, the state of Iowa has contributed little to the world besides a truck-load of toe-tapping country music artists, serial killer John Wayne Gacy and a whole procession of Jerry Springer regulars. Having said that, Des Moines spawned the greatest band in the world. How bad can it be?

Some facts about the town. Its population is around 225,000 people, featuring the second highest concentration of elderly folk in the whole country. The last two decades have seen its high-school students lead the nation in terms of test results. Less impressively, the town has in recent times experienced problems with its over-full asylums.

It is said to be a difficult place to leave. In his book *The Lost Continent: Travels In Small-Town America*, travel writer Bill Bryson – who was born in Des Moines – described it with humorous hyperbole as 'the most powerful hypnotic known to man ... the place does get a grip on you. People who have nothing to do with Des Moines drive in off the interstate, looking for gas or hamburgers, and stay forever. There's a New Jersey couple up the street from my parents' home whom you see wandering around from time to time looking faintly puzzled but strangely serene. Everybody in Des Moines is strangely serene.'

Not the 'Knot. There were many reasons why a band like this would rise from Des Moines' primordial ooze. You could even attribute it to something as superficial as the weather, which mirrored – or perhaps even helped breed – the band's love of extremity.

'In the middle of winter you can die if you're not dressed properly,' Slipknot member #6, Shawn 'Clown' Crahan has said. 'In the summertime, you can take all the showers you want, then walk outside and be soaking wet from the humidity.'

The often adverse conditions have helped forge the band's unbeatable determination.

Shawn: 'Where we're from, when the snow gets four-foot high, everything's shut down for four days. I'm looking out of my window thinking, "How am I getting to practice? I'm gonna find a way." Then if the snow's really too much and we can't practice, I'm like, "What am I gonna do?"'

It was this isolation and adversity, courtesy of Mother Nature, which inexorably drilled its way into Slipknot's collective subconscious. They were born fighting the very elements. And they wouldn't have it any other way.

Shawn: 'Iowa *is* a beautiful land. It has the four seasons. If you want the hot summer, the beautiful springs and falls and snow for Christmas, that's what we have.'

There was also, perversely, a lot to be said for growing up in a town where there's nothing much to do.

Joey Jordison once said: 'We were raised in an environment where you had to develop your own sense of individuality. I had 16,000 imaginary friends. I had my own fucking army.'

Corey told the website *IGN For Men*: 'In a town like Des Moines, a lot of people are so full of pent-up energy, it's just amazing. If you get them in a party situation, you do not know what the fuck is going to happen. Especially when you're growing up – there's nothing for kids to do. You develop destructive behaviour, just from the fact that the only thing to do is break shit. It also pisses the old people off, which is pretty cool.'

While fans of metal music have always been accustomed to feeling like outnumbered underdogs, trapped in their bedrooms listening to records that no-one else cares about, this was never truer than in a conservative, isolated town like Des Moines.

Joey: 'You don't really have an outlet to let go. There's nothing there as far as music's concerned. You really have to develop a sense of self, super-early on, to make sure you can take the music and have enough substance. If you can make it in Des Moines, or come out of Des Moines, I think you can pretty much do it anywhere. That's why we stuck with this band.'

It's important to note that, while certain frustrating aspects of Des Moines spurred Slipknot into existence, they do not hate the town. Far from it.

Shawn: 'I have nothing bad to say about the place I was born and raised. The morals here are good, the educational system is good and you don't get a lot of the bullshit here that you get in other places. In Los Angeles, so many people don't know who the fuck they are. In New York, they're all fucking cattle. I'll take Des Moines over those places any time.'

Maverick film-maker David Lynch would no doubt appreciate the strangeness which bubbles away beneath the calm, strait-laced exterior of Des Moines. This is smalltown America as seen in *Blue Velvet* – peel off the wholesome surface and you'll find Satanic cults, speed dealers and all manner of oddities.

'It's not as nice as you think it is,' Shawn has clarified, 'but it's not gangtown LA or New York. There's a big section of Des Moines that's cool, then there's the white-trash *Springer* side. There are parts I won't go in because it angers me.'

The downside of small town life is that few people want to see anyone else get out. In their numerous pre-Slipknot bands, the members would suffer everything from scepticism to blatant ridicule from peers and elders alike.

Shawn: 'There's a lot of love in this town, but there's a lot of hate and fucked-up emotions too. Our detractors told us we were diseased from a very young age. Instead of dying, we created our own vaccine in Slipknot.'

Joey: 'When someone constantly tells you to get a real job and quit spending your money on new drum pedals, all that shit circles around in your head. There's a constant hate in me: it never leaves and it comes out every day. We were degraded for so long and had fingers pointed at us. When you get that middle finger as much as we did, you just want to throw it back in their faces.'

WOMB WITH A VIEW

Appropriately enough, the first thing Joey Jordison ever remembered was darkness.

'I don't know if I had conscious thoughts while I was in the womb, but I was in a black cell. Looking up in the corner, I could see a tiny square window, letting in a little bit of light. That was it.'

Joey was born on 26 April 1975 in Des Moines' Mercy Hospital. He grew up in a country area outside the small town of Waukee. In turn, Waukee was ten miles away from Des Moines. Joey would barely leave this microcosm until he was old enough to drive. Thanks to his folks, he wasted little time in embracing music. 'They always sat me down in front of the stereo, rather than the TV. I latched onto music at a young age and it was all I cared about. I was a day-dreamer, thinking about these larger-than-life possibilities that could happen if I worked hard.'

As you might expect, the youngster hated the whole concept of school, from the moment he was dragged to the pre-school along the street, aged four.

'School always felt like someone had their thumb on me. I got horrible grades. I was really introverted and didn't have many friends. There were only one or two people who I hung out with. I just stayed by my locker with my headphones on, and concentrated on my own little universe of music.'

Kings in Joey's universe were US rockers Kiss. In America, the band were an institution: larger-than-life superheroes who booted some serious backside.

Joey: 'When I was that age, they seemed so fucking rad. I was obsessed with '70s Kiss, even though I got into them in the early '80s. Them and Black Sabbath were the bands for me.'

Despite being hardly tall enough to reach a door-knob, Joey started his first band while in primary school. As is the case with most school-age bands, members were recruited largely by virtue of the equipment they owned.

Joey started off playing guitar with a friend. They briefly tried out another local kid who owned a drum-kit.

'He sucked!' winced Joey. 'He was going nowhere. So I said I would go ahead and play drums for now, until we got a guitar player.'

Unfortunately, Joey didn't have his own kit. At least, not until he reached Fifth Grade.

One day, the eight-year-old Jordison came home from school to find his mom and dad sitting at the kitchen table.

'Go downstairs and get my Elton John record,' said his mother. 'We're having an argument about one of the songs.'

Joey slouched off down the stairs to the basement. When he got there, he did a double-take. A brand new drum-kit sat in the middle of the room, all set up and ready for punishment. Stunned and delighted, Joey grabbed the Elton John album and took it back up the stairs.

His mother laughed. 'I didn't *need* the record!' she said.

Joey gave them both hearty hugs, then ran back downstairs and hopped aboard the kit.

There was work to be done.

FIEND WITHOUT A FACE

Mrs Jordison was clearly one for practical jokes – a leaning which would rub off on her son and his future Slipknot band-mates.

One Halloween night in the mid-'80s, she leapt around the corner of the house at Joey, wearing a mask best described as a 'spooky Kabuki' – a Japanese creation reflecting gods and mythology. Joey can still remember how she 'scared the fucking shit out of me!' But he liked the mask.

By now, Joey and friends were the house band at Waukee Middle School, playing a selection of Kiss, Sabbath, Led Zeppelin and Deep Purple cover versions at dances.

Joey: 'We became the rock stars at school. Everyone thought we sucked, which we did, but we thought we were bad-ass!'

Despite the pre-teenage kicks Joey was experiencing, his youth would not be all fun and games. When his parents divorced, his dad moved out of the house, leaving Joey with his mother and two younger sisters.

Joey: 'All of a sudden, I had to be the man of the house, in a weird way. I was helping my mom with my sisters all the time. It turned me into a more mature person at a really young age.'

Over the next few years, the Jordison kids would visit their father at weekends. Joey would draw considerable inspiration from seeing how his mother coped with this testing new set-up.

'Her determination was incredible,' he said. 'She got us up in the mornings, made sure we went to school, then she went to work. I would have to take care of the girls after school and she would come home, make us dinner and get us all in bed. She would sleep for the mere couple of hours she was allowed, then wake up and do it all again. She taught me really good morals. Even though I do a lot of fucked-up shit and I play in the most fucked-up band in the world, she did raise me really well.'

THE DEAD ZONE

Joey's mom eventually remarried and set up a funeral parlour with his new stepfather Mike. Joey would often help them with their work, which involved embalming and generally making the deceased look more presentable.

Joey: 'I've seen more dead people than you can possibly imagine. I used to help out with a lot of that. I never used it as a publicity thing though. It was just a job.'

Now at Waukee High, Joey was the great metal-loving outcast.

Shaggy hair?

Check.

Pale demeanour?

Check.

Slayer T-shirt?

Check.

Walkman headphones glued to ears?

Most definitely.

Every American high school seemed contractually obliged to enrol a cluster of these insular misfits.

Joey: 'I couldn't talk to anybody, because they had no clue what I was talking about. They were all too busy playing basketball and making football teams at recess.'

While Joey was never physically bullied as such, he received abuse for being vertically challenged.

'I'm still only five-foot-five,' he told me in late 2000, 'and in school everyone was taller than me. I got shit for many years. No chicks would go out with me! I needed Gene Simmons' seven-inch heels. And his tongue too, so I could make them come a lot faster.'

While Joey jokes about those taunts, perhaps as a self-defence mechanism, you can see that such mockery added to the whole sense of wanting to show everyone what he was truly capable of. What better way to piss off people who made fun of your size, than by forming a band who became huge?

It's no accident that most rock stars you meet are surprisingly short. God bless the Napoleon Complex.

NUMBER ONE SICK BOY

Corey Taylor knew there were only two choices left: get out of town or die.

Now 15 years old, he had recently suffered two cocaine overdoses. Having looked death in the eye twice, he was experiencing a sudden blaze of clarity.

'I knew what I had to do,' he once said. 'The environment around me sure as hell wasn't going to help me, so I knew I had to take care of it myself.'

Corey would never describe the exact circumstances which led him to drug problems. One painful thorn in his young side, however, was undoubtedly never having known his father. Later on in life, he would confront this emotional void by tattooing the Japanese symbol for 'death' on one side of his neck and the symbol for 'father' on the other.

Right there and then, he was numbing the hurt by snorting white powder up his nose.

His mother had raised him in Waterloo, a one-horse town around two hours out of Des Moines. Corey has neatly described the place as 'a hole in the ground with buildings around it'.

In a place like that, movies were a great source of escapism. One night in 1979 proved momentous, when Corey and his mother went to see *Buck Rogers In The 25th Century* and got more than they bargained for. Before the main feature, they witnessed the trailer for 1978's *Halloween*. Not only did this seminal movie provide the blueprint for a thousand slasher flicks, it planted a dark seed in Corey's head.

'I'd like to think it developed some sense of Slipknot in me,' he would reflect. 'I didn't get to see the actual movie until about five years later, but that trailer scared the hell out of me. The fact that this guy's in a mask and he's running around, totally destroying people? That's some powerful shit.'

Corey joked that *Halloween*'s homicidal Michael Myers character is the tenth member of Slipknot. He said: 'I'd like to think he's our guardian angel, watching over us...'

If *Halloween* introduced Corey to masks and extreme behaviour, his grandmother introduced him to rock 'n' roll. She would play Elvis Presley tunes all the time on the eight-track format, and the youngster developed a natural liking for The King.

Corey: 'I didn't understand his infatuation with banana and peanut butter sandwiches, but Elvis was a great singer. I grew up with "In The Ghetto", "Teddy Bear", "Suspicious Minds" ... those were good moments.'

The first metal song he heard and liked, however, was Black Sabbath's self-titled tune. An eerie piece of work from the band's self-titled 1970 debut album, awash with a doom-laden atmosphere aided in no small part by portentous bells, it established both rock's funereal minor-key tones and its often misconstrued love affair with occult, horror-film imagery.

'"Black Sabbath" gave me chills,' he said. 'I was living out in this old dilapidated farmhouse with my mom. It was the middle of autumn and there were no leaves on the trees: nothing but desolate farmland all around. On a real downcast day, it looked like the cover of a Black Sabbath album!

'I was walking outside with my headphones on, and all of a sudden the bells started ringing. I almost shit myself – I was scared to death! I loved the song, though.'

Corey started collecting Spiderman figures when he was knee-high to the Green Goblin. Even when he later hit teens, he would blow all his spare cash on comics and action figures, along with booze. Like most kids, he had a fascination with the dark side. At the age of 12, he and a friend decided to dabble with an Ouija board. It would be the first and last time he did so.

'The board moved on us,' he later claimed. 'We were just asking stupid questions, like "Can a thermos flask really keep hot things hot and cold things cold?". Dumb shit like that – we were only 12! When it moved, we realised we were definitely not using this tool the way it was meant to be used, and it was getting pissed off. We never messed with it again.'

Corey and his friends were similarly curious about an old spooky house which sat beside the woodland path they took to school each day. 'We would always tease each other about going in. One night, we all grabbed flashlights and went over there.'

When the miniature posse arrived at the house, they were surprised to see that the whole place was lit up, as though lived in. 'We were like, "What the hell!" There was all this old furniture inside, but we knew that nobody lived there because we'd been there during the day and it was all burnt out.'

When the kids heard footsteps on the top floor, their hearts jumped into their mouths.

Corey: 'We just ran away screaming! That was an eye-opening experience – the fact that there's some shit going on in another dimension. It seemed like an onion layer over another realm, that could completely fuck your mind up, if you're a kid. It's stuck in my head for the longest time. They tore that old house down though, and we never got to go back and see if it happened again.'

Taylor never had much time to make solid friends at school. He, his mother and his sister were always on the move. For two especially heavy-going weeks, the beleaguered family found themselves homeless in Florida's Fort Lauderdale. They also spent a year in Minneapolis. If anything good came of Corey being bounced around America like a pinball, it prepared him for the foundation-free existence of a band's life on the road. Like Joey, Corey retains nothing but admiration for his mother's strength.

'My mom kept me alive for a long time. She went through a lot of hell just to make sure we had food, clothing and a place to live.'

At the age of 15, Corey found himself back in Waterloo, addicted to cocaine – his rootless existence having done little to help his problems. Realising that the grave was beckoning, he left town and returned to the homeless existence which he had tasted in Fort Lauderdale. He eventually turned up at his grand-mother's home in a trailer park on the outskirts of Ohio. She ushered the boy in, and subsequently took legal custody of him.

'If it wasn't for that lady,' admired Corey, 'I wouldn't be alive today. She had to deal with a snotty little fucking asshole. When you've got off drugs you think you know it all and you've been through everything.'

While living with his gran, the teenager ditched narcotics and his attention turned once again to rock 'n' roll. 'I knew I had a gift for music, but that's when I really started to work at it,' he said. 'My gran taught me a lot about responsibility. She did a lot of things that other people wouldn't have done in her situation, like helping me buy equipment.'

She also tried to get him to go to church every Sunday, like she had always done.

Corey: 'Growing up, a lot of shit was forced on me. If I didn't get up to go to church, I got my grandmother's finger-nails in my arm. I was a psycho, hyperactive kid, so I ended up with a lot of scars. But I didn't wanna sit in someone else's house and listen to some preacher guy.'

When he turned 18, Corey headed out on his own, keen to explore life and the world. He drifted through places like Denver and Phoenix, spending some time in Carlsbad, New Mexico with his uncle.

'I kept coming back to Des Moines, for some reason,' he once mused. 'And now I know what it was. Everything happens for a reason: that's always been a mantra for our band.'

HELL'S WHEELS

Joey hated the school bus. It was, after all, a vessel which transported him to an educational institution every day. One day in 1990, he was waiting for the bus to arrive when his new next-door neighbour Tim appeared. After the pair had exchanged 'What's up?'s, Joey immediately lunged in with the most important question.

'What kind of music do you listen to?'

Despite Tim being a saxophonist, he claimed to like rock. Joey remained unconvinced, however, that he liked the right kind of rock. That night, after school, Tim walked the few feet to Joey's house and sat in his bedroom as his new friend hauled out a never-ending procession of thrash metal albums for his inspection, slapping a few on the stereo.

Thrash began in 1980 with Satanic Brit metallers Venom and the Danish Mercyful Fate, and was taken to the masses by Metallica in the decade which ensued. By 1991, it was a major commercial force, considering how extreme it seemed at the time. The genre derived its monicker from its speed and general ferocity, along with the fact that its disciples generally went completely mad while watching bands play. It was 78rpm metal for adrenaline junkies, who had no interest whatsoever in ballads. 'Overkill, Nuclear Assault, Exodus ...' murmured Joey, handing the garish album sleeves over, with apocalyptic titles like *Bonded By Blood*, *The Plague* and *Scum*.

'Have you heard of Napalm Death, dude?'

Tim went home that night with some tapes to listen to. The next time he came back, Joey gave him some more.

Now in his freshman year at Waukee High, Joey was drumming in a band called Avanga. Being the most intense 14-year-old in the world, Joey found his colleagues' lack of motivation frustrating.

'The dudes were partying and smoking weed, which is cool at high school, but I was fucking strict,' he said. 'I didn't smoke, drink or do any drugs. I was so focused on music and making music happen for me, so I could get out of school. I was getting shitty grades and my mom was drilling me.'

Joey also had to deal with his dad ordering him to cut his long locks, along with regular detentions from his principal. He knew he needed to find a way out of the education system and the depressing rat-race which presently stretched out into his future. The only way he could think of achieving this was through music.

Avanga clearly wasn't his ticket out.

Modifidious might be.

NEW BEGINNINGS

Joey's jaw hit the bedroom carpet. His friend Tim had only just bought a guitar, and he was already playing along to Metallica's 'Master Of Puppets' track, note-perfect. The song was a classic, lasting for more than eight minutes and highly complex in nature, requiring the kind of right-hand wrist action in which only a teenage male would be well-versed.

Joey: 'I immediately quit Avanga, and started a new band called Modifidious with Tim. We wrote 15 songs, right off the bat. It was total speed-metal thrash – a full-on assault.'

The remaining members of Avanga clearly didn't bear grudges, as they came to check out this new duo in action. They doubtless soon wished they hadn't, as the ever-ruthless Joey took the opportunity to poach their guitar player Jay.

After placing adverts locally, the Modifidious boys found a fine bassist in a kid named Ryan.

And then there were four.

Tragically, this situation would be short-lived. One night, Jay was driving home when he fell asleep at the wheel. He died in the ensuing crash.

'That fucking sucked,' Joey told me, wincing at the thought. 'He was 16 and he'd just got his licence. He was one of my best friends and I still miss him so much.'

FIGHT CLUB

Today, it's called Runway II. Pre-Slipknot, at the turn of the '90s, Runway was *the* rock club for bands to play in Des Moines. The town's lack of musical outlets had led to a modest underground scene, with shows and raves going down at key locations like the Central Skate Park. People would take their own alcohol along to these private parties and watch bands play. Despite this subterranean subterfuge, it was important to support the clubs which did make an effort. Shawn Crahan, a local metal enthusiast with a big heart and bigger dreams, would visit Runway on a regular basis, gladly handing over his seven bucks at the door – even though he knew he would leave disappointed.

'Runway was where all the hardcore people came,' he said. 'Anyone with any belief in original music would spend their time hanging out there.'

It was difficult for many of the local bands to get gigs, as even Runway was heavily biased towards outfits who played cover versions of other people's songs.

When Crahan said he was 'in awe' of these copycat bands, he didn't mean it in a good way. 'I'd get really drunk and frustrated as I watched all these people just lose it over bands doing Warrant ballads and Skid Row songs. After Metallica's *Black* album came out, you'd have six bands covering "Enter Sandman". Before an album even came out, bands would hear the songs on the radio or on a video. These cover bands would be in competition with each other, to see who could start playing these new songs the quickest.

'Runway would pay big money, depending on how good the cover band were,' he continued. 'That always blew my mind – some of them would make something like five grand a week! Another band would come in and get 1500, because they didn't look the part as much.'

Runway's owner finally caved in to Crahan's incessant demands and allowed all-age shows on Sunday. It was cleaning day for the club, so he figured he might as well hand the place over to this new groundswell of original bands. After all, he was making enough money from the weekly cover bands to subsidise it.

Shawn: 'We all met at those Sunday shows, when we were in different bands. We'd put together a huge line-up and charge as few dollars as possible. We would hand out tapes and flyers. Not only did we meet each other there, but it installed the whole philosophy of the 'Knot.'

That collective credo would include hard work, self-belief and the continuous drive to render their dreams and ambitions.

Shawn: 'We'd play and get that five bucks per person. The headlining bands would get a little bit more. I still thought, "Fuck this, man. Why isn't Des Moines interested in making a local scene? Why isn't original music important enough that it can be played on a day-to-day basis?" Even at those illegal parties, bands injected a lot of cover versions into their set, along with their own stuff.'

Crahan's manic exasperation was set to continue for some time. Des Moines was not about to be rebuilt in a day. In 1991, Shawn received the finest consolation prize, when his wife Chantal – of whom he has never been able to speak highly enough – gave birth to a baby girl. The couple were destined to produce another girl, two years later, and a boy three years after that.

Crahan supported his family by working in the welding business. Besides regular jobs, he would produce metal sculptures which hinted at the insanity which was to characterise Slipknot.

ONWARDS AND UPWARDS

On 1 December 1991 the biggest band in Des Moines hit the Runway. Named Atomic Opera, their line-up featured James 'Jim' Root on guitar, who was destined to become Slipknot's demonic jester, #4.

They were being supported by Modifidious.

After dealing with their loss, Joey Jordison's posse had decided to forge ahead. They had recruited a new guitarist named Bruce, who turned out to be something of an entrepreneur, organising this Atomic Opera support slot for the band.

Joey felt unworthy of merely sharing the same stage as Jim Root. 'Jim was the king,' he recalled. 'I've been looking up to that guy for so long.'

Modifidious' performance went well enough. The band's feel-good factor only subsided when their new acquisition Bruce jumped ship to join Atomic Opera. He primarily did this, Joey has always believed, because Atomic Opera were a bigger band than Modifidious.

Joey's crew were not to be so easily outdone. Resourceful Ryan again flicked open his phone book and contacted a friend named Craig Jones.

This future #5 made the grade and took up the vacant guitar spot. He would, of course, one day model a diver's helmet adorned with spikes, handling Slipknot's samples and generally bizarre sounds. Modifidious continued to be plagued by musicians dropping out. In the summer of '92, Tim left the band. Joey would claim, 'We all had outside pressures to deal with at the time.'

NEW GUNS

While Modifidious attempted to plug its leaks and keep itself afloat, a new band, Inveigh Catharsis, had sprung up in town. It featured three Slipknot-members-to-be: the LA-born Paul Gray (#2), Josh Brainard (#4, prior to Jim Root) and Anders

Colsefni, who would not last long enough in Slipknot to be assigned a number.

Joey paid a visit to Inveigh's rehearsal place and jammed with them. He enjoyed this, because their music reminded him of New Orleans thrash heavyweights Exhorder, whose excellent *Slaughter In The Vatican* and *The Law* albums were on maximum rotation in his CD player at the time.

Out of curiosity, Josh came over to check out Modifidious in rehearsal. What happened next was scarcely a bolt out of the blue, given that Des Moines' band scene already resembled a game of musical chairs.

Joey: 'We stole him. Josh took over Tim's spot, singing and playing guitar.'

Before 1993 was out, this new line-up of Modifidious recorded a demo tape named *Visceral*, which was laid down in Joey's basement and mixed in Craig's living room. It featured the tracks 'Indisposed', 'Sprawl', 'Drown', 'Into A Shadow' and 'Ritual Circle'. The following year saw them teaming up for shows with Heads On The Wall, a Primus-like combo featuring Shawn Crahan.

Modifidious' second demo was dubiously titled *Mud Fuchia*. The track-listing for this one ran 'Virus 808/Fist', 'Henry', 'Everything' and 'Drop'.

The band eventually combined their two demo tapes onto one self-financed CD and named the whole thing *Sprawl*. While the sleeve notes were handwritten, you could tell that Joey Jordison already had a big-picture head on his shoulders. Two of the songs featured samples from the movies *Body Parts* and *Helter Skelter*, and Joey had been sensible enough to acknowledge these lifts in the credits.

Young Jordison thought all his life's ambitions had already been fulfilled.

'We were the kings of Des Moines!' he said. 'We had a CD out and we were playing all the time, drawing 200 people. That time was really, really good.'

As with all the best tales, however, it wouldn't last.

SCHOOL'S OUT

'Yesssssss!'

This was destined to become Joey Jordison's victorious battle-cry. Right now, it was being used to mark the end of school. Forever.

As the final bell rang, Joey ran screaming, all the way to his car. Bizarrely, this former poster-boy for the 'could do better' set had graduated with fine honours. Surely inspired by the relatively strong achievements of Modifidious, he actually devoted some effort to his educational home-run.

'Just to mentally fuck with everyone, I got As and Bs in the last two years. I got all these awards for having a good attitude, too. I did it to show people. I could do the work – I just hadn't wanted to, before.'

Post-school, Joey's mother told him to get himself a proper job. The teen's thoughts instantly turned to something in the music field. Something to keep his foot in the door. He headed over to Musicland, a Sam Goody-esque store he would regularly visit, over in west Des Moines. Being a familiar face, Joey got the job.

He had mixed feelings. 'It was cool working around music, but on the downside it was so retail and non-underground. It was cheesy! I wasn't buying anything from there – all my shit was coming from metal catalogues and tape-trading.'

Joey's friend Scott Ingram was working at a 24-hour garage, over in the district of Urbandale. One night in March 1994, Joey paid him a visit and was amazed by the scene before him.

'Scott had all his friends there, drinking, with a stereo cranked! I was like, "What the fuck? You *work* here!" I told him to get me a job at the garage, whatever the hours were.'

Scott did. Joey ended up working four nights a week, for ten hours at a time. A typical shift saw him sitting in Sinclair's from ten at night until eight in the morning. As it left his weekends free, Joey didn't mind at all. He could hang out with friends and listen to paint-stripping metal.

His mother was pacified.
Life was good.
Then his band dissolved.

DAWN OF THE DEAD

As 1994 wore on, the once fiery beast of thrash metal wheezed to a halt. After three waves of bands, the best had progressed into the big-time (Metallica and, to a lesser extent, Megadeth), mellowing with age. Grunge had succeeded in killing off the worst acts, and even some of the better ones.

Thrash was out. Death metal and black metal were in.

An even less palatable sub-genre than thrash, death metal's hallmarks are gargled, evil vocals; ultra-violent lyrics; churning, down-tuned guitars which exude morbidity; and lashings of incredibly fast double-bass work from nimble-footed drummers. Black metal boasts many of these features, throwing in lashings of grand Nordic atmosphere and a philosophical allegiance with Beelzebub. Around this time, black metal was hitting big headlines across the Atlantic, as bands like Burzum and Emperor appeared to endorse the burning of Scandinavian churches.

This all spelled doom for Modifidious. While their name made them sound for all the world like a death metal act, they had ironically morphed into a less extreme band, influenced both by the sludge of obscure noise-makers Melvins and the lumbering, mathematical groove of the New York band Helmet.

Paul Gray, on the other hand, had formed his own full-on death metal outfit in Body Pit, again featuring Anders Colsefni on vocals, along with guitarist Donnie Steele and drummer Danny Spain.

Joey: 'Body Pit came in and started taking over. Death metal was booming in America.'

And so it came to pass that Modifidious became yesterday's news. In early 1995, they disbanded due to lack of interest. Clearly, audiences were fickle, even in the extreme metal microcosm. Partly relieved, Joey picked up a guitar and starting jamming with new locals The Rejects, whose frontman Ryan McMurry was nicknamed Dizzy. In Joey's own words, they dealt in 'gutter-slut, trashed-out, drug-rock, super-charged rock 'n' roll. It was something different for me to do.'

Joey played a couple of shows as an honorary Reject, while resisting Paul's repeated attempts to coax him into the Body Pit. He was having too much fun, simply playing guitar. Jordison was vindicated when Body Pit's limelight-hogging glory proved short-lived. They split up, shortly after recruiting man-mountain Mick Thompson, a guitar teacher and the future #7. Paul Gray moved back to California, and Mick retreated back to his bedroom, severely depressed.

'It was weird how all the bands started breaking up,' Shawn reflected. 'My band, Paul's band and Joey's band all broke up within a short period. Des Moines' metal and hardcore scene went down to nothing.'

And so Crahan returned to his life of frustration, welding to cover the mortgage and consoling himself that he at least had a wonderful wife and kids. Still, the town's plague of cover bands, and the public's blind acceptance of them, drove him to distraction.

'I just couldn't understand why people didn't want more than this. Then I decided I was going to do something different.'

Crahan insists that the basic concept of Slipknot came to him one day as he dragged one of his cage-like sculptures out to his driveway, in order to spray-paint it.

'I'm starting a band,' he told Chantal. 'It's going to be really big.'

KEEP THE FAITH

One evening in Sinclair's that summer, Joey was idly watching *The Conan O'Brien Show* on the little TV on his counter. When it was announced that Faith No More would be playing the show that night, he almost leapt out of his skin.

'I called my mom up and got her to tape it. They were one of my favourite bands. I remember watching Faith No More and thinking I was gonna play that show one day. I'd always wanted to play that show, because Conan always had cutting-edge bands on there. He had Anthrax, Faith No More, Fishbone, Smashing Pumpkins, Deftones ...'

Four years later, Conan O'Brien would invite Slipknot, too.

2
Surfacing

> We were walking around with our wrists open,
> going, 'Please look at what we're trying to do,'
> and no-one answered.
> *Joey Jordison, #1*

TRANSFIXION

4 April 1996
'I need a little Christmas in my drink.'

The crowd's faces were even blanker than the mask of the small figure on stage.

'I need a little Christmas in my drink.'

As this was supposed to be the first Slipknot show, onlookers could only assume that this diminutive demon, who stood before them, clutching the microphone, was Joey Jordison.

'I need a little Christmas *in my drink*!'

Ears cocked. Eyebrows raised.

'*I need a little Christmas in my drink!*'

People frowned.

'*I need a little Christmas in my drink!*'

People grinned. Nervously.

'*I need a little Christmas in my drink!*'
When, exactly, would this band start playing?

THE BEGINNING

Come September 1995, there was a new sickness in the cooling Des Moines air.

Joey Jordison, Shawn Crahan and Paul Gray were all thinking along the same demented lines. They just didn't know it yet. Shawn and Paul had started a new endeavour named The Pale Ones, after the misfiring launch monicker Meld. Shawn was on drums, while Anders Colsefni sang and an ex-Body Pit guitarist named Donnie Steele riffed it up. Paul remained determined to get Joey involved with this malevolent new creation. Visiting Sinclair's one night, he repeated his offer. This time, Paul's efforts yielded more results, as he caught the drummer at a vulnerable point.

Joey: 'I was lost. I didn't know what the fuck I was going to do. But I told Paul that we should form something completely new and groundbreaking.'

Paul invited Joey down to witness The Pale Ones rehearse at Anders' house. Due to the disorientating nature of his night shifts, the drummer subsequently failed to turn up for two practices. Finally, on 15 September, Joey managed to show. He was led down to Anders' basement, where all the equipment was set up.

'Okay,' he said, affecting his best nonchalant expression. 'Play your shit!'

Glancing down, Joey noticed a clown mask lying discarded on the floor.

Cue flashback ...

COMPULSION

A 15-year-old Shawn Crahan wandered around in a Des Moines shopping mall with his then-girlfriend. It was a week after Halloween, and stores across America were attempting to shift their surplus ghoulish gear at appropriately slashed prices. Crahan was drawn to the clown mask like a moth to a flame. It sat there all by itself on the rack, gazing eyelessly up at him. He grabbed it from the shelf.

'That mask stood out like a sore thumb and spoke to me immediately,' he has recalled. 'I didn't really know what I was feeling. I just saw this thing and had to check it out.'

As his girlfriend looked on bewildered, Shawn yanked the mask back over his head and started behaving like, well, a clown. Unfortunately, all Shawn had in his pocket was 50 dollars that he had worked hard for. His young lady reminded him that they were supposed to be going out to dinner that evening.

So Shawn reluctantly placed the mask back on the rack, and they walked on.

The only problem was, he couldn't stop thinking about the thing. Later, he came back to the store, picked it up and handed over the money.

BLAST CHAMBER

Joey's ears were pinned back in that rehearsal space, as The Pale Ones burst into action.

The song was called 'Slipknot'. Ultimately destined to be recorded as '(Sic)' three years later, in a greatly improved version, it was nevertheless enough to assault his senses.

'I remember trying so hard not to smile, so I didn't look like I wanted to join,' he said. 'I remained poker-faced, but I thought they ruled.'

The band played two more songs: 'Gently' and 'Fur'.

Joey told himself that he would either have to join the band, or destroy it. Finally realising that it would be futile to maintain his indifferent facade any longer, he finally let his excitement flood out. Grabbing the clown mask from the floor, he pulled it over his head and sat behind the drum-kit.

'I memorised all the songs right there and then, and blasted through three of them. Shawn immediately jumped up to percussion. Suddenly, we had a band.'

ONES TO WATCH

The thrilling momentum which The Pale Ones gathered was unlike anything they had experienced with their previous endeavours.

Joey: 'We started banging songs out immediately. We had songs called "Part Of Me", "Some Feel", "Confessions", "Killers Are Quiet", "Do Nothing", "Bitch Slap", "Tattered And Torn"...'

Sinclair's Garage was immediately transformed into a strategic headquarters. As Joey worked his night-shift, Shawn and Paul would join him, plotting out schemes for world domination.

Joey: 'We planned every detail. We wanted to create the band of whom we'd be jealous if we went and saw them. We dug deep inside and pulled out every ounce of creativity. My rules were: we didn't answer to anyone, we didn't worry about trends, we played what we wanted and we wouldn't allow people to have any sort of influence on the band. I wanted three drummers, of which I would be one, because I thought one on stage left and one stage right would add a really hardcore power to the music. We wanted to let people know that original music could exist in Des Moines, Iowa.'

The musical soundtrack to these fiercely ambitious meetings was provided by Joey and his magical CD collection.

Shawn: 'I'd always drive past Sinclair's Garage, see Joey headbanging and air-drumming behind the glass and wonder what CD he was listening to. He'd bring a different selection of CDs to work every night, and have them arranged in order of favour behind the counter. He had his own listening chart. I'd come in and see that Fear Factory got moved down to Number Three, or whatever. We did a lot of talking in that garage.'

One of the issues that arose during The Sinclair's Sessions, as Joey and Shawn developed their instinct-driven masterplan, was the need for another guitarist. The boys wasted little time in getting Josh onboard, augmenting themselves to a six-piece. At this point, bands with more than five members were scarce

– one of the few outfits boasting eight musicians were Boston's The Mighty Mighty Bosstones, who played ska-punk, as opposed to ravenous metal. The band's Pale Ones monicker didn't last long. Joey suggested re-naming themselves after their song 'Slipknot'.

'It was our favourite song,' he explained. 'It was an easy title with two syllables and it sounded cool as fuck. Everyone agreed.'

Corey Taylor would tell *Kerrang!*: 'When I think of a Slipknot, I think of somebody tied to a stake, and there's all this evil swarming around them. The slipknot is what's holding them to that situation. It's kind of like our music. It holds you down and you can't escape.'

Part of Slipknot's gameplan involved not revealing themselves to the world – not even Des Moines – until they were a thousand per cent fantastic. This was partly a reaction to the weight of expectation which rested on their shoulders.

Joey: 'Everybody wanted to see the local supergroup playing together, and we never let them see it. We just sat in this basement, getting different kinds of drums and perfecting our art. Everyone knew who was jamming in the band and they were like, "Fuck! Have you heard who's in this band?" Everyone had heard about the band but no-one had heard us or seen us.'

Nevertheless, Slipknot couldn't resist putting on a small Halloween show for a select gathering. In the run-up to this low-key event, the band began experimenting with suitably spooky looks for themselves. At this point, they were toying with weird cosmetics, à la Kiss.

Joey: 'I remember coming to practice and Shawn and Andy had this make-up all over their faces, done up all fucking crazy. It looked great.'

Slipknot played what was effectively their first ever gig in a mood-lit room with glowing green lights.

Joey: 'There was a great feeling of something new. Shawn had great make-up on that made his eyes look sunken. Andy had this grotesque face, painted all crazy. I was looking at them while we were playing and thought it fitted with the music.'

Afterwards, Joey told his bandmates that this look should become uniform. 'I remember making a joke,' he said. 'I said, "When it comes to playing a real show, we're all wearing masks!" Everyone was like, "Whatever..."'

Nevertheless, Joey and Shawn started talking about the mask idea, shooting ideas back and forth. Over several long nights at Sinclair's, the mask concept slowly began to solidify.

Joey: 'Shawn was totally down with the mask thing, and so was Andy. Paul said he'd do it. Josh's favourite band was Kiss, so he could totally understand the whole anonymity thing. But Donnie didn't want to do it at all.'

That one vote didn't halt the proceedings. Joey recalls taking his mask to the rehearsal room for the first time – the same mask his mom had scared him with, all those years ago.

'It was completely white back then. That thing literally fit on my face – it *is* my face. We started getting into the idea and it, and everyone was excited. We started wearing our masks during practice.'

While the masks were far from fully developed, the effect on the band members was remarkable.

Joey: 'We could hardly play songs at rehearsals because we were smiling and laughing so much. I knew this band would take more work than anything I'd ever done, but also be more rewarding to my soul than anything I'd done.'

Shawn: 'The mask thing was never a joke. But I don't think we ever thought it would go the distance.'

Nevertheless, the notion of having an anti-image appealed to the band.

Joey: 'Lately, metal has become almost like a fashion show, with clothing endorsements and shit like that. The whole hip-hop clothing thing is fine, except it seems that bands have to make sure they wear the right clothes. We wanted to get away from that. All we cared about was creating the most aggressive, intense ball of energy possible. Being faceless was the best way to drive it home.'

Shawn: 'It all comes down to one fact. I don't give a fuck what I look like and I don't care for you to know what I look like. You are paying money to come to a show and hear some music.'

THE PROJECT

Mike Lawyer had to look twice. Even the second time, he had trouble figuring out what had happened here.

One third of the parking lot was covered with chalk outlines of prostrate humans, as though some terrible massacre had occurred during the night. These roughly-sketched figures boasted huge genitals.

As Lawyer got out of his car, he remembered that some crazy new band named Slipknot had started recording in his studio. Lawyer had been involved with recording studios since 1980. His last studio had been based on a farm to the south. SR Audio was a relatively new endeavour, having laid claim to 3,500 square feet of Des Moines in 1993.

Earlier that year, a major flood devastated the city's downtown area and forced many businesses to move to the western side. SR was planted in the middle of a new industrial strip-mall, sharing its parking lot with various other creative agencies: film production companies, photographic studios and office complexes. While most of these offices followed the nine-to-five regime, SR tended to be open for around 20 hours a day, due to the nature of the recording beast.

As Mike Lawyer smirked at the chalk outlines, he wondered what the other offices might make of them. He told me: 'I saw all these people coming in to go to work at the photo studio the next day, and they were like, "Where the hell did these things come from?" That's when I knew it was going to be an interesting ride.'

Shawn Crahan had called Lawyer a few weeks beforehand. 'He said they were looking to do some work in the studio,' said Lawyer. 'I put them in touch with Sean McMahon, who at that time was working for me full-time as a producer-engineer. He went to see a rehearsal that night. The next day, he came in with his eyes wide open.'

The Wisconsin-reared McMahon had spent years working as a freelancer in San Francisco's metal-heavy Bay Area, as well as Nashville and Memphis. Come 1993, he settled at SR.

The softly-spoken McMahon recalls being invited to a rehearsal in Anders' basement. While most of the band appeared normal, compared to their modern-day looks, the frontman was sporting a decidedly unusual outfit.

'He was playing in a wolfskin loincloth, complete with fur, with sandals,' said McMahon. 'That was pretty much the extent of it. It became his trademark. He was, and still is, a big burly kind of guy – a rather formidable looking gentleman.'

McMahon barely had time to come to terms with the ludicrous nature of Anders' attire, before Slipknot opened fire.

'I was blown away by how tight this band was,' he continued. 'They had three drummers, and the music was very tribal. They were all basically playing in group unison, as far as what they were doing drum-wise. It was powerful and incredibly violent – I didn't really claim to understand what I was hearing, but I could tell that they were obviously extremely good at it.'

Mike Lawyer: 'Sean came back to me and said, "I've never seen anything like these guys in the Mid-West, ever."' Slipknot's mission was to record a demo-album – which would eventually be titled *Mate Feed Kill Repeat*.

Joey: 'We did everything backwards. We recorded some songs first and started tape trading underground and got the buzz going that way.'

Shawn: 'Other bands were worried about playing live. We were worried about coming in here and recording, because we knew the day would come when we were going to be signed and we wanted to be comfortable in a place like SR. We learnt so much there, that when we did finally record our *Slipknot* album at Indigo Ranch, we brought a lot of knowledge, whether it be microphone placement or whatever. We never wanted to be puppets, because we've always been real adamant about our art.'

This particular piece of art would be seven months in the

making, involving studio time in excess of 1200 hours. It would also cost more than $30,000. Not having been born with silver spoons jutting out of their mouths, Slipknot naturally struggled to cover this gargantuan amount. As the year progressed, Shawn would borrow more and more money from relatives and end up seriously in the red.

'He ended up in debt for almost $40,000,' estimated Mike Lawyer. 'He's probably only just paying it back now! Without Crahan, there would *be* no Slipknot. He put his credit on the line – partly because he was the only member of the band who could borrow money.'

Shawn: 'We have nothing but props for our folks. My dad can't stand the music we play: he listens to George Jones, yet he's one of the biggest Slipknot fans ever. My parents never downgraded the fact that I wanted to be an artist. They just said, "Have a job while you're doing it." They would say, "Please work. But oh, you need $150 for a cymbal you broke? I don't understand why you broke it, but here it is." Our families have been nothing but supportive. They're the kings and we love them for it.'

When work began on the album at SR, Sean McMahon discovered pretty quickly what he had let himself in for.

'"Driven" would be one word which would accurately describe most of the guys in the band,' he later judged. 'Two other words come to mind: "angry" and "violent".'

These driven, angry, violent characters moved into the studio and swiftly customised it to their own atmospheric tastes.

Mike Lawyer: 'They did all sorts of things to dress it up. Everything from really hardcore pornography hanging on the wall, to all sorts of lighting. They would build things inside that looked like one of Salvador Dali's nightmares or an HR Giger piece.'

Sean McMahon: 'Each one of them would bring in these select photographs, shall we say. Joey would bring in a photo of some naked female and stick it up next to his drum area, which was right next to where Anders was doing his vocals.'

Then there were the videos.

McMahon: 'I don't know where they got this stuff. They would bring in these max hardcore videos. The band were like, "Come in here! Take a look at this!" I was like, "Okay, this is more than I need to see, guys. Thanks for sharing!"'

Slipknot would book out every available hour they could, in the evenings or at the weekends. After all, a few of them worked for a living: Shawn was still welding and Anders poured concrete.

Shawn: 'Our whole lives were in that studio. It was non-stop there, all the time.'

Initial sessions, in which the band all played together, were an ongoing learning process.

McMahon: 'They wanted something very primal-sounding. We built fake walls, trying to isolate the drums from each other, but some parts were stepping on each other. What started out sounding like a tribal unison, under the studio microscope, was exposed for having miniscule timing errors which weren't necessarily complementary.'

This is arguably where the seed of Slipknot's percussive genius was sown.

McMahon: 'We re-arranged some of the parts, just so it wasn't all the same drum part times three. We also went for some more unorthodox instruments. Initially, Clown had a timpani, congos, bongos and a 55-gallon oil drum. Eventually, we ended up moving over to an oil drum, beer kegs and garage-door-opening springs – big coils which they scraped with "re-rods". Those are the reinforcing rods that go in concrete when they lay it. These things are in highways, all over the States! It's a pretty unorthodox drum-stick and it makes a nice "ting" sound when you strike metal on metal like that.'

With the band's temperament being somewhat volatile, the pseudo-walls which McMahon had erected to divide the room up soon got damaged.

Shawn: 'I'd put holes in it. I'd get really frustrated and throw my equipment at it.'

McMahon: 'We put Shawn over in the corner. When he

would screw up, either his drum-sticks or his fists would go into the wall.'

Lawyer and McMahon were also forced to implement a no-smoking policy inside the studio, due to the sheer volume of carbon-based fog which managed to float the 50 feet down the corridor from the smoking lounge to the control room.

Lawyer: 'When you've got so many people in a band, along with a few roadies and girlfriends, and everyone's chain-smoking, it can do some damage.'

McMahon: 'There was almost as much smoke in the control room as there was down the hall! Eventually, they had to go outside.' Somewhere along the way, the producer developed cunning diversionary tactics. Such as those chalk outlines.

'We were doing guitar over-dubs,' he recalled, 'and having everyone in the room was not helping matters. I had my intern run up to our local grocery store and purchase some chalk. I told the band, "Hey, it might be fun if we did some chalk-line markings, as though drive-by shootings have fallen out in front. Why don't you go and do that?"'

Like the big kids they were, Slipknot ambled off to draw some corpses.

'I didn't know that they would make them anatomically correct,' laughed McMahon, adding that, luckily for him, the outlines were swiftly covered up by snow.

The winter of '95 was merciless. Iowa saw some of its worst blizzards in years. Not that a simple setback like the whole of Des Moines shutting down could hinder Slipknot.

McMahon: 'There was one day when the schools were closed and people weren't getting out. I was snowbound at home – I wasn't going anywhere, because I couldn't make it out of the driveway. Anders picked Shawn up in his station-wagon, then picked me up from my duplex in Urbandale. We got to the studio and worked through the night.'

Lawyer: 'There were four-foot snow drifts in front of the door, and they were still here recording. The shitty weather just made them play better!'

McMahon: 'At two o'clock in the morning, we tried to leave, but basically a drift had developed. It was clear we were not going anywhere, so we just kept working. It was about five or six in the morning when we were eventually able to go home. I don't think we actually slept.'

McMahon further recalls a particularly humourous moment during the album's recording.

'Joey was having a problem nailing one song, so he took off his clothes and played it naked. Then he nailed it. It was where he needed to be, in order to get that power. I don't know what the logic was, but it worked!'

EXIT STEELE

In February 1996, Donnie left the band. According to Joey, this wasn't because the guitarist didn't much care for the mask notion, or even because he had seen the drummer in his birth-day suit.

'Donnie found Jesus, like you wouldn't even believe. Him and our producer start having these God talks, when we were supposed to be working on shit. They were holding our project up! Donnie completely lost his mind in Jesus. We were prepared to keep him on, but he didn't want to stay.'

Remarkably, Sean McMahon believed that Donnie had always been a devout Christian, but was rather slow to realise what kind of band he was in.

'When they were rehearsing in the basement,' said the producer, 'Donnie would be on the other side of the room from Anders and had no idea of what the lyrics were about. When they got to the studio, we'd be recording and Donnie would say to me, "Did he just say what I *thought* he said?!" He eventually got to the point where he said, "Guys, I love you but I can't be a part of this." He politely withdrew and they respected his decision.'

While McMahon himself also had a strict Roman Catholic upbringing, he wasn't so bothered by the album's lyrical content. Whereas the band's lyrics today are swamped with profanity, hatred and generally irreligious behaviour, the words which Anders wrote had more of a basis in dark fantasy.

McMahon: 'Anders had a bit of a werewolf fetish. Most of *Mate Feed Kill Repeat* is all about the role-playing game called *Rage*, which is based on werewolf lore. So at least I was able to justify my involvement with the project by saying it was partly social commentary and partly fantasy. Their newer material definitely draws the line, though.'

Pressing onwards, Slipknot chose Craig Jones to pick up Donnie's fallen guitar, on account of his being, in Joey's words, 'sick in the mind'.

By far the most enigmatic member of Slipknot, Craig seems content to remain in the background both physically and verbally. His mask reflects this distance he likes to keep from the rest of civilisation, featuring vicious-looking nails that jut out from his helmet.

In a rare speaking appearance, he would later tell *Kerrang!*: 'Sometimes, when we're working our way up to the stage, we'll shove our way through the crowd. When people see me coming, they mostly get out of the way. But sometimes they don't ...'

He also told *Rolling Stone*: 'Everything makes me mad. Life sucks. If I wasn't doing this, I'd probably be going out and killing people – just like the other guys in the band.'

A computer genius, Jones would years later erect the band's www.slipknot1.com website, while Shawn helped commandeer its evil sister site (www.slipknot2.com).

By the time Craig arrived, the album was being mixed. Which was when the real fun began.

The band's first proper show loomed on the horizon.

THE UNVEILING

A central Des Moines reggae club placed right next to a Word Of Christ church, the Safari was hardly the most likely of places for Slipknot to reveal themselves to the public.

The bar's floor resembled a filthy patchwork quilt. Some of it was red, some was black, and some seemed to be made of rubber. All of it was littered with dirt, broken glass and the sticky residue of wasted alcohol. The volume of cigarette smoke made the place resemble fog-ridden Victorian London, and if you could find a chair which didn't wobble, you could consider yourself very lucky indeed.

'It was a piece of shit,' judged Joey. 'And it fucking ruled.'

Since Runway closed down, fans of alternative rock had nowhere to go. They began migrating to Safari, when the club's owner Tony – possibly seeing the gap in the market – began staging shows by the occasional guitar-toting band. At present, Corey Taylor's band Stone Sour were occupying the live throne, dominating what little circuit there was to play.

Corey: 'Our sound was pretty mellow at first. It got more aggressive when I started experimenting with all this hip-hop shit I was into, like Public Enemy, Ice Cube and NWA. I still hadn't found my voice, though. I didn't find it, either, until we made the *Slipknot* album. Thank God I've kept it.'

Stone Sour partly conformed to Des Moines' unwritten law of bands playing cover versions.

Corey: 'We did half covers, half originals. To get anywhere in this fucking town, you had to. A lot of bands who played only originals were basically playing to the floor. We were a good bar band – we'd do some Top 40 crap, but then impress our originals on people. It was cheesy, but once we started to get into songwriting, it started to come out really fucking good. We released a tape, burned off 400 cassettes and sold out of them. We had a good following, but once we started to get into the heavier shit, people said, "What are you doing?"'

Little did Corey know that Slipknot were about to steal whatever thunder his band had accrued. The ever entrepreneurial Shawn had a word in Safari owner Tony's ear. 'I told him we were done with all the other venues and we wanted to start something somewhere new. So he gave us the Thursday night.'

Slipknot were booked in for 4 April 1996. Naturally

wanting to ensure an audience for this grand opening cere-mony, they set about distributing as many posters as possible around town. When the big night rolled up, Safari contained a very healthy 200 people, who were initially set upon by local alternative crew 12 Gauge Floss. This kind of attendance for a local band was unheard of. It was an even more impressive feat when you considered that the word 'metal' barely remained in Des Moines' vocabulary by this stage. Thrash and death metal were virtually obsolete, with praise instead reserved for country bands and coffee-shop poets. Anticipation and excite-ment ran high among the band's ranks as they got ready for the show at Shawn's house.

Finally, the six members clambered into Joey's rusty Chevrolet Suburban and drove down to Safari. The drummer parked and the engine fell silent. The masked sextet sat motionless, gazing out at the club.

Time slowed to a crawl.

'Ready?' said someone.

Slipknot were as ready as they would ever be. They got out and strode towards the entrance. Joey was vaguely aware of his legs wobbling. When this long-awaited supergroup walked into the crowd, they didn't look anything like people expected. Paul, for instance, was modelling a look inspired by one of the Cenobites in the movie *Hellraiser III: Hell On Earth*.

Joey: 'He had this wire strung all over his head, through his piercings and through his tongue. Andy had tape strung all over him. Josh had an executioner hood. Craig had stalker-type pantyhose over his head, which meant he couldn't even see when he was playing. Shawn and I had the masks we'd always had.'

The crowd parted like the Red Sea as Slipknot made their way to the stage.

Joey: 'We had so much energy and excitement. We got up onstage and got this feedback going from our amps.'

Then something unnerving happened. Joey Jordison grabbed the microphone and informed the audience, 'I need a little Christmas in my drink.'

Then he said it again and again, increasing the volume and intensity of his voice with each repetition.

'I got maniacal with it. I went ape-shit and started scream-ing. People were losing their minds. I had so much energy that first show, that I tripped the whole band out. They had been nervous, but immediately they were all jacked. They were ready to kill.' When the feedback and his own ranting had reached fever pitch, Joey moved back to the drum-kit and the band slammed into the song 'Slipknot'.

'That,' Joey still believed in October 2000, 'was the best feeling I've ever had.'

As for the origin of the '...drink' phrase, the drummer picked it up during his childhood. At Christmas, his grandfa-ther would raise a glass of Coke and utter those magic words. Shortly afterwards, a bottle of Jack Daniel's would be ferried in his direction.

That expression stayed in Joey Jordison's head. Exactly why, almost two decades on, he decided to use it as his opening gambit at Slipknot's first ever show, is a mystery on a par with the Easter Island statues.

IN DEMAND

The barbed wire look had been cool enough, but Paul Gray knew he needed a proper mask. He finally found it in the shape of a stern-looking pig's face.

'I thought it was kinda sick-looking, in a weird way. It didn't look like a normal little pig. It kinda represents my indulgent personality, but not in a drug way. I just like to go out and experience stuff, and get the most out of life.'

He snapped up the mask just in time for Slipknot's second night at Safari – the day after their first. This time, they were playing with Corey Taylor's band, Stone Sour.

That night saw another fine performance from Joey and co, introduced once again by a scary '...Christmas in my drink!' rant from the drummer.

Slipknot would go on to play five more shows at the Safari

that month, including one with semi-legendary hardcore mob DRI. At midnight after another show, on 25 April, Joey celebrated his twenty-first birthday.

'I still didn't drink or do anything,' he would note. 'But I did have a beer after we played.'

Slipknot steamrollered onwards, enticing more fans every time. Their publicity campaign was relentless and, at times, controversial.

Shawn: 'At one point, we were putting up thousands of posters all over the place. The bar owner would get a call from the city saying they were going to fine him for every poster. He'd call us and we apologised, but he said, "Keep it up!" So we started bringing a lot of people and kind of started a new scene.'

While, on the face of it, the band's constant live presence ran the risk of making them overly familiar to local fans, they constantly reinvented their show with new twisted antics. One notable stage routine of Shawn's employed his bizarre fetish for deceased crows.

'I had the same dead bird in a jar for five weeks. Every week, I would come out with my dead bird, which was starting to liquify. I would open the jar lid, then puke in my mask all over myself – I made sure I ate before the show. Then I'd hand the jar out to the kids and they'd put their hands in there, touch this bird, then wipe it on their faces, stick it in their mouth.'

Sadly, if Slipknot pulled this kind of stunt today, they would probably be sued by parents for poisoning their offspring. Back then, however, it was innocent excitement.

Even if people *did* get complacent about the band, Shawn wasn't about to be ignored. 'We would throw tables at people and say, "Are you paying attention? We're here now."'

Paul: 'Shawn would pick out a group of people, then taunt them and mess with them. There'd be moments when we'd think, "Oh man, maybe we're going to end up in a fight." But then they'd come up after the show and go, "Oh, that was the greatest!"'

WHEN JOEY MET COREY

'You ever had clamidia?'
    'No.'
    'You don't want it. Ever had gonorrhea?'
    'No.'
    'You don't want it. Ever had hepatitis B?'
    'No.'
That's an approximation of Joey Jordison's first ever conversation with Corey Taylor at Sinclair's Garage, in which the latter quizzed the former about various sexually transmitted diseases. All that's missing in this reconstruction is Corey's vivid descriptions of each ailment's symptoms.

Corey was a fiery young man. Despite playing in Stone Sour he remained an energy ball with little focus and even fewer outlets for his hyperactivity. All Des Moines could offer socially were watering holes. The choice of adolescent hangouts was simple enough: either the skating rink or Woodland Cemetery.

No prizes for guessing where Corey would go. 'The graveyard's not too far away from downtown,' he later recalled, 'so we'd hang out there. We'd get so drunk sometimes that we'd actually contemplate digging up a skull and drinking wine out of it!'

While Corey had been to see Slipknot play – he attended their debut 4 April show – Joey and Corey had yet to meet. They finally did when Joey's best friend Isaac Christiansen brought the singer down to Sinclair's.

Joey: 'I remember Corey getting out of the car and jumping up and down, spazzing out. He had long, long blond hair. I was like, "What is that dude's problem?" It was like he was on crack – he was stomping around, headbanging. I told Isaac: "Take Dave Mustaine, put him back in the car and get him the fuck out of here!"'

Of course, Isaac didn't. So Joey watched bemused as this madman grabbed a procession of candy bars from the racks, shoving them in his mouth.

Then came the seminar on sexually transmitted diseases. After that, Corey popped the billion dollar question. 'Do you think my band's cheese?'

Joey shook his head. 'No, dude, it's cool.'

Joey was lying. 'I *totally* thought it was cheese,' he later laughed. 'It was heavy, but we were a lot heavier. And Corey was completely into what we were doing.'

LUCKY SEVEN

It occurred to Joey that the band still wasn't complete. Their recordings featured a lot of samples that they couldn't pull off live. While electronic sounds and hip hop beats were increasingly in vogue for rock, what with the increasingly common-place cross-pollination of rap and metal, Slipknot didn't just want their effects to be automatically played from a DAT during gigs.

Joey had an idea. Craig Jones promptly received a sideways promotion, becoming Slipknot's full-time samples man.

Joey: 'He liked doing that anyway, coming up with all these noises and sounds.'

Big Mick Thompson came in on guitar. Having seen Slipknot play, he hardly needed much persuading. After all, Mick had recently spent most of his time sitting at home prac-tising guitar and being utterly despondent.

A massive Jimi Hendrix fan ('He was the whole reason I got into music'), Mick has always been renowned for intimi-dating folk on first contact. And sometimes second, third and sixteenth contact.

Corey: 'Mick is the scariest member of Slipknot: him and Craig. Mick is very overwhelming if you don't know him. He doesn't say a word, and he's complete death when he's onstage. Craig is the quietly scary type. You don't even know he's in the band, but he knows what's up. If you don't know either of those guys, it's best to back out slowly, saying, "Sorry to have bothered you, I just wanted to use the bathroom!"'

Mick: 'I'm usually quiet ... unless I'm pissed off. It's one or the other. The I'll-rip-your-fucking-head-off side of me comes out when I'm onstage. I'm not always like that. I'm a nice guy, but at the same time, don't mess with me!'

A self-confessed 'night person', Mick unsurprisingly shared Craig's morbid fascination with serial slaughterers.

'If I were a famous killer,' he has ruminated, 'I'd take some of the finer points of quite a few of them – Albert Fish and Ed Gein spring to mind.'

Fittingly then, Mick ended up wearing a heavy-duty mask which resembled the joint handiwork of screen death-dealers Dr Hannibal Lecter and Jason Voorhees.

'It's weird,' he said of his choice of headgear. 'You do something, and there's a reason, even though you don't necessarily know why. Your subconscious gravitates towards something – it's revealing yourself, in a way. My mask just really fits me – I couldn't possibly wear anything else. I'm not a clown – that's Shawn's whole thing and it suits him really well.'

Joey's decision to recruit Mick had initially been based more on musical concerns than personal ones. 'Me and Mick used to hate each other,' Joey told me. 'We just never knew each other and we thought each other were dicks. To me, Mick just seemed to be about macho shit. Then I got to know him properly.'

Mick slotted into the band well, despite his initial jitters.

'One rehearsal,' laughed Joey, 'Shawn set up a video camera to film us playing. Mick was so paranoid, he thought the camera was on him the whole time, to see how he played and the way he looked. He thought that if he fucked up, he'd be kicked out!'

MIXING WITH THE RIGHT PEOPLE

When the time finally came to mix *Mate Feed Kill Repeat*, Sean McMahon learnt the full extent of Slipknot's obsessive behaviour.

'We mixed and re-mixed some of the songs a number of

times, what with Joey being very "persnicketty",' said the producer, sounding for all the world like Ned Flanders of *The Simpsons*. 'I'd worked with a lot of bands and my modus operandi was respecting the fact that most people don't have much money to spend recording. I tried to get them from point A to point B expediently, without sweating the small stuff. There were some details that I saw as small things, but were major issues to Joe. So I would mix and remix stuff to keep him happy.'

Interestingly, the yardstick for how good the album sounded was Joey's single-speaker boom-box at Sinclair's.

McMahon: 'It was horrible, but that was the standard. The key was, we would go to Sinclair's with a test CD. We would play it, and to use Joey's vernacular, if the speaker farted out, it didn't pass the test. So essentially what we kept mixing and mastering for, was a situation where the speaker did not fart out. It was a challenge to get it there, but we did eventually.'

Not without a great deal of arguing, however.

McMahon: 'Let's put it this way: at that point, there were eight guys – seven of whom were extremely intense individuals. Joey and Craig were the smallest people in the band! When we tried to get something mixed, I was getting seven or eight different opinions thrown at me. The conflict resolution was initially a violent process! It was downright scary – I wanted to crawl underneath the recording console and hide!' The producer stressed that while there was never physical violence among the band members, time and money pressures led to 'very intense voicings of opinions, often punctuated with profanity. People bickering was making things go along very slowly.'

Mike Lawyer: 'Sean is a such a straightforward, focused, mellow guy. Slipknot thrive on tension. It took them a while to feel each other out. To Slipknot, their fighting was creative. They weren't being inspired by drugs or alcohol – they were being inspired by pushing each other's buttons and going for the aggression.'

'We're human,' defended Shawn 'Imagine Salvador Dali and Picasso collaborating on a painting. Picasso would be like,

"Hey, that bitch needs three tits" and Dali would be like, "Why does she need three legs?" There'd be fucking war, dude, but at the end of it there'd be a beautiful surrealistic creation that would blow everybody away.'

During one confrontational episode, Shawn somehow managed to lose a ring his wife had given him. He subsequently admitted: 'We were arguing in SR one time and I was swelling up, so I had to take my ring off. I slammed it down somewhere and I haven't seen it since. My wife made it for me. She bought me another one, but it wasn't quite the same.'

Three years later, someone found the ring, much to Shawn's delight.

'That ring is the one thing that reminds me of who I really am in life,' he said. 'No matter how bad it gets or how cut up my face gets, or how many dead cow heads are all over everybody. When it gets like that, I look at my ring and realise that I have something that most people don't have: happiness with a family who love me very much.'

One night in the studio, Slipknot's bickering became too much for Sean McMahon.

'He got so fucking mental on us that he kicked us all out!' Shawn laughed. 'The whole band got mad and told me to go see what was up. I snuck back in and he was laying on the floor, looking up at the sky and wondering why he was working with this weird-ass band!'

McMahon: 'I went into the studio area, shut off the lights, lay down on my back and took three deep breaths. I tried to regain my composure and get myself together, so I could go back to work.'

Crahan managed to sweet-talk McMahon and Lawyer into allowing Slipknot's vital project to continue.

'I'd have to come in for private little meetings with them,' said Shawn. 'They'd be like, "Enough is enough!" I'd say, "Dude, we're gonna take this all the way, we're gonna make it. Please believe in us." They stuck with us the whole time and here we are today.'

Mike Lawyer: 'We just had to realise that this was going to

be a completely different type of band to deal with than anybody I'd ever experienced anywhere else. It was frustrating and nerve-wracking, but we knew there had to be something there. A band like this had never come out of Iowa, that's for sure.'

In June, when the mixing process was completed, there was still the mastering to contend with. In all honesty, no-one without a degree understands what this process entails, but it's said to be tricky.

McMahon: 'We had this manufacturing company do it three times, and we were not happy with anything that they did. So the band just said, "McMahon, *you're* mastering it!" I was like, "No, you don't understand – I'm not a mastering engineer." I contend that someone who has engineered and produced something is without question the worst possible person to master it. Part of the glory of mastering is being able to throw it at a fresh ear.'

Nevertheless, the producer buckled under the band's persuasive ways and gave it a try. For a while. 'I eventually withdrew. The band were making a lot of changes and I really felt like we were beginning to castrate the project. We'd over-processed it, and lost what I felt was the rawness and energy. I believe that Mike Lawyer ended up doing much of the mastering.'

The album ended up bearing a hidden bonus track called 'Dogfish Rising'. By all accounts, it was a less-than-serious affair.

McMahon: 'It was partly a spoof on Kurt Cobain. At least, that's what it started out as. It rapidly deteriorated into something quite different. Joey set his drums up, not in the studio but in the control room. We had a great time.'

The 'Dogfish' experience involved the band and a posse of pals scribbling down ad-libbed lyrics, then taking it in turns to sing them.

'There were probably a good 15 to 20 of us,' said McMahon. 'When it came to someone else's turn to do a vocal line, we would literally throw the microphone across the room to this person. They'd either catch it, or in some cases not and it would hit the floor. All that stuff was left in the final track – it's hilarious. There are all kinds of references to sphincter muscles.'

THE LAUNCH

On Halloween, *Mate Feed Kill Repeat* was unveiled with a party at – where else? – the Safari. People peered intently at the sleeve of the new record, which depicted Joey naked in a metal cage. The cage had been made by Shawn, Joey and Anders. It was a piece entitled *Patiently Awaiting The Jigsaw Flesh*.

Joey: 'We took that album sleeve photo in Indianola in minus 30 degree weather. That cage was so rusty. Jesus, I should have had a tetanus jab before I got in there.'

The cage also became known as the Death Cage, and would become part of the band's stage show, with various willing victims sitting inside it while they played.

The *Mate Feed Kill Repeat* release party drew 400 people. This attendance blew the band's minds.

Joey: 'It seemed like the height of our careers. We thought it couldn't get any better than that.'

The album itself stands today as a promising first effort, featuring a few rudimentary versions of tracks such as 'Only One' and 'Tattered And Torn' which would eventually come to their ultimate fruition on the *Slipknot* album three years on.

Only 999 CD copies were reportedly pressed up, and Shawn Crahan admits that even he doesn't own one. 'At the time, that first album was the best thing ever,' he told *hiponline.com*. 'It's a sick, demented, magical album. But we don't support it anymore. It really didn't have any structure. We'd try anything as a band, as long as we felt it belonged to Slipknot. We had songs that go from total death metal to grindcore, right into funk and disco. But we made it so it wasn't a joke. It was really powerful and it was really us. We were basically soul-searching for our true entity and trying to figure out exactly what we were going to be.'

Joey admitted: 'Our style was kinda disjointed at first, because we had so much we wanted to do, but didn't know how to get it all out.'

Nevertheless, original copies of the album have since changed hands on the eBay website for as much as 400 dollars. Slipknot could have done with that kind of money at the time. Shawn was by now up to his eyes in debt.

In January 2001, Mike Lawyer told me: 'The band never considered collecting a dime from any shows they did. Everything went back into merchandise, equipment and so on. I don't know Mick or Craig very well, but I know that no-one in the band came from privileged families. Paul and Corey particularly came from poor families. They've all slaved and worked for pretty low pay. That's what set Slipknot apart. If you believe in what you do enough, you'd better be ready to eat peanut butter sandwiches for two years.'

GUERRILLA RADIO

After the release of *Mate Feed Kill Repeat*, Sean McMahon set about sending copies of the album out to around 120 people at record and management companies.

'I knew I had no power to make Slipknot's career happen, so I at least wanted to try and put them in the hands of people who *could*. The response ranged from interest to "Are you out of your mind – what *is* this crap?" I wonder how many of those people have sold the album on eBay!'

McMahon put the band's passion for crows to good use, turning the bird into a promotional item.

'They definitely had a crow fetish,' said the producer. 'It's a dark, ominous bird that appears out of nowhere and is some-what known for being a cunning or wise creature. Whenever we had an A&R rep who was hot on the band, we made a point of sending a very realistic-looking life-sized theatrical crow to them. We put the crow in the package with the CD and the bio – it was the kind of thing that you could get to sit on your shoulder or whatever.' On occasions, the crow would grab people's attention. To some, including McMahon, it became a symbol of their tenacity and conviction.

'People became curious as to what the crow fetish was,' he said. 'Something which was evident early on was that the band believed in itself. Their attitude was, "We *are* breaking out of Des Moines – we *are* making it." They were convinced of this. It was much to their credit – what they were trying to show their other musical peers was: do something unique, be willing to be yourself and you *will* make it.'

On a local level, McMahon made a point of playing *Mate Feed Kill Repeat* to Sophia John, who was Assistant Programme Director at the relatively new Des Moines radio station KKDM 107.5.

Recalled McMahon: 'Sophia was like, "These guys are amazing – this is a *local* band?"'

'The station played cheesy alternative rock,' said Joey, 'but Sophia loved our band and she knew we had something.'

It just so happened that KKDM 107.5 were staging a 'Battle Of The Bands' competition, with outfits playing on air through several heats over several weeks. The panel of judges included people from local TV stations and newspapers. The first heat saw Slipknot pitted against none other than Stone Sour.

Joey: 'We thought we'd lose, because Corey was the king of Des Moines. He was the beautiful singer-guy with the nice voice – he didn't do any screaming or hard vocals back then at all.'

Nevertheless, Slipknot emerged victorious over the Sour boys. They had a few weeks to get over the shock before the second round, in which they went head-to-head with a band named Maelstrom.

Joey: 'We wiped their asses! Killed 'em dead.'

By the time the finals arrived on 18 December, it was just Slipknot and an improvisational jazz-rock band called Black Caesar in the running. A difficult one to judge.

Joey: 'We still weren't confident enough to think we were gonna win, but we went absolutely ape-shit bonkers on that last show.' It paid off. Slipknot walked away with the prize.

'We were so happy,' recalled Joey. 'We won this extra recording fund, so we went back and started demoing some more material.'

After this, Slipknot's future record label Roadrunner started showing more interest in the band. The company dispatched a scout to check out the band. Ultimately, Roadrunner Records' A&R supremo Monte Conner expressed interest in seeing where the band were in a year's time.

Joey: 'We started having label negotiations, but Roadrunner weren't interested all that much. They thought the music was good, but the singer needed a little work and a little melody.'

On New Year's Eve, Slipknot played the first gig to earn them a significant amount of money. This was still only 1500 dollars split between them, but it was better than the 10 bucks to which they were accustomed.

The show saw the band dressing up in ludicrous outfits. Mick wore a Little Bo Peep costume.

Shawn: 'Mick is almost seven-foot tall with long black hair. He looks extremely brutal. When you see him dressed like Little Bo Peep with the bonnet, that's twisted.'

At that time, Slipknot would often sport outfits which veered towards the comical. One night when they supported Brooklyn goth-core merchants Type O Negative, Shawn dressed himself up like Barney, the TV dinosaur character. During a live chat at *twec.com* the percussionist said: 'It was probably one of the hardest things I've ever done in my entire life. I felt like I was underwater. But the whole time, I made Barney look like he was on crack.'

Shawn would also wear a nun's habit on occasions. While this more humorous side of the band would later be abandoned in favour of a united serious front, it felt pretty damn good on that New Year's Eve.

Joey: 'We were freaking out! There were about 600 or 700 people at that show. That night, we even had our own hotel rooms.'

Finances aside, Slipknot's main problem was being fat fish

in a small pond. Vacating those waters would prove the hardest challenge of all. To prove the point, those rejection letters were starting to pile up.

Joey: 'We were ruling Des Moines and having fun, but everybody else thought we sucked.'

Sophia John became Slipknot's first manager, at their request.

'She was helping us out so much towards the end of '96,' Joey explained, 'that it soon became apparent that she should manage the band fully.'

Sean McMahon: 'It was very much against Sophia's will. She went kicking and screaming. She was the Programme Director at a radio station – she had a lot on her plate already. She really didn't feel that she had the time or resources to put into managing a band. But she had developed a really good rapport with people at record and management companies.'

John told the *Iowa State Publications Board*: 'I saw a lot of pieces to the puzzle that make a band good. They have good writing, solid shows, publicity in newspapers, and even now some airplay. What they're doing is so unique and there are a lot of signs that they're "in".

'I'm gonna do what's best for the band,' she continued. 'Our first goal was to make one million copies of its new album – now it's three million. I want the whole thing for them – I want the dream. I want to see Slipknot on the cover of *Rolling Stone*, playing at Ozzfest and having its own record label. Then they can come back and grab the local bands that supported them.'

For all her enthusiasm and goodwill – not to mention fairly accurate predictions – John couldn't work miracles. The lack of reaction from the outside world conspired to send Slipknot into a slump.

At the end of January, Shawn bought Safari. Of late, it had seemed like he practically ran the place anyway.

Shawn: 'I would come down and mop the floor before the shows. I would tell Tony which drinks to have specials on and totally get involved. It got to the point where he went, "Dude, just buy the bar!" So I did, and I opened it up to everyone in local music. I built a new stage and a huge dressing room. We had "battle of the bands" competitions and benefits for local hospitals.'

While we can presume that this acquisition took Shawn up to the $40,000 debt mark, he was doing this as an investment to eventually claw back some funds. And by all accounts, he did it well.

Praised McMahon: 'Shawn brought in some very good bands during his tenure as owner there. It obviously worked well for Slipknot too, because it gave them a place to play.'

Secretly, however, Joey saw Shawn's purchase as a bad move. 'I hated it. It took Shawn's time away from the band.'

To make matters worse, in February, the band were kicked out of Anders' basement, leaving them with nowhere to rehearse. This situation lasted four months, during which time they barely played together.

'I was pissed off.' Joey admitted 'I went to start jamming with The Rejects again. Eventually, I told Shawn that he should be concentrating on the band – not the fucking bar.'

There were no immediate results. Tension grew.

Then one day, Joey Jordison left Slipknot.

3
Resurrection

Biding my time, until the time is right
Corey Taylor, #8, 'Scissors'

THE STORM

3 June 1997
Joey and Shawn bundled off stage screaming blue murder at
each other.

Slipknot had just played in front of 18,000 people at an
outdoor festival called Dotfest in Ankeny, a short distance
from Des Moines.

'We sucked so bad,' winced Joey. 'Everything went wrong,
in front of a crowd that size. It was supposed to be The
Moment. I got off stage and me and Shawn ran into this huge
fight. I quit the fucking band.'

This wasn't as severe a measure as it sounded, however.
After sinking into a huge depression, triggered both by the
disappointment of playing such a bad show and the thought of
the Slipknot-free future which stretched out before him, Joey
reconsidered. He inevitably patched things up with Shawn
and returned to the fold.

Dotfest would not have been an event fit for inclusion in Slipknot's history book had it not also been the day that they first laid eyes on Sid Wilson. Wilson, who was destined to become the band's #0 – the maddest member of them all – was spinning records at a T-shirt tent on the festival site.

'I remember looking at this kid,' said Joey. 'He had Elvis glasses on and his hat was turned 'round some whack-ass way. He had a Michael Jackson shirt on and shorts hanging half-way off his ass. He looked crazy. He was slamming to all these records he was playing.'

Neither Joey nor the other 'Knotters spoke to Wilson that day. But he stayed in their heads. The next few months would see vital changes in their line-up, cementing the Slipknot which would break through and bite chunks out of the cosmos.

THE LOST ALBUM

By the summer of 1997 Slipknot were back at SR, working on their second record – a little-known project which would never be released. Slipknot were continuing to hone their craft – at least as far as they were able with the present line-up. Despite their boundless enthusiasm, they had started to run into problems with Anders.

'We were writing new songs which required a little more vocal melody,' recalled Joey. 'Andy was trying, but it just wasn't working.'

It seemed that many of the rejection letters from various companies cited the vocals as a sticking point.

Sean McMahon recalled a 100-minute argument in the studio, concerning the pitch of one of Anders' vocal lines.

'Andy was great for growled vocals,' said McMahon. 'But I felt he had some intonation problems.'

That night would prove key in Slipknot's timeline.

Recalled McMahon: 'After Andy left the session that night, Clown and Joey were shaking their heads going, "Man, that was a lot of work." Clown asked Joey outside, saying he wanted a smoke. When they came back in, they said,

"McMahon, what would you think if we got Corey to join the band?" I was like, "*What*? Corey from Stone Sour?!" He had a great voice and I could imagine it, but wondered if they could actually get him onboard.'

The duo were already out the door.

PORN AGAIN

As Stone Sour was hardly paying the rent, let alone keeping him in Spiderman action figures, Corey Taylor had needed a job. He settled on a Des Moines sex shop named Adult Emporium.

'It ruled. I'm always drawn to the sick and disgusting, but I didn't see the shop in that light – just a natural way of expressing your perversion. I worked the midnight-to-eight shift. It was really only busy at the weekends, when all the freaks came in.

'Sometimes people treated *me* like a freak,' he said incredulously. 'I thought, "You're in a porn shop at four in the morning, looking for something to give you a toss – what are you looking at *me* for?!"'

Corey made a point of ensuring that his customers didn't feel embarrassed about selecting their 14-inch dildos. The way he saw it, the world was already flooded with enough sexual guilt, courtesy of religion and moral crusaders.

'That was important for me. People are made to feel dirty every day, and that's bullshit. Most of my customers eventually got past the fact that I had really long hair with about eight different colours. I was a pretty psychotic-looking guy, but I ended up having a lot of regulars who would say hi when they came in.'

One night at the Emporium, Corey was paid a visit by three people he didn't expect to see: Joey, Mick and Shawn. Their message was simple enough.

Corey: 'They basically told me that if I didn't join the band, they'd kick my ass!'

'Corey was shaking,' recalled Joey. 'Freaking out. We said we'd get in touch with him, and left. We were deliberately trying to make him mental.'

'Singing in this band was something I really wanted to do,' Corey told local journalist RH Michaels. 'Ever since I saw those guys there was this thing in my head going, "What would it be like to be in Slipknot?" I loved the guys in Stone Sour, but I felt like I could expand more here.'

The idea of joining Slipknot represented a great opportunity for Taylor, in many ways.

For one thing, he was miserable. 'I was all pent-up,' he admitted. 'I was hurting myself and drinking a lot. There's a lot of pent-up aggression in Des Moines, and a lot of people who don't have the facility or the mentality to form a band like Slipknot. They're stuck in a drug hell, a job hell – they can't express themselves like we do, so they destroy themselves bit by bit.'

The masks also held great appeal for the singer. 'I had my long hair and I was a pretty-boy, whatever. But with Stone Sour, nobody really got into my writing – I wanted people to hear the music. That was one of the reasons I wanted to join Slipknot. For one thing, you don't know what the band members look like. In Slipknot, there's no more wondering if you should wear these jeans with this shirt tonight. It's like, "Here's my fucking uniform – here's my music." It's about complete expression, rather than image.'

Just about the only downside of joining Slipknot was that Corey had to abandon a work-in-progress Stone Sour album which the band had been recording with Sean McMahon at SR.

'That came to a screeching halt,' McMahon laughed, 'and Corey's grandmother was paying for it! We had quite a few songs done. It got shelved and nothing's been done to it.'

From the material on this half-formed melodic rock project, McMahon would single out two tracks in particular, 'Monolith' and 'Tumult', as songs which could still stand up in the new millennium. He described another tune entitled

'Covetous Me' as having 'kind of a White Zombie-meet-Nine Inch Nails feel'.

We'd have to take his word for it.

GET IN THE BOOTH

Inevitably, Corey ended up coming down to SR Studios.

'We threw him in the vocal booth,' said Joey, 'and he wrote some lyrics right there on the spot.'

The words Corey scribbled that night were for the song 'Me Inside'. The moments before he sang them were suspenseful, to say the least.

'They didn't know what the fuck I was gonna do,' said the singer 'so I just went for it. They all sat up and went, "Holy shit! That *works!*"'

Joey: 'The moment he started singing, me and Shawn looked at each other and said, "That's our boy." He could do the really good melodic singing and he had a great personality.'

Shawn had mixed feelings about this development.

'It wasn't that he didn't like Corey,' Joey noted. 'It was just that we'd have to move Andy, who was one of Shawn's best friends.'

Shawn also had the task of breaking the news to Anders. The singer would now contribute backing vocals and percussion.

Anders later told the local press: 'If I didn't like it, I wouldn't be here anymore. At first, it was a little bit of a shock. My thing was, "Let's see how it sounds."'

'It was hard, but we were thinking about what was best for the band,' said Joey. 'We knew the sky was the limit and we weren't gonna accept anything less. No prisoners.'

Corey described his first practice session with Slipknot as 'kinda weird. Stone Sour and Slipknot were pretty stiff rivals. I really wanted to get into this band and they were again looking at me, going, "Let's see what happens." I didn't give a shit. By the end of the practice, we were all slamming.

Nobody normally did that in Slipknot. We were so into it, that this power was coming out of us.'

In a town the size of Des Moines, and in a microscopic metal scene, nothing could be kept secret. Word soon spread that Corey had been practising with Slipknot.

Joey: 'People flipped. There was this big drama about Corey's arrival. People said it would ruin the band, or they said it would make the band better, or they said we were assholes for breaking Stone Sour up. Whatever it was, everybody had something to say about it.'

Slipknot quickly integrated Corey into the band. After a while, even Anders had to admit it was sounding more than viable.

'We practised and everything just clicked,' he told the local press. 'A lot of bands do vocal overdubs in the studio to make everything fuller, but live they can't do it because they don't have enough people who can sing. We can get five going at once.' There was confusion in some of the local rags as to exactly what Slipknot were doing, back at SR Studios. Speaking to Lori Brookhart, Joey clarified that they were not re-recording *Mate Feed Kill Repeat*. Not exactly, anyway.

'We are focusing on the way things are now in the band,' he said. 'Everything is gelling differently and we've learnt how to write songs differently. Through playing live, we've experienced a lot of different sounds. We have come up with new ideas for songs we originally recorded. When we started out we came up with a lot of kick-ass ideas that most bands go their whole career without coming up with: that's something to be proud of. Slipknot has become more now than ever before.'

Joey also explained the latest incarnation of the band's triangle of percussive power.

'I play the main set which is all acoustic drums, and I am the main drummer. I sit in the back and I am the glue that holds the band together. The Clown is a total power drummer; he is all aggression. Now, we have acquired electronic drums to work with the samples for a different element to the music. The third drummer is taking care of a tribal, auxiliary sound while also doing his vocals. We want three perspectives for an auditory overkill.'

Indeed, in all the excitement over the band's image and overall musical assault, the importance of Slipknot's unique percussive configuration is often under-played. As is the skill which it requires.

'I'm a big fan of Joey's drumming,' Shawn has said. 'There's not a day in practice, or during a show, that I'm not amazed. Standing up and playing drums isn't as easy as it looks, either. Try it some time – it's extremely brutal.'

TECHNICAL AGONY

On the night of 22 August 1997, Joey Jordison would be re-christened Superball by his bandmates. This was due to his bouncing around in a fit of blind, miserable rage.

Slipknot felt that their first show with Corey Taylor did not go well. This was not down to a poor turn-out or lack of interest. On the contrary – the Safari was packed with folks struggling to breathe in the arid summer heat. Even the bar's fish-tank was layered with steam.

This was a benefit show, for the local Blank Children's Hospital. The cause couldn't have been closer to Shawn's heart, as the hospital had saved the life of his newborn son.

'They are a godsend,' he told one journalist on the night. 'I'm gonna take my little clown-boy up there tomorrow and deliver the cheque in person.'

Charity aside, the show was ill-starred from the outset, due to massive expectations riding on it. Although Anders was still in the band, tonight was in essence the launch of Slipknot Version 2.0. Corey took to the stage without a mask. Instead, he had grotesque make-up all over his face and latex exes over both eyes. Add long, bright-red hair and you're talking supreme strangeness.

'I was really nervous at first,' Corey told the local press, 'but I put all that into the aggression because I wanted this to go over and I wanted people to accept it. I've never pushed that hard in my life – there were times when I had to cut back and I missed a few lines, but I came right back in. Luckily I had guys onstage to help me out.'

Unfortunately, the band were beset by technical problems.

'Josh's amplifier fucked up horribly,' Joey later remembered. 'We had all kinds of feedback problems and the heat was so intense we couldn't breathe. We were trying to work out the bugs in our first show with Corey, in front of 500 local people.'

Hence Joey transforming into Superball.

Anders told the press of his first show *sans* spotlight: 'It was crazy, it was weird. I'm not singing as much, but I am moving more and beating on the drums more. I thought I was going to be a lot less tired than I normally am, but I was wrong.'

After the show, Joey 'completely bugged out. I couldn't believe it. I was so depressed.'

Insult would later be added to injury. That night, Joey sloped into his house and went to his room. He saw that there were some messages on his personal answering machine and pressed the button.

'I can't believe you guys fuckin' cheesed out,' sneered an anonymous caller. 'That dude sucks! Go back to your old singer.' Click.

Right there and then, Joey Jordison was truly crestfallen. Today, that whole moment still pisses him off, but he has reason to thank whoever left that message. It was those kind of detractors who continually spurred Slipknot on to rage so hard.

FIGHT OR FLIGHT

Despite the fierce self-belief which had propelled them this far, Slipknot experienced a moment of collective doubt.

'We were wondering whether we'd made the right move with Corey,' Joey later admitted. Thankfully, their resolve would strengthen. 'Finally,' said Joey, 'we decided it was just a bad show, and Corey was just getting started.'

Interestingly, the local press reviewed the show favourably. 'Most of the crowd wanted to see if Corey Taylor could pull it off,' wrote RH Michaels. 'He did. By appearances, you'd think Corey died and came back as a different man. The old and the new meshed well. Vocals contained all of the passion and emotion that fans have come to expect from Slipknot. They also attained a crisper sound.'

By the time the next Safari show rolled around, on 17 September, Corey was wearing an actual mask. His new band-mates had found him the basic face-piece, and he dreaded up his hair, shoving the ropey snakes through holes in the mask. He would later cut the dreads off, but attach them to the mask for that medusa touch. This time, the show was far better and – contrary to the band's fears – the turn-out remained healthy.

Joey: 'We were glad people were still interested. We came out and completely ruled. It was a great show.' It was also a very strange, and pivotal, one. When Slipknot started the gig, they had eight members. When they ended the show, they had one less.

AND THEN THERE WERE SEVEN

'I've got an announcement to make. This will be my last show.'

Anders' sudden declaration took both band and audience by surprise. Slipknot were, after all, standing onstage, about to launch into their closing tune 'Scissors'.

'I was pleased he wanted to go,' Joey would admit. 'I didn't give a fuck if that was rude of me or heartless. I felt Andy didn't fit – he wasn't even wearing a mask, he was wearing tape.'

Shawn was less jubilant about Colsefni's decision.

Joey: 'I remember Shawn pacing back and forth, shaking his head, as we played the song. I tried to tell him not to let it show. They were really good friends, so for Shawn it went deeper.'

Corey: 'Anders wasn't feeling fulfilled in Slipknot to begin with. If he hadn't left, I don't even know what the band would sound like today. I don't even think about it anymore.'

With Anders gone – he would later form the band Painface, in 1998 (see www.painface.com) – Slipknot threw their efforts back into their second demo-album. They erased their ex-frontman's vocals, recording Corey's in their place.

Songs on this new untitled album included 'Slipknot', 'Gently', 'Do Nothing', 'Tattered And Torn', 'Scissors', 'Me Inside', 'Coleslaw', 'Carve', 'Windows' and 'May 17th' – the latter's lyrics apparently written by Shawn, concerning a dispute with his father-in-law.

Joey: 'That album was never released. We still have it, and we might release it some day, because I'd still stand by it now.'

Judged Mike Lawyer: 'There's some stuff on there which is every bit as good, or better, than anything on the *Slipknot* album. This is one of those bands that never looks back. Even if they've recorded great material, it may take them a couple of years to finally realise that it's so good. They're such worka-holics, that they always wanna be doing something new. Once they do a song, they don't care about it – they want to be working on the next one.'

ENTER DICKNOSE

To maintain that percussive power triangle which they so believed in, Slipknot again needed fresh blood. After testing a few people who didn't fit the picture, the band tried out a guy from Ankeny named Chris Fehn, who had previously come to see them play – and had even asked if he could roadie for the band.

There is a scene in the excellent turn-of-the-millennium movie *Fight Club*, in which various applicants stand outside rebel leader Tyler Durden's derelict house for days on end, suffering verbal abuse which is secretly all part of the test. You'd swear the scene was based on Slipknot's cruel vetting process for Fehn.

Joey: 'We made him so mental! We made him come to prac-tice at Shawn's house, then we sat out on the front porch having drinks and laughing, while he sat around the back by himself with the mosquitoes. We were talking about him, to see if he would fit into Slipknot.'

Fehn's ordeal stretched out for a month. Finally, Joey asked Josh to go and get Chris from the back garden.

'Alright, dude,' Joey told Fehn as the others looked on. 'We've been talking and we know you've worked really hard. But we're just gonna have to say no.'

Fehn dejectedly looked down at his own Sepultura T-shirt. 'That's cool, man,' he murmured.

'Just kidding!' blurted Joey. 'You got the gig!'

Fehn exploded into laughter, along with his new band-mates. 'You fucking cocksuckers!'

Chris subsequently opted for a perverted zipper-mouthed mask with a highly phallic nose. Depending on which Internet site you believe, it's seven or eight inches long.

'This mask reflects my comic personality,' he would tell *Kerrang!* 'Plus, I chose it for the bondage factor. When you put it on, it takes you to another place. It's very hot, it's very tight and it hurts. Which goes along with the aggression we create.'

INTERVIEW WITH THE VAMPIRES

Slipknot seemed very fond of mischievous, testing behaviour. One of their first interviews, with a local female journalist, proved highly memorable.

Shawn: 'We got her to come to the basement of my house. I opened the door in my mask and she immediately shit herself. She was scared out of her fucking mind, shaking like a leaf.'

Downstairs in Shawn's basement, the rest of the band were waiting with their masks on. The darkness was softened only by a few strategically placed candles.

Joey: 'That basement was pretty scary in itself. It had stinking mildew, jagged bricks, water leaking. It looked like the place out of *Pulp Fiction*, where they keep the gimp.'

The journalist had yet even to see this basement, but she was terrified. She asked for something to drink.

'You know,' Shawn teased her, 'You don't *have* to do this interview.'

Recalling the incident, he said: 'I got her some water and I heard this weird music from the basement. It sounded like one string on an acoustic guitar being scraped. There was shit being dragged across the floor. I took her down there and this lady was in her hell. I was actually kinda freaked out myself!'

To her eternal credit, the writer sat down and began the interview.

'By the end, she was *so* into us,' said Shawn triumphantly. 'She became a Slipknot fan and came to all the shows.'

THINK OF A NUMBER

Having assembled their dream line-up, Slipknot set about creating a uniform for themselves with *those* coveralls – each adorned with a barcode. Somewhere along the line, the idea came up of assigning a number to each person.

Corey: 'Originally, we were just going to wear the jumpsuits with the barcodes. We figured we might as well take that further and number ourselves. If we were going to be wearing the barcode anyway, we were basically saying, "Hey, we're a product!" But it was more than that. It's a symbol of how far people take commerciality in the world today. The real reason we started doing music in the first place was to say, "Fuck you, your symbolism is bullshit!"'

Once the numerical concept was agreed on, everyone had to pick one. Corey chose the number eight.

'It's always been what you might call a lucky number for me. Shawn grabbed six because it meant something to him.'

Shawn: 'It was highly unusual that everybody fell into a number. No one even thought, "It's zero through eight." Everyone had different reasons for picking their numbers. It really felt good.'

This ease of number selection is, admittedly, hard to believe. You would imagine that, for instance, numbers two or four would have been the undesirable equivalents of Mr Pink and Mr Brown in *Reservoir Dogs*. Still, who would dare brand Slipknot liars?

NICE BEAVER

It soon became apparent that Corey didn't merely fit into Slipknot by virtue of his voice. He proved more than a match for Shawn when it came to playing with dead things onstage.

'Corey and I got a severed beaver tail from a fan,' Shawn told *hiponline.com*. 'It actually came from a police officer. In Iowa, beaver tail are extremely illegal, unless you have a permit to trap beaver. This officer said we were the only people in the world who would appreciate something like this.'

At the time, Shawn had no idea what to do with the item. So he gave it to Corey as a present, before they went onstage.

'Next thing you knew,' Shawn continued, 'we got out there and – boom – we were gone, dude. Corey and I pretty much started digesting this tail. We were squeezing the juice; oozing the fluids all over us ...'

Corey: 'We got offstage and we were puking our guts up. What the fuck were we thinking? But when you're onstage, in that zone, you'll do anything and everything possible to bring all the negative stuff out of your system. I don't know if that's good or bad ...'

HAPPY HALLOWEEN

This year, Slipknot played an unusual show at the Safari – and not just because it was one of their first shows wearing the coveralls. They were beginning to sense that a certain percentage of their audience were coming to see the band because it had become trendy. Trends were anathema to Slipknot.

Shawn: 'We felt we were getting too big and that a lot of people were just jumping on the Slipknot bandwagon, who had no idea about what we really were. It was getting to the point where it was cool to go to a Slipknot show. That made us furious.'

It was time to separate chaff from wheat. 'Joey and I made

a video of some of the sickest shit you'll ever see in your life,' said Shawn. 'Shit, piss – you name it.'

'That video was like shock therapy,' said Corey. 'It was insane. We had two huge console televisions, up on our PA speakers.'

That day, Slipknot played two shows at Safari. For the first, which was an all-ages gig, they wisely toned the visuals down.

When darkness fell, however, 400 people got more than they bargained for.

Half of them walked out.

Laughed Corey on reflection: 'We lost half our friends because of those fucking videos, man. People freaked out. One friend of mine in particular was exposed to a suicide a long time ago. The clip with this one guy shooting himself in the mouth was too much for her. She lost her mind, and I only found that out later.

'That's the problem with this band. We charge in, we don't give a fuck. Then we process the pain later. Something's always gonna offend somebody. You can't please everybody, and when I think about it, I don't want to. The only thing I wanna do is stay away from lawsuits ...'

This would prove difficult.

SPITTING IN THE WIND

Shawn eventually decided to hone down his priorities. He sold the Safari to some good friends who re-christened it Hairy Mary's II.

'We were at the stage where we just wanted to shove this fucker home,' he said. 'I had been doing all these different things. I was this crazy guy who went out onstage; I was a bar owner; I was a husband and father. Eventually, I asked myself what I really wanted to do. Did I want to own a bar? Absolutely not. Music was all I wanted to do, and everything else revolved around it.'

Slipknot wrote a new song called 'Spit It Out', which was written about a bitter dispute the band had with a local radio station, which led to the odd bar-room brawl. They recorded the track at SR with Sean McMahon.

'That was the band's re-birth,' said Shawn. 'We sent a copy of "Spit It Out" to Monte Conner at Roadrunner, along with a letter saying, "Hey, we're still doing our thing."'

Interest in Slipknot was reaching an all-time high – and now it wasn't confined to Des Moines.

Joey: 'All of a sudden, we started getting people into town to see us play. A&R guys were flying out to see us.'

A lot of the attention Slipknot received was on the basis of good word spreading across the Internet.

Joey: 'We got one call from Hollywood Records. They said that if we matched up to reports on the Internet, they'd sign us. We were like, "Yes! We'll take anything!". We were stupid. Naive and vulnerable.'

Slipknot were, however, smart enough to know that they would love Ross Robinson to produce their album. Having heard the band talking about Robinson all the time, Sophia John decided to put her feelers out on the industry network. She phoned one of her contacts, John Rees, who managed the punk band Goldfinger. Slipknot had once supported them in Des Moines. The conversation went something like this.

'John, do you know how I can get hold of this producer guy, Ross Robinson?'

'Ha. You're kidding, right?'

'No. I'm serious. I really need to get hold of him.'

'Well, I *manage* Ross Robinson.'

Destiny beckoned.

THE PRODUCER

As a spiritual kind of guy, Robinson firmly believes in fate – the idea of things being meant to be.

So, in early 1998, when Sophia John called his manager, the coincidence involved raised his eyebrow. 'It was a fluke,' Robinson told me, 'and whenever something like that happens, it always perks my interest up. That's how I find bands – through the obscure.'

An excited John rushed over the band's latest three-track demo for Ross's perusal.

'The tape had way, way different versions of everything,' he said. 'Apart from "Spit It Out", a lot of the stuff later changed totally. On the final album, there's more vibe, more energy and that really demented ghosty thing you feel. But the demo tape wasn't really the thing that inspired me.'

Neither was Ross overly taken by the enclosed promotional photograph. 'The mask thing didn't mean too much to me,' he insisted. 'It wasn't like, "Oh my God! They wear masks!" To me, At The Drive-In's afro haircuts are more effective than those masks. If I describe Slipknot, I don't ever talk about the masks. I'm about music. The masks reflect their attitudes and they turn into different beings with them on, which is cool. But when I work with them, the masks aren't sitting on their faces.'

A few weeks later, Robinson flew to Des Moines with his manager – an endeavour which, he later admitted, was 'partly a favour for Sophia'.

The idea was for the pair to check out a Slipknot rehearsal at Shawn Crahan's parents' house and then a big show they were playing at the Safari.

They would get more than they bargained for.

MEETING OF MINDS

As Robinson and his manager drove towards the snow-capped Crahan residence on 1 February 1998, they saw tiny figures clustered on the front porch. As they got closer, they could tell it was Slipknot unmasked.

'They were all smoking and hanging out,' chuckled Robinson. 'Then, when they saw my car coming, they all ran into the house. That was pretty cool!'

Joey would claim that he was sitting inside the house, in the computer room, trying to remain calm.

'I said to the others, "Dude, you just made yourselves look *so* nervous, by running into the goddamn house!" But we were all shitting ourselves. We recognised Ross straight away, from Korn's home video.'

Even back then, Slipknot were a tightly-knit unit, shunning outsiders unless it was deemed absolutely necessary.

Shawn: 'We didn't want people in the practice room, going, "Why don't you play that riff a couple more times?" We've always cared about what *we* think, first and foremost. If people watch us rehearse and say, "Hey, I really like that bridge part", we'll probably get rid of it. We don't want any influence.'

When strangers did venture into their space, Slipknot had a standard procedure.

'Whether you're male, female, animal or bird,' said Shawn, 'when you come into the basement, everybody will say in unison: "Girl in the practice room!"'

But this visitor was different.

Joey: 'Of course, Ross was the tenth member of Slipknot without even knowing it yet. He was an honorary member. He could come in.'

As Ross and his manager descended the stairs to Slipknot's hallowed basement, the tension was palpable.

'I stood by Joey's drum-kit,' recalled Ross. 'Everyone was totally nervous.'

Joey: 'I was thinking, "This sucks. Why do you have to pick me to stand by? My God!"'

Ross: 'They were so nervous. Joey counted the first song in, and when he hit the first drum the sticks flew out of his hand!'

'I didn't even get the one-two-three-four count off,' said Joey. 'I thought we were done for, but Ross just said, "Don't worry about it, man. I hate this part too. Just do your fucking thing."' Slipknot proceeded to do just that, hammering through eight of their finest compositions.

'Corey was rolling his eyes in his head, contorting and tripping out,' said Ross. 'I was, like, "Whoah, check out the freak!"

When you put the mask on that guy, it's kinda disappointing, because you can't see all that crazy, weird shit that he does. When they were playing without the masks, you could see all these facial expressions. I think that's why the mask thing doesn't really thrill me – I know what they look like without the get-up. I like to look at people's face and read the fire.'

Concurred Shawn: 'The few people who are allowed to watch us rehearse, they fucking flip. Our practices are so destructive. You can see the pain on our faces, whereas onstage you can't. People get mental and look at us differently after that. Our tour manager and our stage manager and our manager were like, "Whoah, you guys!" This isn't a fucking joke – this is the real deal.'

Recalling the moment, Joey told *Metal Update*: 'Ross had a smile on his face from ear to ear. He said, "I've been waiting for a band like you guys. You've got the elements covered of music today, but you come from the same school as Morbid Angel and Carcass."'

Amid the post-showcase adrenaline buzz, Ross instantly clicked with the band. 'They were the same as me, in terms of what they experienced growing up,' he said. 'I look at Joey, he looks at me and we're the same person. We're both Beavises, and we both grew up in white-trash small towns. I think Corey had a more fucked-up childhood than I did, but I've gone down some serious roads and I understand life on the other side.'

The ever enigmatic Craig Jones, on the other hand, said nothing to Robinson for quite some time.

Ross: 'I would go up to him and say, "You know what, dude? You're the sickest guy in the band, I can already tell. You're the secret jacker!"'

The first thing Robinson noticed about Slipknot was their all- consuming passion.

'You look in their eyes and all you see is hunger,' he admired. 'They're the hungriest band in the world. They were completely isolated from the rest of the world and all the music business bullshit and completely on their own trip. I knew right there and then that we'd do good work together.'

LA STORY

Having spent his early years in the desert towns of Needles and Barstow, Ross Robinson could easily relate to Slipknot's sense of isolation and frustration. He moved to Hollywood at the age of 17, having been 'dying to get away. I had to get out. It was the same exact thing that Slipknot felt in Des Moines.'

When Robinson arrived in the City Of Angels, he was arrogantly optimistic about his prospects. 'Everything seemed brand new. I thought in my brain that I was the chosen one. I was a 17-year-old ego from a small town, thinking I could rip everything apart!'

After answering a small-ad in 1984, Ross ended up playing guitar in a metal band named Detente, which featured the late Dawn Crosby on vocals. After releasing 1986's *Recognise No Authority* album through a fledgling Roadrunner Records, Ross jumped ship to the ill-fated Catalepsy.

'I still thought it would be easy for me to get a record deal, no matter what,' he said. 'I was living in la-la land, because after that I couldn't find the right combination of people for it to happen. It's really rare to find that chemistry.'

In the early '90s, Ross formed a couple of bands with a drummer named Dave McClain. Destined to join Sacred Reich and then Machine Head, McClain remains Robinson's best friend to this day. After Dave landed the Reich gig, however, Ross was left somewhat high and dry.

'I was living in the practice room that we had been rehearsing in,' he recalled. 'I had a pad and a blanket rolled up in a cardboard box. I'd pull them out of the box every night and go to sleep, then get up in the morning, go to the gym, take a shower and go work at Blackie Lawless' studio for free.'

The Blackie Lawless in question was the frontman of OTT rockers W.A.S.P, and the studio was Fort Apache. In the words of *This Is Spinal Tap*'s director Rob Reiner, don't go looking for it today – it's not there anymore.

'I used to go on the roof and throw eggs at cars for fun,' said Robinson. 'Then I'd record stuff, late at night.'

Robinson learnt how to produce bands from an engineer friend who worked with Detente.

Eventually Robinson produced Sex Art – a band featuring Korn's singer-to-be Jonathan Davis and guitarist Ryan Shuck, who was destined to play guitar in Orgy.

'I did the same thing with Sex Art as I did with the other band,' said Ross, 'except I had them sign a really small agreement. Two years later, Korn signed their record deal. They stuck by me and that opened the door for all the brand new bands that I found. What happened to Korn gave bands the opportunity to make it, through me. And that totally opened the door for Slipknot. It started the whole thing ...'

LIVE EVIL

On the night of 2 February 1998, Robinson witnessed Slipknot in masked form for the first time.

Safari was packed. Not exactly the tallest man in the world, the producer stood with the rest of the crowd – some of who had clearly recognised him.

Shawn: 'We don't like to talk about things we're involved in, so we didn't tell anybody in Des Moines that Ross was there. It was funny to watch people shit themselves. They were like, "That guy looks a lot like Ross Robinson!"'

Finally, everyone in the crowd peered at the dark, vacant stage as one. As it turned out, they were facing the wrong way. Slipknot were approaching from behind.

'They barged through the crowd like destructors,' Robinson would describe, still awestruck by the memory. 'Joey was on Mick's shoulders, kicking people and hitting them on the back of the head. They were ready to rip their audience apart.'

The show was frenzied. While Robinson preferred the mask-less rehearsal he had seen earlier, it was nevertheless an amazing spectacle.

'The Clown was using an angle-grinder to shoot sparks into the crowd,' he said. 'I thought he was going to take somebody's eyes out with that thing.'

After the show, Robinson ended up hanging out backstage with a sweat-soaked Mick. Being a stubborn, dyed-in-the-wool metal-head, Mick was the member of Slipknot who was most suspicious of Robinson and his nu-metal hocus-pocus.

'I produced the first Limp Bizkit album, and that wasn't exactly a cool thing on my resume as far as Mick was concerned,' conceded Ross. 'He was wondering what I was about, because he hates that kind of music. He hates anything that isn't pure metal! His nickname is Molten Metal God.'

Wisely, Robinson began by discussing black metal with the broody giant.

'I went on to let him know how I felt about Slipknot,' Ross recalled. 'I said, "Dude, your shit's so fucking real. It's old-school, kick-ass metal shit." His eyebrow went up. He was thinking, "Okay, I think I like this guy now!"'

'Mick is that way with everybody,' he added. 'I love that guy so much it's ridiculous. If you open up and give yourself to someone, they'll be open back.'

Later that night, Slipknot were taken out to dinner by a host of record company representatives, including major players from Sony and Universal.

Joey sat next to Ross, and the two like-minded souls proceeded to talk each other hoarse.

'We definitely had a connection,' said Joey. 'There's not many people I feel that much of a connection with. Me and Ross are the same guy. We've been through the exact same things – stuff happened at the exact same points in our lives. These days, we can pretty much complete each other's sentences.'

Just as the main course was about to arrive, Ross made the mistake of telling Joey that he had just finished the new album from Soulfly – the band formed by ex-Sepultura frontman Max Cavalera.

Straight away, Ross and Joey left the restaurant, just as the food arrived. They headed towards Joey's Chevy Blazer, their breath misting in the air.

Laughed Joey: 'We listened to the whole Soulfly record,

then came back and our food was completely cold. We'd missed the whole conversation.'

The night was still young, and the party's next stop was the strip club Beach Girls. After the revelry there had finished, Joey decided to give Ross a parting gift of friendship. The band had just had some Slipknot wind-breakers manufactured, and Joey took his off.

'Here dude,' he told Ross. 'This is my favourite jacket. I want you to have it.'

'Fuck yeah!' responded Ross, possibly worse for wear.

As Ross and his manager stumbled off into the night, Joey turned to Shawn and pointed after them.

'Check *that* out, dude,' he breathed. 'Even if we never see him again, Ross Robinson is wearing a Slipknot jacket.'

GOOD NEWS, BAD NEWS

It all arrived on Monday. Slipknot had just finished rehearsing when Sophia John turned up with the information.

'I just got word from John Rees,' she told them. 'Ross Robinson wants to produce your record, even if you don't have a label.' The band might have been tired from rehearsing, but their reaction was both deafening and unanimous.

'Y*essss!*'

Joey recalled: 'The feeling I had at that time was insane. You could never replace it.'

The band's elation was slightly tempered when Joey called Ross, with everyone huddling around, ears eagerly pricked.

'So when can we start?' Joey asked.

'Not for another eight months, dude,' came the heart-stopping reply.

'*What?*'

'No, dude. I'm committed to these other records.'

This was the last thing a band like Slipknot wanted to hear. To them, spontaneity and immediate action was all. Nevertheless, they decided that the best would be worth waiting for. Having been laid off from Sinclair's Garage since mid-1997, however, Joey was forced to explain to his mom that it would be a while longer before he had any money.

As for Sean McMahon, he greeted Ross Robinson's arrival on the scene with understandably mixed emotions. 'The band and I had developed a friendship,' he told me, 'and, yeah, I was a little hurt that I didn't get to go along for the ride. At the same time, I also realised that what Ross Robinson could do for them, was more than I could. What's interesting is that I've had a lot of people tell me that "Spit It Out" is the best-sounding song on the album.'

At the time of writing, McMahon and Robinson had never met. 'I've heard stories about him,' said McMahon, 'just as I'm sure he's heard stories about me! I do know that his aesthetic is different to mine – he's more organic and dry. I like feel, but I also like technical excellence.'

McMahon would subsequently migrate to Alexandria, Indiana, working at a studio owned by southern gospel luminary Bill Gaither. The producer would jokingly suggest that this change of musical and spiritual gears represented some kind of penance for his time with the 'Knot. He eventually returned to roost at SR, where he was destined to work with individual members of Slipknot. More of which later.

THE ZERO BOY

In February 1998, Joey and Shawn visited Safari as customers, to check out a night by the local DJ collective known as the Soundproof Coalition.

Sid Wilson was one of them.

Joey: 'By some chance, he came up to us and introduced himself. He said he saw us at the Dotfest and thought we ruled. We said we needed a DJ. He said, "Look no further!"'

The duo told Sid to call Shawn. They didn't think he would, however, writing their exchange off as mere bar-babble.

'He started calling Shawn ten times a day,' Joey would marvel. 'He wouldn't get off Shawn's ass!'

Having more than proven himself keen, Sid started attending rehearsals. The band began working his turntable scratches into their sound and he started listening to *Mate Feed Kill Repeat*. When Slipknot played a local gig supporting The Urge on 11 March, Sid was still not entirely integrated into the line-up, but came along anyway for (im)moral support.

'I went to see that show to get an idea of what I'd be in for,' he said.

As it turned out, it was more a question of what his new bandmates would be in for. Right before Slipknot went onstage, Sid entered their dressing room. Whereas most right-minded folk would simply wish the band good luck with the show, Mr Wilson took it upon himself to assault them all with his skull.

'He headbutted us all!' exclaimed Joey. 'He almost knocked me out, before I had to go onstage. We were looking at each other, thinking "This fucking dude's lethal!"'

That night during 'Tattered And Torn', Shawn went into the crowd to rile them up and get in their faces. Unfortunately for him, he encountered The Wilson.

'I fell right into it,' Sid recalled. 'I grabbed the Clown and headbutted him a few times.'

'Sid headbutted Shawn 16 times while he was out there,' estimated Joey, still shocked. 'He put Shawn down, the crazy fucker!'

Clearly, Sid Wilson was Slipknot material. Born in America, his English parentage surely accounts for his renowned grip on sarcasm. Before joining the 'Knot, he had spent seven years as a hip-hop and jungle DJ while enjoying metal and punk.

'The first stuff I loved was punk rock,' Sid has said. 'After that, I quickly discovered The Beastie Boys and a lot of b-boy type stuff. I got into punk rock, Beastie Boys, hip hop, dance music...

'When I first saw Slipknot,' he added, 'I knew I was born to be in this band. There was something going on with it – I belonged.'

'Sid's phenomenal,' praised Joey. 'I've never seen a DJ be so punk rock. How many DJs do you see spinning records while wearing a Slayer shirt?'

Sid would go on to claim that he suffered from 'organic brain syndrome' – an invention which is more than likely tongue-in-cheek. He would adopt a variety of effective-looking gas masks, which clearly didn't aid his condition.

'Wearing the mask prevents the oxygen from going to my skull. I get hallucinations and stuff. Half the time, I don't know what's going on around me. It's up to the Clown to intimidate me and keep me in line.'

Joey claimed that Sid's madness is due, at least in part, to the fair quantity of drugs the boy has apparently consumed in his time.

'You can't get him to focus on anything, day to day. The only time you can get him to sit, focus and do something right is when he's DJ-ing. Otherwise, the dude's a loose cannon. He makes everyone nervous!'

Asked what he brought to Slipknot, Sid Wilson would say, 'I bring youth and energy. I'm the youngest in the band and I'm always ready to go for it. I've got that child's sense of not being serious about everything all the time. It allows people to lighten up about stuff, I guess.'

Sid's appointment provided Slipknot's cake with its cherry. They now had someone to contribute turntable work – and a total psycho. It also meant that Slipknot now comprised an unprecedented nine people.

'Everyone freaks out that there are nine guys in the band,' Joey would tell *Rolling Stone*. 'I didn't want nine guys in the band – that's too many fucking people! But that's what it took to get the sound we wanted.'

BIDING TIME

As Slipknot jubilantly rehearsed with their unhinged new DJ, business deals were afoot. Ross Robinson signed them to his own record label I Am. They were his second acquisition, following in the heavy foot steps of LA hardcore-metallers Amen.

Joey: 'We had a lot of label interest, but Ross was the one who really stepped in and said, "Even if these other people aren't interested, I'm going to self-finance your album. We're going to do it whether someone likes it or not." He made other people interested simply because of who he was – but we could tell who was genuine and who wasn't. We had heard that one guy at Epic Records said, "If Slipknot are the future of music, then I don't want to be alive!" We knew we were doing something right when we heard that! For Ross to take us out of Des Moines and put us on the map was a great thing.'

Shawn: 'As it turned out, Ross didn't have to fund our album himself, because he ended up signing us to Roadrunner. But that's how much he believed in us.'

Slipknot ending up on Roadrunner Records was a result of Robinson doing a production deal between the label and his I Am imprint.

'He chose Roadrunner for the deal,' said Joey, 'so that was where we were going. Ross was pretty much the one getting us out of Des Moines and we owed a lot to him, already.'

Robinson described starting his own record label as 'a calling' which he had felt for quite some time.

'Whenever I was driving somewhere and there was silence, my heart was going, "I have to start a label!"' he told me. 'If I had done that years beforehand, I would have signed Deftones, Limp Bizkit, Korn and all those bands, plus more.'

It would still be six months before the producer was available to produce the band's all-important worldwide debut album.

Ross: 'It seemed like an eternity for Slipknot. Having to wait was really, really hard for them. They kept calling me, apologising for bothering me all the time. Even the contract took a long time to do – Roadrunner are very, very careful.'

That summer was a business-heavy period for the 'Knot. For one thing, July saw them amicably parting ways with Sophia John. 'She knew she took us as far as she could,' said

Joey. 'It was time to get someone new. We still talk to her once in a while.'

Some members of the band often visited New York, for meetings with Roadrunner. On their first trip to Manhattan, they had an experience which provided them with the chorus of their song 'Eyeless'. Stepping out from the label's Broadway offices to get a bite to eat, the Slipknot posse bumped into one of the Big Apple's many lunatics, outside the legendary hardcore punk club CBGB's.

Joey: 'This crazy-ass bum was stumbling all over the place with a glassy look in his eyes. He came right up to me and said, "You can't see California without Marlon Brando's eyes!" Then he just stumbled away into the darkness. I was like, "Okayyyy..."'

'He was running around, screaming it at everybody,' said Mick. 'I think his choice of actor was pretty cool.'

Later, when Slipknot were writing 'Eyeless' – the last song they would create before starting work with Ross – they needed a strong line for the song. For some reason, the episode sprang to mind.

Joey: 'The song itself is actually about Corey's dad and how he doesn't know him. We just used Brando as a figure that everyone knows, to amplify it.'

The song's demented chorus literally ended up being "You can't see California without Marlon Brando's eyes." Somewhere in New York City, there's a bum who's owed royalties.

Slipknot decided to close their Roadrunner deal in a fairly extravagant fashion. They phoned all the local press and told them, 'We have a story you'll want to see.'

Various hacks descended on The Axiom, a local tattoo-and- piercing parlour run by the band's friend Davo. They interviewed the band, who then signed the deal right in front of the assembly. The journos went away that day with a story about the first metal band ever signed out of Des Moines. It was a real triumph.

Meanwhile, Ross Robinson was busily producing Amen's

self-titled debut album, as well as resurrected cred-free rapper Vanilla Ice's nu-metal album.

'I did Vanilla Ice to fuck with everybody,' said Robinson. 'I started the Adidas rock thing with Korn and ended it with him!'

At this point, Robinson was keen to distance himself from the already clichéd rap/rock aspects of nu-metal. His protégés Korn had decided to try out different producers for their third album *Follow The Leader* – even though they ended up drafting him in at the eleventh hour to help out.

Ross: 'I'm totally proud of what I did with Korn and I'm grateful that they didn't wanna work with me anymore. It pushed me to create a new thing. I just wanted to express something amazing and radical. Moving people is everything to me. That, and standing for something while I'm here in the world. The question is: when I'm gone, did I stand for something great or was I a bunch of shit?'

Come the autumn of 1998, Robinson was, indeed, about to be part of something which exuded sheer brilliance. On 23 September, he received a call from the ever-enthusiastic Joey. As usual, the drummer was wondering exactly when work on the album would start. After all, Christmas was getting near.

'You know what, dude?' Ross told him, suddenly. 'Fuck it. Drive out here right now.'

TO LIVE AND DIE IN LA

You'd never seen Slipknot move so fast – not even on stage. Right after Ross told them to come to Los Angeles, Joey put the phone down and Slipknot left Des Moines.

Joey: 'There was no planning. Nine guys packed up their shitty cars and everyone left my house.'

The guys hurriedly stowed away two coolers full of lunch meat, along with bread, water and some sodas. They set off in three cars, owned by Chris, Craig and Shawn – the latter Hundai belonging to the Clown's wife.

Joey: 'We put this trailer on Chris' brand-new Toyota Tachoma, completely fucking it up. We loaded it too much, and as we left, Chris almost flipped the truck. The trailer started wobbling back and forth, real bad. Shawn was yelling out of his window, "Slow the fuck down!"'

Later, as the Slipknot convoy hit an exit to head south on the Interstate, Chris almost totalled his truck again. All in all, the trip would take three days.

'One time, me and Chris were driving late at night, listening to Slayer's *Reign In Blood*,' laughed Joey. 'He got an adrenaline rush and drove the truck a little too fast. He attempted to pass this semi and barely made it. That was a near-death experience right there. Shawn yelled over that he was going to kill us!'

Even when the posse finally hit Hollywood, the danger didn't end.

Joey: 'Chris was trying to drive his truck and trailer through the LA traffic. It was a disaster. He almost got into wrecks left and right – he was getting mental.'

Somewhere in Slipknot's private video collection is a camcorder-captured account of the whole wacky road trip.

'It was,' Joey later summarised, 'like *Fear & Loathing in Las Vegas* without the drugs.'

HOLLYWOOD BABYLON

When Shawn Crahan casts his mind back to that time, he has abiding memories of, 'driving away from my family for the first time in pursuit of my dreams. Me and my brothers had a ball – stepping up to the reality of being a signed band, being scared as hell, facing all the nightmares directly in the eye and realising that you only have one chance in this business to come out completely true.'

Despite sincere offers of accommodation from Ross, Slipknot chose to squeeze themselves into two hotel rooms at an Econo Lodge in one of Hollywood's less desirable ghetto areas.

'They were so hardcore,' recalled the producer. 'They just didn't want any help!'

Joey: 'We didn't wanna intrude. We were just aching to get shit on tape and get working.'

LA's relentless sunshine and showbiz glamour generally means that people spend a lot of time talking bullshit about the various projects they're supposed to be working on, but in reality end up sitting by the pool with a marguerite, flicking their hair. Not Slipknot. The next few months wouldn't even see them touching a drink.

Their first week in California was spent rehearsing hard for what lay ahead, while existing on a daily diet of wallet-friendly Taco Bell.

Ross Robinson had booked them a space in Hollywood's Cole rehearsal complex. It wasn't overly expensive and would accommodate all nine members and their equipment. At that point, Cole was also enjoying the patronage of Kiss, who were preparing for their latest world tour, named after their new album *Psycho Circus*. Joey and Josh, in particular, were stoked to see and hear their ultimate idols walking around the place.

Laughed Robinson: 'Josh had all his Kiss dolls and his Kiss shirts with him every day. When the real Kiss came in, he was like, "Fuck!" Slipknot would stand outside of the Kiss rehearsal room and be so excited. Then we'd go practice.'

The room's acoustics were far from ideal.

Ross: 'You couldn't hear Corey at all! He would be screaming at the top of his lungs and nothing would be coming through. But he'd still do it and blow himself out. It was amazing – those rehearsals had the best vibe ever.'

Joey: 'It was magical. Ross kicked my ass so much during that week and really improved my playing.'

Advancement came at a price, however. After a mere few days, Joey ended up sporting 17 blisters on his left hand and 19 on the right.

'Chris became my tape-tech,' he said. 'He would have to wrap up my hands every day, because they were bleeding. Every time I hit a cymbal, blood would fly on my toms.'

In between sessions, Joey and Josh would sit outside Kiss's rehearsal space, as if making a pilgrimage to some sort of shrine. One day, Joey got his heroes to sign a cymbal which he had broken. Today, it sits inside his bedroom closet. He also bagged some plectrums which remain in his wallet.

Looking back in December 2000, Gene Simmons was genuinely touched that Slipknot found so much inspiration from Kiss' presence.

'That's very sweet,' he said. '[Metallica drummer] Lars Ulrich used to tell me how, when he was still wet behind the ears, he used to sleep outside the Stockholm Hilton and wait for us to come out in the morning. He didn't even want an autograph, he just wanted to look.

'I hope that magic thing never goes away, or out of style,' the megastar continued. 'If Slipknot really reach the heights and start playing the stadiums, raking in the money and every girl wants to have their children, and the next band comes up, pointing to them as inspiration ... I hope it *means* something. I hope the legacy continues. You've got to be aware that if you reach the heights, you have a moral and ethical responsibility to encourage the next new band. Over the years, we hope we've done that by taking out all kinds of groups on their first tours: AC/DC, Bon Jovi, Iron Maiden, Judas Priest ... I can't even think of all the bands. The best part is that we did it because we were fans. You can't lose your love of being in the audience and watching that magic happen.'

One day at Cole, Slipknot were thrilled to see their rock gods have a very mortal punch-up.

Joey: 'The tour almost got called off and we witnessed it! We were sitting in the lounge when Peter [Criss, drummer] and Ace [Frehley, guitarist] came flying out of the rehearsal room. All of a sudden, Gene and Paul came out, going after them. There was a huge fucking fight and we were like, "*Yessss!*" We thought we were seeing the demise of Kiss.'

By the time Slipknot's week at Cole came to an end, Kiss and the Des Moines crew were nodding acquaintances.

'Maybe we'll open up for you guys one day,' Paul Stanley told them.

When they were out of ear-shot, Shawn grabbed Joey's arm. 'Dude, he just passed the torch! We're the new band!'

Ozzy Osbourne had passed over one torch, back in 1982. And here was yet another from Kiss. Fate was beaming down on Slipknot.

'That's what it's all about, isn't it?' Gene Simmons told me. 'You never know, you see. It goes up and down. But whether you're opening the show or closing it, just be thankful: it beats working for a living. Every band should realise that. Passing the torch is okay – it's not yours forever.'

4
How to make a monster

Ross Robinson is fucking nuts.
He's probably nothing like you'd expect him to be.
Mick Thompson, # 7

EXTREMITIES

Autumn 1998

Ross Robinson knew he had gone too far. His obsessive methods of producing Slipknot records – yelling and jumping around and throwing plant-pots – had finally backfired.

He and Slipknot were here at Indigo Ranch studios to record the band's vital first statement to the world, and Robinson wanted it to succeed almost as much as the band did. To this end, he had pushed them almost to the limits of human endurance. One musician stood bleeding before him, physically and mentally unable to play another nano second, following a spate of heavy-duty goading from the producer.

In a way, this temporary breakdown had been inevitable – much like a stuntman getting hurt in a violent action flick. If you set out to make an album of this magnitude, you would have to crack some heads. Still, it slightly altered the relationship between Robinson and the band member.

'Looking back,' Ross would admit, 'some of my prodding on that record was just too much.' Ross was referring to his now-notorious methods of channelling and purging musicians' negative feelings. It produces results, but requires serious physical and emotional investments from both band and producer. Ross Robinson, as you'll swiftly gather, is a million miles away from the traditional bespectacled 50-year-old who sits glued to his chair, murmuring suggestions.

'When we're recording,' he said, 'I try to create this really intense, full-on heart-opening where everyone feels so vulnerable and awake and aware. The moment stands still. I feel chills. Then this invisible ball of energy happens in the middle of the room. It's very ... therapeutic.'

Given the violent nature of the music he has captured on numerous mega-selling metal CDs, you might be surprised to learn that Ross Robinson believes in God. Or, at least, in something he refers to as 'the source'. He attends a non-denominational Los Angeles church named Agapé. In the spiritual profession, his mother is the equivalent of a rock star, operating heavy-duty self-help sessions.

'She cruises around and has these intensive workshops with 500 people at a time. It's not spiritual "woo woo" garbage, like evangelism. It's more about breaking it down to the core. In France, I saw her work with an interpreter and have a whole room in tears. People were broken.'

Robinson's father is an electrical contractor in the Nevada desert. 'Before anything happened in my career he'd be like, "When are you going to get a real fucking job?" Now, he has people handing him CDs, trying to get them to me. That rules!'

Despite the technical nature of recording music, Robinson's chosen profession owes more to his ma than his pa.

'I use a lot of her tools to get to the core of the artist. It's pretty deep shit – prodding and prodding away ...'

ROAD TO INDIGO

The ocean twinkled merrily at Joey Jordison as Slipknot chugged along the Pacific Coast Highway in their battered vehicles. The drummer gazed out of the window and thanked his lucky stars. They were finally going to Indigo Ranch.

To fans of contemporary, hard sounds, Indigo Ranch was a utopian nu-metal factory. This was the genre's rightful birth-place, where Ross Robinson recorded the first two Korn albums (1994's *Korn* and 1996's *Life Is Peachy*), Sepultura's classic *Roots* (1996), Limp Bizkit's debut album *Three Dollar Bill, Y'All$* (1997) and more recently At The Drive-In's *Relationship Of Command* (2000).

Tucked up in the Malibu hills, the studio was at least an hour away from Los Angeles. The drive up there was perilous and occasionally nerve-wracking; especially if you weren't the one driving. Perseverance brought its own rewards, however, because the views were spectacular, with beautiful hills stretching hazily off towards the ocean.

The studio itself was a single-level, visually old-fashioned affair – all ancient wood in the midst of picturesque scenery. Take a brief stroll away from the front of the place, past the cacti, and you'd come to a steep drop, plunging down into a valley. Many a photo session had taken place at that precari-ous edge.

The Ranch buzzed with wildlife – some cuddlier than others. Besides coyotes, skunks, mountain lions and the studio's own blue-eyed dog Cheetah, at certain times of year you'd encounter rattlesnakes, tarantulas and black widow spiders. Robinson found the place by chance in the first half of the '90s. He had been looking for a place in Malibu where his latest demo band could rehearse and write material.

'This realtor told me there was this little recording studio in Malibu that might have a rehearsal place. I went up there and it was like, "Whoah!" It freaked me out – it was amazing.'

More than anything, the Ranch felt like home to Robinson. 'It had the whole Colorado river vibe. It's isolated and it's quiet. You have to face yourself and be courageous to face those feelings. It changes people.'

The silence and isolation of Indigo Ranch has clearly made a huge contribution to the records made there.

'If you stay up there for a month-and-a-half, in that sort of silence,' said Ross, 'you have to grow. You don't have a choice. The vibe of the records made there is really special and unique.'

Over the next couple of years, Ross virtually became the Ranch's in-house producer, by virtue of bringing in constant business.

'I just liked it here, so I started dragging everybody in.'

Slipknot barely even made it up to Indigo.

'Chris was forced to drive up there at about three miles an hour,' related Joey. 'We thought we were never going to get there. We could hardly even find the place – it's located about 2000 feet up in the mountains. The engine was burning up in the truck – it was practically on fire.'

When the band finally crawled into Indigo's parking area, the trailer sank into the ground, as if issuing its final death knell. Slipknot were definitely moving in. They instantly warmed to the place – and not just because it was a residential studio which would afford them a little more personal space.

Shawn: 'We're a very disciplined group. Everything we do, no matter what, is very thought-out and dissected, down to its nucleus, and then put back together. Indigo Ranch was a beautiful time, because it was so surreal. If most people in Los Angeles went up there, they probably wouldn't like it, because of all the bugs and stuff. Us being from Iowa, we appreciated the landscape, the view and the rocks, the flowers, the smells and the trees that shed bark. It was very comfortable.'

Some members of the band stayed in the Ranch's cosy cabin, while others opted for the living room space in the studio itself.

Ross: 'It was a free-for-all. Pick a spot!'

Joey opted for the living room, making a home for himself on the couch. He would confess that most band members were unsettled by some of the wild-life. 'We ended up with nine burly, insane-looking dudes, scared shitless of the wolves and crazy bugs. The first night, we were hearing all sorts of weird stuff. We went outside, to the top of Indigo Ranch, and all you could see were the glowing eyes of raccoons. It was scary, all these eyes looking at you.'

LET'S GO TO WORK

'There was a real sense of a lifelong dream being realised,' Ross Robinson told me of the initial recordings. 'They were so grateful to be there, and we were all so open to suggestions, just wanting to take it as extreme as possible without caring what people thought. There was a lot of magic around.'

Once the highly excitable 'Knot boys had settled in, Robinson approached the mammoth task ahead of them with military precision. His responsibilities included making sure this psyched posse didn't burn themselves out in the first 24 hours.

Joey: 'When we started recording, we were so on fire and so insane. I just remember everyone playing like it was a show. We recorded eight songs in one night. Ross had to stop me, because I was gonna get it all done.'

While Indigo Ranch isn't the kind of place you'd expect to receive complaints from neighbours, Joey somehow managed to provoke them.

'I was playing really loud. That was the first time I met the owner of Indigo Ranch, Richard Kaplan. He looked like Santa Claus, with a big beard. He said he'd been getting complaints from the neighbours and all that shit!'

Shawn: 'Ross told us we were the hungriest band he'd ever witnessed. We did all the drums in three days. We were just so hungry for this album, because we had been so fucking sick of waiting to be signed. I don't know if bands talk about the anxiety they go through, trying to make this happen. Sometimes it can put people against each other.'

Robinson wanted Slipknot to be fully prepared to give their all, and more besides. To this end, he considered it vital that everybody in the band understood what Corey would be yelling himself hoarse about.

Ross: 'I had Corey explain his lyrics to everybody, before we started jumping into it. I wanted people to dig into the meaning of his words – and, for him, it's pretty desperate shit. Everybody needed to feel it.'

To the producer, music was all about expression.

'We were there to express something deep and emotional about the lyricism,' he said. 'You can get that same feeling that a singer's feeling through hitting a hi-hat. It's about everybody expressing one mind. It's a prayer.'

It's these kind of quasi-religious methods which Robinson attributes to the success of the albums he has commandeered.

'People haven't heard anything like these records before. They haven't heard anything like this on the radio before, but the records are selling. All of a sudden, people are like, "What's going on?" It's because this music has the heart connection. And that's all it is. I don't make records for radio; I make them for the soul.'

Slipknot discarded their masks during the sessions which ensued.

'When you're so close and you're connected with somebody,' Ross would theorise, 'whether they're wearing the masks or not, you're not seeing a body. You're seeing a spirit.'

With all the band primed to simultaneously blast through a song, Ross would set the tape rolling ('I record everything – I don't wait for *shit*!') and lead them through the first rendition. Then he would set about systematically intensifying their performance.

'I mainly do that with the lyrics,' he stressed. 'They give their input, I give mine and it goes back and forth, deeper and deeper. There was constant prodding and digging. I let everybody know that their sole purpose on this planet was to play their music as if their life depended on it. It was as if their parents would die unless they did it as hard as they possibly could, every single moment.'

'Ross is insane,' admired Shawn, in a pot/kettle moment.

'If you're tired, he'll tell you to run down a mountain to get your blood flowing. He didn't have to do that with us, though, because we're mental.'

Ross was unrepentant about his hard-line regime. 'When you're pushing the limits of your body, spirituality and mind, it's got to be the most important thing in your life. There's no holding back and it's not second to anything. It's number fucking one.'

Despite his own undoubted contribution to Slipknot, Robinson would acknowledge Shawn as the band's true ring-leader.

'Shawn is absolutely essential to the band,' he said. 'The whole time we were making the album, Shawn was the one who was really bringing everybody together. He did all the bullshit-talking, too: the industry things. It takes a lot of pressure off of everybody else. He's an amazing, heartfelt person – very supportive. He's also a loony – totally out of his mind.'

Under Ross and Shawn's combined tutelage, Slipknot were soon going seven shades of ballistic as miles of tape steadily revolved.

Mick: 'You can go to our websites and download video of us recording. We were like we are in the show. Full-on slamming. It's a very live-sounding recording. What you see me do onstage is what I did in the studio, just without my gear on. It's the only way. You can sit there and play lightly, or you can just bash the fuck out of stuff. It definitely translates.'

For Ross, conducting the madness was a religious experience in itself.

'It's incredible, watching everybody all at the same time,' he marvelled. 'They're ripping it so hard, with shit flying through the air. Things are exploding. You have no idea what it's like to be me, in that zone! I'm in the middle of it, while they're playing harder than they have in any show. And nobody knows about it – it's just us. It's so private and so amazing.'

Joey: 'I'd never felt that much emotion from playing music. Something happened. Ross made me play to my fullest ability and beyond. Everyone really came into their own while we were making that record, because it was so hard to do.'

Joey: 'I remember him coming into the room the first time. He had this look in his eyes and he was completely different. I thought, "Oh shit – what did I do?"'

Shawn: 'Ross is so into what you're doing that his pants are falling down and he's throwing plants at people and pushing people down on the ground. People are trying to film us and he's smacking them in the face! It's absolutely true. We're extremely violent people and we wouldn't want it any other way. To work with him was an absolute honour.'

Adds Joey: 'Once, when we were recording, Ross threw a potted plant at me. It exploded on the wall over my head and the dirt went in my mouth and all over the cymbals while I was playing. It was awesome!'

'Joey almost gagged,' recalled Shawn, 'but he fucking loved it! He was just slamming harder and harder. We kept the whole session. From the beginning, Ross was just an amazing producer and he's part of us. He grabbed something and knew it was there. He was like, "I am here to unleash it!"'

Ross: 'You're feeling all these emotions, and everybody's expressing the lyrics. Your body just wants to explode and so you do something fucked up. Or if I see that somebody's not on point with what me or everybody else is doing, I'll whack 'em. Like, "Get back! Bring it back!"'

While Ross was highly demonstrative in pushing Slipknot to the nth degree of focused insanity, the band appreciated the fact that he barely changed the musical content of their songs.

Mick told *Ozzfest.com*: 'Whereas a lot of producers will come in and go, "Here's where we'll put your chorus...", that really wasn't the case for us. Ross is the biggest inspiration. I've heard the comparison of Sepultura starting to sound like Korn when Ross did their *Roots* album. Well, they wanted to achieve that kind of sound, so that's why they enlisted his services. The main thing he did with us was strip down shit, mainly in the drumming department, so it's just straight power.'

Shawn: 'Ross lets the band be the final decision makers on their art. All you have to do is say, "Man, you added this effect on the guitars and we're not really digging it," and he'll just go, "Done." He's behind you as an artist, which is an incredible feeling. Ross is the most spiritual human being I know. He's *the* purist producer out there.'

Chris Fehn, on his own memories of the sessions: 'We were going crazy! You can nearly tell that on tape. It's a very raw album. Ross is a great guy, who's there for everybody all the time. It was a really smooth album to make, even though we were nervous and all that stuff.'

Joey: 'The great thing about Ross is that he's our friend, so there was no extra pressure on us. He's a complete dork metal head just like we are!'

Corey went so far as to credit Robinson for renewing the band's faith in itself. 'Before recording the album, we were so stressed out and screwed up in the head from people wanting us to go commercial or "radio up" our songs,' he confessed. 'Everybody saw an opportunity; everyone saw they could make money on this. But we've never written anything for a specific anything. For a while, we forgot we could write real killer songs.

'Ross brought back out of us the music we'd been trying to write for the longest time,' continued the singer. 'He was like, "Dude, bring it back, go fucking old school!" He brought some of the sickest shit out of us that I've ever heard us do.'

Ironically, one of the tracks which really takes you inside the atmosphere of the recording sessions, 'Get This', didn't make the initial release of the album – it only surfaced later on digipack CD releases. Arguably the band's most intense track to date, 'Get This' sees Corey railing against all the envy Slipknot had experienced from other bands. At the beginning of the song, we hear Robinson prompting Corey to give the opening scream. Then, at the end, both producer and band members whoop with joy at this incredible take.

There was one day, however, when Robinson's extreme therapy went overboard. He refused to say which member of the band he almost drove over the brink.

'It turned out bad,' he said, on reflection. 'I was going through a hard time at that point and I just kept craving more and more. I was pushing and pushing and the poor guy was bleeding. He was taking the wrath of Ross! I think that guy is uncomfortable around me, even today. But it goes both ways, and I learned a lot from it. And so did he.'

Joey was understandably vague about the specifics of the incident. 'It happened,' he shrugged. 'It might have been me, when I was bleeding from my hands. I almost had to go to a doctor, because I was afraid they were gonna get infected. The insides of my hands were completely raw, like I rubbed them on concrete.'

SKUNKS AND RELIGION

When the band weren't recording, they would be dabbling with the Internet, watching movies, hammering a Playstation or driving down to Sunset Boulevard to catch a band at the Troubadour club.

Shawn: 'It was all new to us, because we weren't big LA boys. We didn't get a lot of attention, because people weren't betting on Slipknot's work. We were left alone. Now, I can't *be* left alone. There's a million people who want a million things.'

Between recording blow-outs, Robinson would employ subtle motivational tactics to keep the band pepped up.

'The guys were broke at the time,' he would recall. 'There was a skunk around the Ranch. I told Mick that if he caught the skunk and gave it a "death growl" in its face, I'd give him 300 dollars.'

Joey: 'Mick got in his underwear and tucked his hair all up in his hat, then went out trying to dig for it.'

Ross: 'Oh, fuck. He couldn't find the damn thing ...'

At the time, Robinson was driving an 850 BMW. He offered to hand over the keys to any member of the band, in exchange for a 'point' on the Slipknot album – that is to say, a percentage of the profits.

Ross: 'I would never have actually made the trade, because I knew that was their full-on income if it ever blew up, like it did. I threw that out there partly to rile them up, but also to back them up. I was saying I believed in them so much.'

Despite inflicting such light-hearted torments on the band, Robinson conceded: 'The main tactic was loving them – being there for them and being open and caring. Creating that environment and being fucking radical. It's all about attention and love.'

During the sessions, Robinson even took three members – Paul, Chris and Corey – to his church of choice, Agapé.

'The music there is so high; they're singing about the real deal,' said Ross. 'They're singing about The Source. No matter how sick and demented the lyrics may be, or how brutal and nasty the band may look, or how it sounds, it comes from the same source: our lifestream. The deeper you go into the lifestream, the deeper the album will go into the heart of the person who listens to it. That's the thinking behind what I do. Even though somebody may not be into that kind of thing, it makes a lot of sense.'

The visiting Slipknot trio seemed to understand, on the day Robinson introduced them to the church.

Ross: 'It was great. There were 3,000 people there. Anyone who was coming for the first time was asked to stand up. It was so cool to see Paul stand up with his Slipknot shirt with "Fuck" something written on it! They totally accept it in that place – everybody knows that it's all good and all the same.'

Ross claimed that the Slipknots 'got all high' during the session.

'Then we went back and chilled out,' he said. 'I've taken Korn and all the different bands to Agapé, too. They're all into it.' Corey would later visit one of the workshops operated by Ross's mother.

'He got blown away,' enthused the producer.

Both band and Robinson have insisted that the only 'highs' employed during the Slipknot sessions were of this spiritual nature. Alcohol and drugs were outlawed for the duration.

Ross: 'We didn't drink at all. The whole band was sober. We did it up on the high level. If Slipknot drank, it would suppress what they are. It wouldn't be as good. They're proof that rock 'n' roll excess is a bunch of bullshit. Drinking and stuff doesn't do shit but knock you down.'

SPIT ROASTED

One of the few brick walls which the band encountered during the recording came as they repeatedly attempted to lay down the ultimate version of 'Spit It Out'. The version which Ross recorded with the band was faster than the original which they had laid down at SR Studios in Des Moines.

Ross: 'The record company wanted to make it this whole other thing. We were going back and forth with them. But you can never, ever, reproduce what you do on a demo, unless the music is completely electronic! It's really stupid to try, but we tried.'

Three versions of the song ended up floating around – the SR Studios take, a faster one and a slower one. In the end, both band and Ross conceded that they couldn't top the original.

SR Studios owner Mike Lawyer: 'They could not capture the magic of that recording, back when the song was fresh. It was written and recorded within a couple of days. When they tried to go back and re-record it – even working with a great producer like Ross – they couldn't get the feel that the label liked.'

Ross: 'That was a good lesson for me. I'll never play that game with a record company again.'

Trivia fans may care to note that Robinson's slightly speedier cut ended up appearing as a single B-side and an extra track on the US CD digipak in 2000, labelled the 'Hyper Version'.

On 11 November the recording of the album seemed to be complete. Slipknot returned to Des Moines for the holidays. They had found themselves a new manager in Steve Richards. The former manager of mega-selling popstress Paula Abdul, Richards had originally attempted to sign Slipknot to Epic Records.

Joey: 'When we were recording the album, Steve kept coming up and listening to the mixes. He was so adamant about him being the guy to manage the band. He literally thought we were the best band in the world. We thought that if he was really that excited, we should take a chance.'

As Richards entered the family, however, someone was on the way out. Over the Christmas period, Josh did a lot of thinking. Early in the New Year, he told the rest of the band that he wanted to hand over his bondage hood.

Ross: 'Josh was married with a stable job. While we were making the record, he was on the phone with his girl the whole time. For him, in his heart, it wasn't good.'

Joey: 'The guy was getting too much heat from his wife. He knew he would not be able to commit to the touring schedule in 1999. It would just cause too many problems. I knew it was coming, so I was relieved. I would have loved him to stay, but I knew it wasn't going to work. He wanted to pursue more of a chilled-out home-life. He likes coming home, playing on his computer, playing guitar, spending a little time with his wife and going to bed. That's what he likes doing, and that's fine. I don't think we understood a lot of that, back when the vision was set on the dream. We understand it now. '

Josh would continue to contribute to various songs and albums by other bands – often getting jobs on Robinson's recommendation.

'If anyone ever needs a guitar player,' said the producer, 'I always make sure Josh comes out. It's always good to see him.'

ONE MAN DOWN

This left Slipknot, yet again, with the problem of finding a new nutter. And once again, as had been the case with Mick's recruitment, they knew exactly who to set their sights on.

'Jim Root had always been the baddest guitar player, besides Mick,' said Joey. 'When it came time to get a new guitarist, we knew we wanted Jim.'

Jim's old band Atomic Opera had recorded a self-titled

album at SR Studios a few years back. After the disc's limited release, however, they learnt that they weren't the only Atomic Opera in the world, on being contacted by the originals. This bombshell would prove fatal to the band's morale.

Mike Lawyer: 'They got so upset, they all kind of fell apart. They said, "If we can't call ourselves Atomic Opera, we're not going to call ourselves anything!"'

For a while, the band laboured on under the somewhat eccentric monicker Flying Ass Cannon.

Lawyer: 'We have tapes of the album lying around in SR Studios which have "Atomic Opera" crossed out and "Flying Ass Cannon" written over the top!'

After the Cannon was wheeled into retirement, Root returned to the fray with a new band with the more sensible monicker Deadfront. They self-released a budget album and, in Slipknot's absence, stepped up to the plate as the new Kings of Des Moines. They had recently started to receive interest from a few record labels.

Then Slipknot made Jim an offer and completely screwed it all up.

Joey: 'We asked him if he'd be interested in playing for us, and he was so confused. He wanted to, with every ounce of heart, but he also wanted to stay true to his friends.'

Jim's initial answer was a regretful no. Then one night, Deadfront played in Iowa City, 120 miles out of town.

Joey: 'Jim had a shitty show and threw his guitar at the end of it. He called Shawn from that show and said, "Dude, we need to talk!"'

That same night, Jim drove all the way down to Shawn's Urbandale home.

Joey: 'Jim sat and broke down in tears. Then he came to practice and that was it. The band was complete.'

A display of emotion like Jim's truly underlined the difference between Slipknot and a hundred other bands. For some musicians, their band was a hobby, or a half-hearted stab at fame. If it went wrong, daddy would still buy them a condo. For *these* people, it was their whole life.

⬆ Humble beginnings: Joey (left) and Shawn relax outside the latter's parents' house in Des Moines. Ever the handyman, Shawn made this furniture himself.

➡

Joey behind the till at Sinclair's Garage, where much of Slipknot was planned in nocturnal gatherings. You'll find this place on 2970 Douglas.

⬅
Shawn and Joey at the Runway club, where Slipknot members first played in their various baby bands.

↑ Slipknot fight for use of the swings in a Des Moines playground.

↓ Joey and Shawn in SR Audio, the Des Moines studio where their recording career began.

© SEAN PEAKE

→ Slipknot producer Ross Robinson (right) and Amen's Casey Chaos toast Slipknot's success.

The band present their hidden soft underbellies in this touching shot at Indigo Ranch studios, California, during the making of the *Slipknot* album. ↓

© LISA JOHNSON

← Band friction: Sid 'accidentally' sets Shawn on fire during a show.

Shawn enjoys a finger-wrestle to the death with Chris. ↓

© PAUL HARRIES

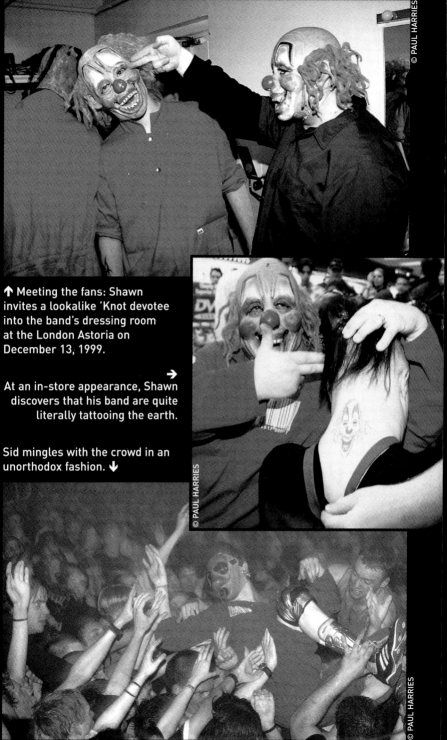

↑ Meeting the fans: Shawn
invites a lookalike 'Knot devotee
into the band's dressing room
at the London Astoria on
December 13, 1999.

→
At an in-store appearance, Shawn
discovers that his band are quite
literally tattooing the earth.

Sid mingles with the crowd in an
unorthodox fashion. ↓

© ASHLEY MAILE

← Corey goes for it at the Tattoo The Earth festival's Portland, Oregon stop-off on July 15, 2000.

Slipknot looking particularly scary at the *Kerrang!* Awards in London, England on August 29, 2000. ↓

© PAUL HARRIES

The live 'Knot experience inspires Christ-like behaviour from one awestruck crowd member. ↓

© PAUL HARRIES

↑ When *Kerrang!* magazine asked Shawn to come up with an idea for its Christmas cover at the end of 2000, they didn't expect him to pose with some decaying cow heads.

↑ Down with the sickness: Slipknot in New Jersey, October 2000.

Contrary to appearances, Jim Root was actually taller than the gigantic Mick, who Jim claimed liked to 'embellish' his height with heavy-duty boots. On joining the band, Jim inherited Josh's bondage hood, attempting to make it his own by pulling his dyed- purple hair through a hole in the top. After the first show he played with the band, he immediately hated that mask.

'It was really painful,' he told *IGN For Men*. 'It trapped all the sweat around my head, filled my ears up with sweat and pushed into my eye sockets. It was like playing underwater. So it was time for me to develop my own thing.'

The thing in question ended up being a demonic court jester creation which fits in perfectly with the other characters. Slipknot – that was Joey, Shawn, Corey, Paul, Mick, Jim, Sid, Craig and Chris – were once again ready to rumble.

FOREVER AND EVER, AMEN

Newly psyched, the latest – and hopefully final – 'Knot line-up rehearsed for a week and a half, then hopped on a plane to Indigo Ranch. They and Ross recorded two extra songs: the old track 'Me Inside' and the soon-to-be-controversial newie 'Purity'.

Next on the agenda, however, was the truly brain-frying part of the recording process. Mixing.

The process was further complicated by the fact that Robinson had arguably overbooked himself with other commitments. No less than two other works were in progress at Indigo: Amen's self-titled debut album and Machine Head's third album *The Burning Red*.

Ross: 'Casey Chaos blew out his voice and would come in after hours to sing. So did Robb Flynn from Machine Head. We had guitars set up, we had vocal mikes set up and we had the Slipknot mix on the table. We were doing everything all at once, and all the bands were totally cool together. It happens – you can't *not* finish a record.'

Amen singer Casey Chaos had met Slipknot once before,

that summer, when both bands played a bizarre showcase gig as part of a Las Vegas music convention.

'We played in a video arcade called Gameworks,' recalled Casey. 'I watched them and thought, "Fuck!" but we didn't get to hang out much. We saw them after the show and they told us we were awesome. I had no idea who they were – all I knew was that Ross was with them.'

A few months later, when Casey hit Indigo Ranch at the same time as Slipknot, he was bewildered by how many people were in the band. 'I couldn't remember who was who, and who did what,' he would laugh. 'It was very confusing – such an army of misfits! When Ross told me that most of these guys were in Slipknot, I couldn't grasp what he was even talking about.'

Chaos immediately formed a bond with the various members. 'I made friends with Craig. He'd always be sitting at the computer, and the other guys would play video games. I had Shawn asking me about where he could get masks, and whether I could get [special effects guru] Screaming Mad George to make him one. We were all real people; we were humans communicating. It was nice to have a new bunch of friends.'

Chaos was fast accruing a reputation for living up to his surname. During one Amen recording session at Indigo, he somehow managed to snap an artery in his arm, spraying the recording console an attractive shade of red.

Cue Slipknot, to the rescue.

Casey: 'Sid and five or six others came running in. They bandaged me up, put pressure on the arm and took care of me. We were friends straight away – there was a basic connection between us because I grew up as an alienated youth in the outskirts of Orlando.'

Machine Head frontman Robb Flynn also recalls hitting it off well with the 'Knot.

'The studio was chaos, but in a good way. We played basketball with Slipknot a few times. I remember them all being very humble and ready to help out with stuff. Mick wanted to fix all our guitars, so we let him. He certainly didn't have to do that.'

While new friendships were being forged, the finished mix of *Slipknot* seemed ever more far away.

Joey: 'Ross was getting burnt out. He'd go home, crash out and come back, then I would get up and we'd start mixing. It was hard enough on me, so I can't imagine what it was like for him.'

Ross: 'Mixing can be an absolute mind-fuck. I mix by hand rather than using computers. When you do that, you're relying on intuition more than your ears and if you're tired or not on point mentally, it won't always work. When I did the first Korn record I jumped straight into mixing, but I guess doing a lot of records had some detrimental effect on me.'

After a week, Roadrunner suggested letting someone else havea try.

Ross: 'I was like, "Cool, let him fucking do it." I was completely fried. Joey went in with another guy and they mixed a bunch of songs. I heard it and thought it was a very average-sounding album. I didn't like what he had done with our rough mixes.'

The story of The Great Slipknot Album Mix is complicated and will doubtless differ, according to whom you speak. At one point, however, it seems that Joey had the master tapes flown back to Des Moines and attempted to mix at SR Studios. Finally, the tapes ended up back at Indigo Ranch. Having taken a much called-for break, Robinson re-examined the situation with Joey and his faithful Indigo Ranch engineer Chuck Johnson.

Said the producer: 'We went back when I was fresh again and blasted it out. We quickly found that our original rough mixes totally blew away all the others. They had the vibe. The difference was like night and day. Joey and I looked at each other and went, "Fuck this!" We grabbed the tapes.'

What followed was a process which both Ross and Joey describe as 'brutally hard'.

Joey: 'I have pictures of us doing that final mix and we look so dead. We were burnt to a crisp!'

The whole studio was almost literally toasted one night in February.

Joey: 'I got finished mixing one night and went to bed in my little living room area, which contains the TV, the computers, the Gold records for Korn and all this antique stuff. It was starting to get cold in the mountains, so I would place the heater right near the couch. I woke up hazy and smelt something. I looked up and all I could see was foggy, cloudy smoke. I had knocked a pillow down onto the heater and it was in flames. I got up and Richard [Kaplan, the Ranch's owner] burst through the door. He tried to open up all these windows, but there's hardly any ventilation at Indigo. I was freaking out, going, "Oh shit, what am I doing?" Richard threw the pillow outside and switched the heater off. There was a burn mark on the floor and the place smelt like smoke for two days.'

Joey's theory as to the origin of the fire involved the Ranch's alleged ghosts. 'I think I was taking too long mixing and one night they got pissed and tried to kill me,' he said. 'I never saw a ghost while we were there, but we heard moanings and footsteps. I would see things that had been moved, when no-one claimed to have moved them. It was odd, odd shit.'

As the mixing sessions wore on, the ever-genial Chris Fehn hung around at Indigo, effectively acting as Joey's personal assistant.

'Chris was my friend down there,' said the drummer. 'He helped me with my peace of mind. He would come in every day when we were mixing and ask what we wanted from Subway. He knows so much about me now – what I like on my pizza, my burgers...'

Techno-heads may care for the specifics of Joey and Ross's mixing ordeal.

Ross: 'We didn't use any automation. It was all live – you're playing the song as you're mixing. We did each song in one pass, all the way through, mixing all the instruments. It was bad-ass, but that will hopefully be the last hand-mixed album I ever do!'

SLIPKNOT: INSIDE THE SICKNESS BEHIND THE MASKS   119

Joey: 'We were like members of the Fantastic Four, dude, or Stretch Armstrong! I was doing all the drums and DJ stuff, and Ross was doing the vocals and guitars. We did it so unconventionally – completely the reverse of how any band does it today. We used dusty-ass equipment and experimental sounds that really don't fit with the way albums are made so slick these days.'

To help break the tedium, Robb Flynn recruited Joey to sing an impromptu backing vocal on the Machine Head album.

Flynn: 'You can hear Joey on the song "Nothing Left". He does this scream in the crazy build-up section. I also remember the whole band watching one time, while I did the vocals for "Desire To Fire". Their own album kicked ass, but I never got to hear it properly, because they were always mixing the damn thing.'

WILDERNESS

The prolonged mixing sessions called for yet another leap of faith on the parts of both Slipknot and the record label. They knew it was vital to make the album perfect – but did other bands ever mix an album this many times? And exactly how much was this costing, by the way?

Shawn: 'I do a lot of business for the band, so I get to see a lot of figures. I was brought up by my father and my mother to always ask why. There was a point when I was hearing stuff from the record label and I freaked out. It sounded like buying a house – and a house is normally the biggest thing anybody buys in their life! I was sitting there looking at the band and we were mixing the album for the third time and I was like, "What are we doing?"'

For a moment there, it seemed that Slipknot's once-unbreakable confidence was about to unravel.

Shawn: 'This is how mental we are: we started asking ourselves, "Are we a joke?" The masks have never been a joke. They were never laughed at. The way society is, if you're a little overweight or something, somebody will always poke fun. There have been individuals who poke fun at the masks. I'm so attached to our philosophy that it hurts my feelings.'

As the mixing wore on, Shawn would retreat to the back of the Ranch every night, perch himself on the same rock and take in the view. 'I would think, "What am I doing?"' he later confessed. 'Because this lifestyle and this whole thing can kill you.'

If this sounded like melodrama, then you would only have to picture Kurt Cobain lying next to a smoking firearm to realise that Shawn had a point. Reassurance came when the band's music was exposed to the world for the first time. *Kerrang!* magazine, already massive fans of the band, placed a rough version of 'Eyeless' on a cover-mounted CD.

Joey: 'I got that copy of *Kerrang!* sent up to Indigo. I was sceptical, because the track wasn't mixed or mastered. I was scared shitless, anyway. I knew Ross understood us and I believed him, but I still didn't know if anyone else was going to like us. "Eyeless" was a great song for people to hear first, but it's not that easily digestible, because there's so much shit going on: jungle beats, insane voice, guitars, super-fast drumming. It doesn't even hit a groove until the end of the song.'

It turned out that plenty of people were going to love Slipknot.

Joey: 'I started reading about that song all over the Internet! People said it was kick-ass. It was very emotional when that happened. We realised that maybe we *were* needed.'

FINAL GRAND SLAM

Slipknot was, and still is, a mammoth piece of work; never less than electrifying. Both band and Robinson were justifiably proud of it.

The album began unmistakably with the eerie drone of '742617000027', which was named after the bar-code number on the back of the *Mate Feed Kill Repeat* album. Craig Jones's computer wizardry generated this remarkable intro, which featured Corey's looped voice saying, 'The whole thing I think is sick', at varying pitches.

The opening moments of '(Sic)', which hammered in directly afterwards, were nothing short of incredible, and viciously stated the band's intent. This was the mother of all Slipknot songs, and it received some stiff competition throughout the album. 'Surfacing' would become the band's best-loved anthem, featuring the 'Fuck it all, fuck this world, fuck everything that you stand for' chorus which would issue from the mouths of thousands, a lot sooner than the band anticipated. Musically, it saw Sid make his presence felt, based as it was on a completely deranged, pounding jungle beat.

Slipknot also ably demonstrated that they weren't all about pulse-pounding aggression. The freakily atmospheric tracks 'Tattered And Torn' and 'Prosthetics', and the epic 'Scissors', truly mapped out the breadth of Slipknot's scope and potential. They also emphasised what unique feels the band could produce with their percussive triangle.

Without examining each and every track, the best thing about *Slipknot* – despite its laboured birth – was its savagely raw urgency. You would have been hard-pressed to fault any of the performances, with Corey turning in an alternately livid and vulnerable vocal performance which raised the neck hairs. This, then, was the finest album of 1999. And no-one had even heard it yet.

WASTED IN AMERICA

As the album went off to get mastered, its creators went off to get plastered. After so much hard work and abstinence, it was celebration time. Ross, Joey, Paul and Chris, along with members of Amen and Machine Head, hit the LA strip club scene like an atom bomb.

Joey: 'I remember me and Ross breaking down in tears. There were all these chicks around, but me and him were sitting there howling. He'd go, "You rule!" and I'd go, 'No, *you* rule!"'

Ross: 'We drank for the first time since we started the record. We ripped it up. People were coming up to me and Joey, concerned, because we were crying full-on, hardcore tears for two hours, but we were like, "No! You don't understand!" We were just letting out all that frustration and hard work. It was finally finished, dude! That was a great, great night.'

Such a great night, in fact, that Casey Chaos could barely remember it.

'That was the night Ross cried?' he pondered. 'I *always* see Ross cry – it's become a blur!'

Robb Flynn's memory was slightly more lucid. 'Joey must have told me he loved me 75 times!' he laughed. 'He kept going on about how influential Machine Head had been on his band. He was all drunk, but you could tell it was genuine.'

When the album was finished, Ross Robinson and Slipknot inevitably drifted out of contact from each other as a Glassjaw album beckoned for the former, and frantic road-work for the latter.

Ross: 'It's like with every band. They go off on tour, do their thing and they're really out there. They have to work and that doesn't really involve me. I kind of lose touch. The thing that stays connected is the heart. We don't stay connected through the press, that's for sure. Stuff can get really nasty and misinterpreted.'

SHIT HAPPENS

In case you're still wondering what the story is behind the album's bizarre nameless hidden track – in which someone appears to be throwing up as a host of other people voice their disgust – the truth can be at least partly revealed.

One night during the band's stay in California, they decided to conduct an initiation ceremony for Chris Fehn – as if the boy hadn't suffered enough. Slapping on a hardcore porn video featuring defecation – bringing new meaning to the term 'shit-eating grin' – Crahan switched on his camcorder and gleefully filmed Fehn's distinctly green-gilled reaction to the tape.

'I wasn't there,' Ross would comment on this gentleman's soiree, 'but I know they were trying to freak Chris out and break him into the band.'

Horrified moans and groans erupted from all present and Fehn brought up his lunch on camera. The audio from Crahan's home movie would later make its way onto the end of the Slipknot album.

'They could sell that video,' chuckled Robinson, 'if only it didn't have the faces in it.'

At least, I *think* he said 'faces'...

5
Summer of hate

The only plan right now is to kill everybody.
Joey Jordison, #1

FINAL DESTINATION

San Bernardino, California, 24 July 1999
'I think the kids are ready for something brand new.'

Shawn Crahan was preaching the gospel, sitting on the back of a golf cart, backstage at the last Ozzfest event of the summer. Slipknot had spent the last two months aboard this travelling circus, playing to more than 650,000 American kids. This was the tour which broke them, unleashing their sickness on a grand scale.

'People are tired of the derivative, regurgitated crap that's out there, which just will not die,' Shawn told one Seattle journalist. 'We've got a great response on this tour, and a lot of kind words from all the beautiful people on the web. I'm glad to see the kids are getting it, and we're just gonna keep taking it to them. You're never gonna get rid of Slipknot.'

At this point, no sane metal fan would want to. The momentum which Slipknot had accrued since the tour's first date on 27 May was unbelievable. Their *Slipknot* album was now selling at an exponential rate.

This, then, is the story of how everything finally went right for the Des Moines posse. The odd bout of plastic surgery aside ...

THE BIG ONE

Slipknot had discovered that they were Ozzfest-bound in March, when their manager Steve Richards called Shawn, who immediately called Joey.

'I was screaming so fucking loud,' Joey told me. 'Finally, we were on a real tour.'

The band spent the subsequent months readying themselves. The Ozzfest was, after all, the elusive break they had been waiting for. The dream. As the event's name implied, it was the brainchild of rock's royal family heads, Ozzy Osbourne and his wife/manager Sharon.

This was Slipknot's chance to finally break out of Iowa and expose themselves – in some cases, obscenely – to the rest of America. Possibly because of his debts, Shawn had been forced to move his family into a smaller house, selling his original house to his parents. *Chez* Crahan was no longer a viable rehearsal pad for Ozzfest preparation, so Slipknot began pounding out the noise in Sid's basement.

Shawn: 'Sid's mom and dad are the coolest. They'd be upstairs entertaining friends and we'd be down in their basement making the sickest noises. They'd never, ever say a word about it. I think our shit is still lying all over the place down there ...'

Three days before the Ozzfest began, Roadrunner Records surprised the band by letting them shoot their first promotional video, for 'Spit It Out'. The clip turned out to be a very obvious homage to *The Shining*, complete with swinging axes, two creepy twin girls (played by Shawn and Chris!) and the band's name written backwards on a door.

The concept was borne of a night at Shawn's house, when he and Joey sat tossing ideas back and forth.

'One of us said that if we ever made a video,' said Joey, 'it would be a parody of *The Shining*. It's always been one of our favourite movies. We've always wanted to make our own version of *Blue Velvet* too.'

Corey gleefully reprised Jack Nicholson's role, while Joey played his psychic son Andy, pedalling frantically around a mock Overlook hotel on a tricycle. Mick turned up as the ghostly barman, while Sid enjoyed an amusing cameo as the scary old woman in the bath-tub. Perhaps as a result of being the new guy, Jim was forced to play Shelley Duvall's role as Nicholson's wife, but did at least get to heave a baseball bat around and knock Corey down some stairs.

'That was pretty surreal, because we had previously talked about doing a version of that movie,' Shawn told *Kerrang!*. 'Horror is fine, but we like psychological horror, and there just happened to be enough parts in that movie that we could carry over. We didn't even have much time to think about it, because the Ozzfest was so close, but it was cool.'

Fans finally got the chance to own a copy of the video when it was released as part of the 20-minute *Welcome To Our Neighbourhood* video, later that year. MTV would refuse to play the clip, on several bewildering grounds, including its supposedly racist overtones.

Slipknot couldn't concern themselves with such matters. They were about to embark on the first tour of the rest of their lives. A few days before the Ozzfest's first date in Florida's West Palm Beach on 27 May, the band sat on their first ever tour bus, cruising down across America. The excitement was such that they didn't mind the fact that their bus was 40 feet long, as opposed to the regulation 45 feet, and it had 13 people crammed into nine bunks. They didn't even mind the bus breaking down in Iowa City, a mere 120 miles out of Des Moines.

Laughed Joey: 'We said, "Yeah, we're definitely on tour now. We're a real band!" We didn't care at all. People were sleeping on the floor of the bus – it was pretty hardcore.'

THE BAND THAT JACK BUILT

'Hi,' said the stranger. 'I'm Joey from Slipknot. We're playing later on the Second Stage. Check us out!'

Being the son of Ozzy Osbourne, Jack was used to unidentified characters rushing up to him, hands outstretched, with kind words or requests for his father's autograph. So when a long-haired, intense-looking character approached through this hazy low-90s heat and 85 per cent humidity, backstage at the first Ozzfest of the year, the 13-year-old scarcely batted an eyelid.

Jack had never heard of Slipknot before. He nodded and said he would try and see the band. As a confirmed devotee of all things fresh and metallic, Jack meant what he said. As things turned out, however, he didn't manage to catch Slipknot's opening assault on America at large.

The Ozzfest was, by now, an institution. 1999 saw the event hit its fourth year, with the excitement amplified by Black Sabbath topping the bill, playing what was said to be their last ever run of shows before their end-of-the-millennium split. As a result, this Ozzfest was being touted as Black Sabbath's Last Supper. The event was rapidly gaining itself a peerless reputation for not only delivering enormous names in rock, but for introducing America to hot new talent.

The Main Stage was an outdoor seated arena mostly dedicated to more established acts. This year, a rock-solid line-up joined Sabbath: Rob Zombie, Deftones, Slayer, Primus, Godsmack, System Of A Down and Static-X. The Second Stage was also outdoors, but you could stand where you liked, in order to catch performances from hungry up-and-comers.

Slipknot had been placed on this latter platform, along with British mob Apartment 26 (who featured Sabbath bassist Geezer Butler's own son Biff), Sweden's Drain STH, LA's Flashpoint, Texans Pushmonkey, Florida-based Puerto Ricans Puya and the cumbersomely-named Californians (hed)PE.

The placing of these bands on the Second Stage bill was set to rotate every day. This meant that, depending on the show,

Slipknot could be onstage any time between 11am and 5pm. On some dates, a Second Stage band would be promoted to the Main Stage, opening up the show. The only given, day in and day out, was that LA cyber-metal veterans Fear Factory would headline the Second Stage.

As the performances alternated between the two stages, there was barely a moment of the day when a band wasn't playing, giving you distinct value for dollars. If, for some reason, you found yourself with time on your hands, you could get a piercing, a tattoo or have fun at the numerous fairground-style stalls. Five dollars, for instance, would buy you a shooting spree with an Ozzy-style machine gun, while other stalls offered bucking bronco rides, a Spiderman-style climbing wall or the opportunity to make a bell ring by hitting something with a hammer. There was even a 'Kara-Ozzy' stand, at which you could croon along to Osbourne's greatest hits, much to the amusement of your equally drunken mates.

The Ozzfest had it all, and as 19,000 metal fans piled into this opening show at the Coral Sky Pavilion, there were no signs of its decline. Indeed, celebrated indie film-maker Penelope Spheeris would be on board with her crew this summer, shooting a racy rockumentary on the event which would eventually emerge in 2001, bearing the Sabbath-derived title *We Sold Our Souls For Rock 'n' Roll.*

Girls at the Ozzfest tended to wear as little as possible, which was understandable, given the overwhelming heat. They also had a penchant for spraying band's names across their chests. Male fans wore enormous shorts with wallet chains that could strangle a rhino and made it their business to modify every available inch of their bodies with ink and/or metal. Nobody's hair was its natural colour.

This was pre-millennial metal, American style. Naturally, the mainstream media considered the whole affair a mystery at best, and horrifying at worst. Following the Ozzfest's first date, the *Palm Beach Post* would sum the event up as 'Unbearable heat. Ear-punishing sounds. And tides of menacing-looking people who've chosen to permanently disfigure themselves with garish tattoos and faces pierced to smithereens.'

In fairness, the writer Frank Cerabino confessed to being a 'stranded island of middle-aged conventionality'. Clearly, anyone who considered themselves conventional was not going to like the Ozzfest, just as most folk who enjoyed the Ozzfest would hate the opera. This was exactly the point. Vive la difference.

HELLO AMERICA

When they hit West Palm Beach's Second Stage in the mid-afternoon, Slipknot stunned the vast majority of the crowd. They hit the ground running with '(Sic)', as they would for the next 16 months, and never let the pace drop. The fact that they had a mere 30 minutes onstage only served to boost their intensity.

Paul Brannigan from *Kerrang!* was present to witness the spectacle. His live review in the magazine, three weeks later, raved: 'The nine-piece's attack is as subtle as a battery acid enema. Tunes like "Purity" and "Spit It Out" are simply staggering. You might as well start cutting their name on *Best New Band* trophies now.'

Joey had the show camcordered. 'That tape is so cool to look at,' he said. 'We're complete virgins, but you can tell the heart that we have. We're going out there and playing so hard, but compared to how we are now, we're under-developed. We're kids out to see the world.'

Without the benefit of roadies, Slipknot settled into a down-and-dirty, hands-on routine.

Joey: 'We would go onstage and set up our equipment without masks, then get changed and go back up there to play a 25 minute set. You can't ask for a better first tour than the Ozzfest – it was a dream come true. We still haven't had as good catering as we had on that tour. We're way better these days, but we still get shitty food.'

REVELATION

To say that the nine men in identical boiler suits and masks caught Jack Osbourne's attention would be a major understatement. They violently hijacked it. It was the middle of the afternoon at the Lakewood Amphitheatre in Atlanta, Georgia, and Jack had been innocently wandering around behind the Second Stage.

He couldn't help but stare at this cluster of weirdos waiting to go on. Suddenly, one of them broke away from the pack and walked towards him.

'Hi,' said this bizarre character, his long hair framing the plain white mask. 'It's Joey from Slipknot, man! Are you gonna come watch us play?'

This time, when Jack nodded, he knew he would be fulfilling his promise.

'I watched them and was amazed,' he told me. 'I thought they were the coolest thing I'd seen in so long. Soon after that, they became my favourite band.'

'Jack was videotaping the show,' Joey recounted, 'which I thought was great. I gave him this little necklace which represents creativity. He still wears it to this day.'

A few days later in Nashville, Tennessee, it was Slipknot's turn to open up the Main Stage. They found it a surprisingly awesome task.

'It was pretty crazy, looking out there at this huge amphitheatre,' admits Joey. 'We were just never used to seeing a sight like that. It was overwhelming, to say the least, but we went about it like it was a tiny club.'

Joey had already become good friends with Jack Osbourne. 'Me and him started hanging out, every day,' said the drummer. 'I remember Jack lighting a firecracker and throwing it at Dino (Cazares, Fear Factory guitarist). It landed right by Dino's ear and blew up. He got so pissed off. He was like, "Where's that little motherfucker?" as Jack ran away.'

He added: 'Jack's a little hellion. He would steal golf carts with us and we'd drive them around, crashing into shit. It was like a big summer camp and it was fun. I'll remember that tour until the day I die.'

Slipknot effectively became Jack's bodyguards; his makeshift older brothers. At one point in the tour, when his motor-scooter was stolen, he went straight to the Des Moines Nine.

'We had no friends on that tour,' noted Joey. 'No bands would hang out with us. (hed)PE was the only band that befriended us at all. Bands either didn't understand what we were doing, or they were a little bit intimidated.'

How strange ...

BLOODLUST

Shawn Crahan was signing autographs. This would not have been unusual, were it not for the fact that medics were waiting to whisk him off to a nearby hospital.

During Slipknot's set in Holmdel, New Jersey, Crahan had injured himself in a frantic display of clowning around. During the second song, 'Eyeless', the percussionist smashed his head on his own oil-drum, cutting a deep gash above his left eye. Despite this injury, Crahan rode the subsequent wave of adrenaline all the way to the set's end.

'When we came offstage,' Joey would recall, 'he ripped his mask off. He had blood all dripping down his face.'

Shawn scribbled his name on a few items handed over by fans, and was taken to the nearby Bayshore Hospital. It took five stitches to close the wound – a mere trifle, compared to what would later lie in store for him.

A few days after the incident, I attempted to interview Shawn over the phone. It was a disaster, on account of the big man wearing his mask. Neither of us could understand a word the other was saying. Whether Slipknot attempted many interviews while wearing masks in those early days, is unclear. Suffice to say, they have probably learnt their lesson since.

When the Ozzfest subsequently hit Columbus, Ohio, the band finally realised they were starting to build some serious momentum.

'People started singing the words back to us,' marvelled Joey. 'We'd never had that before. To hear the audience singing was fucking insane.'

LIVE AT LAST

I first saw Slipknot at one of these Ozzfest shows, in Hartford, Connecticut. Despite the fact that they were playing in the early afternoon, they were everything I wanted them to be, and a lot more besides.

As the band were still, relatively speaking, a secret to be enjoyed by those in the know, you could thread your way through the crowd with ease, scoring a fine view of the Second Stage. Within minutes of the band exploding into action, great plumes of dust rose up, as the initiated and uninitiated alike showed the band some violent appreciation.

Slipknot were unthinkably intense, coming on like a half-hour movie with 10,000 scenes. Your eyes constantly darted from one member to another, trying to keep an eye on what each distinct character was up to. Blink, and you might miss Shawn taking Chris doggie-style – or Chris masturbating his own highly phallic nose. This band were everything you wanted them to be. Just as their pictures had suggested, they really did act like some kind of fucked-up alien superheroes. Surely, these people could not be human?

It was something of a disappointment to meet Slipknot minus masks. Not because you imagined them to look any particular way behind those grotesque creations, but because it broke the air of mystery. When people post mask-free photographs of the band on the Internet, it's unlikely that many true fans thank them for it. Part of the fun of loving the band is not knowing what they look like.

Hanging around outside the band's tour bus with their Roadrunner press officers, before their set, had been an interesting experience. Various people were entering and exiting the bus, but which of them were in the band?

The only one you could be sure about was Joey. As he

walked down the steps he was instantly recognisable, extend-
ing a hand and launching straight into hyper conversation.
The band were highly impressed with *Kerrang!* at this point,
having just read the magazine's highest-accolade five-K review
of the *Slipknot* album.

'The best thing that's happened to us in six months is that
five-K review,' Shawn pointed out when I finally met him.
'That's what we've been struggling for: someone to pay attention to our frustration and our dreams. It was a luxury that
was handed over to us. It was amazing that people could be on
our level, because we expected bad things all the time.'

Joey recalled: 'Our US press officer Maria came and told
me the album had got five out of five in *Kerrang!* I said,
"There's no goddamn way!" I remember getting a xerox copy
of the album review, and that was one of the greatest
moments in my life. I'd been reading *Kerrang!* since I was 15.
It was so cool that someone understood what we were doing.
I got it framed in my room. I'm the most anal guy in the band,
and I think everything I do can be done way better. I'm very
self-critical.'

Writer Paul Brannigan's review of *Slipknot* was indeed one
to cherish. 'This is the most venomous, apoplectic and vein-
poppingly furious album since Korn's 1994 debut,' he furiously scribbled, 'and easily the best metal debut of the year.'

As you met the other members of the band, it was a strug-
gle to reconcile their faces with their respective masks. As you
hadn't seen these people before, it was a case of attempting to
remember nine names, attached to nine roles in the band and
nine masks. We broke the ice by conducting what was known
as the *Kerrang!* Challenge – a 15-question general knowledge
quiz – with the entire band, who all squeezed obligingly onto
the bus. Rather disconcertingly, it transpired that Corey had
been sentenced to silence by the others. This was apparently in
order to rest his all-important voice.

'Corey could talk if he wanted to,' noted Shawn, 'but we
don't let him. This is our first tour and we wanna play our
cards right. All he's got to say is what he says for 30 minutes

every day. And that's total brutality. We're watching him and thinking about the future.'

'Besides,' added Joey. 'Take a guy who talks all the time and tell him not to talk for four days. Then put himself onstage with a microphone ...'

Good point, well made.

While you might have imagined that such an outwardly brutal bunch of characters might lack humour, this was clearly not the case. At one point during the Challenge game, Sid produced a cellphone and, with mock shiftiness, murmured, 'I just gotta call someone!'

'There's no need to cheat,' laughed Mick. 'The book's called *Hannibal*!'

You learnt about the band's personalities from their answers. Mick, for instance, revealed that his girlfriend's favourite character in the Nicolas Cage snuff-themed *8mm* movie was the masked psycho-killer Machine. Which figured.

Corey and Shawn professed admiration for Jim Carrey, after successfully answering a question about *The Mask*.

Joey was first off the mark when it came to knowing how many *Friday The 13th* movies had been made, while Mick soon established himself as a walking serial killer encyclopaedia, answering a question about Richard Ramirez, the killer nicknamed the Night Stalker.

'He was a wuss,' said Mick. 'He shot one guy right in the face with a .22, but it didn't kill him. The guy got up, beat the fuck out of Ramirez and chased him out of the house.'

'I remember living in LA,' added Paul 'and my mom and dad telling me to keep the doors locked.'

Perhaps as a result of there being nine of them, Slipknot scored a mighty 14 out of 15 possible correct answers.

TEARS OF A CLOWN

'I could cry right now,' Shawn Crahan told me that day in Hartford, with a very real sadness in his pale blue eyes. 'Every Ozzfest has a middle row in front of the soundboard, where

they put all the handicapped people. I don't try and pay attention, but I see people who are completely fucked up. It hurts
me, because I don't want them to be that way.'

Good God. Would the real Shawn Crahan please stand up?

Of all the members of Slipknot, The Clown would appear
to be the most complex – and certainly the one who lives the
most extraordinary double life. He is at once a family man
who loves the works of Picasso and religiously reads Edgar
Allen Poe *and* a scatologically-minded maniac who boasts of
eating 'poop'.

One of the encouraging – and confusing – things about
Slipknot is that they have never been afraid to show emotions
other than anger and hatred. Crahan has always spoken
proudly of his wife Chantal and their three kids, stressing that
while he hates being away from them, Slipknot is a mission he
cannot refuse.

'One night, I got home with my wife, who's my best
friend,' he once said. 'I've got three beautiful healthy children.
I was lying in bed with Chantal, staring at her while she slept.
I went downstairs and fixed myself some food, thinking that
though this is the craziest dream I've ever wanted, I need to do
it for my wife, my kids and for myself. Most importantly,
there are a lot of kids who need us. Be careful what you wish
for in life.'

Shawn has, perversely, always espoused what you might
call traditional values in relationships. He has said: 'One band
showed us a home-made rock 'n' roll video, with sex and
stuff. We were astonished – this guy had better porno than
you could buy in a store. This guy had been around for a long
time and we had total respect for him. But he said, "You guys
sell three times more albums than us – you should be getting
three times the pussy." I was like, "No, dude. I make love
with my wife." Laugh if you will, but I don't understand all
that stuff.

'It's so easy to be bad in this world,' he added. 'It's so easy
to take the extra drink; break down and start smoking again;
cheat on your girl. But I get a hard-on from thinking about

being non-drugged with three children, married and in the greatest fucking band on the face of the Earth.'

At the root of Shawn's anger is a deep, dark hatred towards the world's very design. He seems to despise the human condition.

'We don't really like to talk about this,' he told me, 'but there's not a day that goes by where, not only do I miss my kids, but I wish they weren't born. I don't want anything to happen to them and it scares me so much. I'm generally a pissed-off person because I hate the sadness in the world. If you were to kill a bug in front of me, I'd get mental.'

Chief among Crahan's peeves is man's lack of respect for the planet. When he vented his spleen on this subject, offstage and maskless, it was almost as frightening as watching him throw heavy objects around as the Clown.

'I hate this filth that the world chooses to ignore,' he said. 'Dude, I got three kids. Why did I bring my beautiful babies into a world that's fucked up like this?'

Crahan has admitted that he is a mess of opposing emotions. 'My biggest battle has been with myself,' he said. 'I always lose, too. I'm in a constant battle with myself every day – I like to live, I don't like to live, I like to be in the band, I don't like to be in the band. It's a lot of pressure.'

You can see why Ross Robinson identifies this man as the band's ringmaster. The Clown is the member who offers some depth. If Joey and Paul are the band's musical masterminds, Shawn Crahan delivers the black heart and soul.

SPREADING THE DISEASE

After Hartford, the Ozzfest crew enjoyed a six-day break before the next instalment in Detroit, Michigan. Jack Osbourne flew back to LA, taking with him one of the sampler tapes which Slipknot's people had been handing out at shows.

'I had already called my best friend in LA,' he said, 'and told him, "You've gotta hear this band!" So I came home and played him this two-track cassette, which had "Spit It Out" and "Surfacing" on it. He loved it and played it to his friends.'

Picture thousands and thousands of American teenagers doing exactly the same thing, and you can imagine how the Slipknot epidemic spread across the country and beyond. Positive advance word followed the band around the remainder of the tour and hurtled around the web in excited e-mail bursts.

'This is fucking nuts!' Mick told the Ozzfest's own website. 'What's really cool is that from handing out sampler cassettes, people are singing along. I can hear the chorus louder than I do from the monitors onstage. It's just the most incredible feeling.'

At that point, Mick was still recovering from having met his heroes like Slayer guitarist Jeff Hanneman and Black Sabbath's Bill Ward.

'I got to meet the guy who wrote "Angel Of Death"!' he enthused of Hanneman and the opening track of the band's *Reign In Blood* album. 'I ate lunch with Bill Ward. It's surreal, and they're all really down to earth and cool.'

Corey Taylor took advantage of the break to fly to Indigo Ranch. Ross Robinson had an extra-curricular activity lined up for him, involving Onyx rapper Sticky Fingaz.

'I was in a club in New York,' Robinson told me. 'This A&R producer guy said he wanted me to do something with Sticky Fingaz. So Sticky came out to Indigo, and I got Corey and Josh Brainard over, with [Amen drummer] Shannon Larkin on drums. We did two songs – the one with Corey came out good, but the other was really shitty.'

'End Of The World', the aforementioned track featuring Corey, is hailed by those who have heard it as a doozy. Shawn Crahan has described it as 'one hell of a song'. Inexplicably, however, it didn't make Mr Fingaz's solo album on its 2000 release.

'They didn't mix it or anything, so it's sitting in a closet right now,' said Ross sadly. 'No-one may ever hear it. It never even got out on the Net ...'

HERE COMES THE PAIN

While Slipknot had been furiously gaining their hold on the minds of America's youth, there had hitherto been no way for impressed Ozzfest-goers to walk into record stores and buy a slice of their music.

Finally, on 29 June 1999, the album was launched in US record stores. It was promptly snatched up by hordes of fans who were already hopelessly devoted to the sickness.

Joey: 'I remember talking to these kids, who said they'd been trying to buy the album all day but it was sold out. We were like, "Yes! That might be ten CDs!"'

Onstage at the Deer Creek Amphitheatre in Indianpolis, Indiana, the band's innate fury was tempered only slightly by the joyous realisation that their music was finally out there. Part of the battle had been won.

Shawn: 'It was one of our craziest shows. We got to announce that our album was in the stores, so people could go and buy it. That was a beautiful moment for me. It was like a giant weight had been released – it was like giving birth as men.'

An enduring image, for sure.

Joey: 'That day, we met some of the craziest fans we've ever met. They were so into what we were doing, we thought they gonna kill us! We realised that we were infecting people, even though we weren't that big yet. We were selling more T-shits than every other band. When I think back, I can still smell the air ...'

A week later in Chicago, Illinois, Slipknot appeared on MTV as part of an Ozzfest special. They were interviewed by none other than Ozzy Jr.

Jack: 'I was supposed to take the MTV crew around Ozzfest. I asked Slipknot if they would let me interview them and they said, "Sure". That was the first time they ever got mentioned on MTV.'

MTV's interest was more than likely based on the perform-ance of the band's album. A mere week after the release of *Slipknot*, a Soundscan placed it at Number One on the

Billboard Independents Chart. The record had sold approximately 15,500 copies in its first week. For an independent metal band, the feat was little short of incredible. For Joey, the tour became even more triumphant when it stopped off in Vancouver, Canada. Indeed, it was his favourite date on the tour. For once with Slipknot, however, the reasons weren't purely musical.

'It was the first time I ever got a groupie,' laughs the drummer. 'I got a blow-job in the back of the bus. That ruled! I never had one of those in Des Moines ...'

The fact that Joey's groupie philosophy is so opposed to Shawn's only serves to illustrate how Slipknot aren't united on every subject. They're not, after all, a robot army – as much as it would be cool if they were.

CRASH COURSE IN BRAIN SURGERY

Blood was pouring from the Clown's mask. To the crowd, this may have appeared to be part of the fun – the product of concealed blood capsules. But Shawn Crahan had, in fact, smashed his head open on his own oil-drum. Again.

In a bizarre replay of the New Jersey forehead-gashing incident, Crahan once again damaged himself during 'Eyeless'. This time, the song's title very nearly proved horribly prophetic. The wound was serious.

Jack Osbourne watched aghast from the side of the stage. 'I thought it was the craziest thing ever,' he marvelled. 'I saw Shawn fall back from his drum-kit and there was blood all over the place. The crew ripped open his mask and saw he'd cut himself right down to the bone.'

Crahan would relive the incident, telling me: 'I stood up on my drum-riser and crashed down on my kit. I saw blood squirting from my eye socket before I felt the pain. I felt all this warm shit on my neck.'

The effect was so severe, in fact, that Shawn thought he had been shot in the head. 'My mask was full of blood,' he said. 'I must have swallowed two pints. I almost passed out.'

Crahan was hurriedly taken offstage and placed on a stretcher.

'I was aware that he had gone,' said Joey. 'I knew that if he'd got whipped off the stage, he must have a serious injury. I just hoped he was okay. But he was the lucky one, because he got to see us play from the audience's perspective.'

For Shawn, the moment was akin to an out-of-body thrill. He told *twec.com*: 'As the rest of the band played "Wait And Bleed", the ambulance people were trying to get me in the ambulance because I was bleeding everywhere. I told them to chill the fuck out because I wanted to watch the greatest band in the world. It was pretty much one of the most religious experiences I've ever had – the pain and pleasure all in one.'

Crahan was this time taken to see a plastic surgeon, who closed the crevice in his head with 17 stitches, taking his grand total to 22. 'All I can tell people,' he offered, 'is that when I'm onstage and I hear the dive-bomb riff at the end of "Eyeless", I feel like destroying everything and everyone surrounding me. That's how I explain what influences me to be crazy. For me, this music is on fire. When I hear it and I hear the words, I'm free from everything and everyone. I'm going to go mental and I'll kill you if you're in my way.'

Admired Joey: 'When Shawn came back later that day, he looked so cool – like death warmed over, with a huge scar up and down his face. I asked him if he'd be okay to play the next date and he said he would be. I thought, "Well, if that can't keep him down, nothing can." He had to keep going – we couldn't stop. Fortunately, he hasn't done that one again since.'

Shawn: 'When we hit the stage, safety precautions go out the window. We just do what we do.'

Not to be outdone in the self-abuse stakes, Sid also scored an injury, one day on the tour.

Joey: 'He headbutted one of the kegs we use as a drum, and cut his head open. He played the last song with concussion. Afterwards, we had to wake him up every two hours so he wouldn't go into a coma. Then the next show he was headbutting stuff again. He's out of his fucking mind.'

Crahan indeed hit the stage of San Francisco's Shoreline Amphitheatre with all guns blazing. Whereas undergoing plastic surgery would make most musicians drastically reconsider the strategy of their performance, Shawn was only more determined to up the ante.

'I probably went madder than I ever have before,' he told me, of the first few post-surgery shows. 'This is only the beginning. I have really tough bones – I'm a big milk drinker.'

Crahan's actions can sometimes be a worry to everyone from his fans to his family. He told me: 'I do flips onstage, and my wife said, "If you kill yourself onstage, I'll never forgive you. I'll tell your kids that you deliberately loved the band more than them." We all get stupid sometimes.

'I've seriously, sickly, in my own head, thought about breaking my own limbs during shows, then continuing to play,' he continued, disturbingly. 'I play my drums sometimes with my fists, because I've keyed in on someone in the audience and I'm like, "Maybe they understand."'

Crahan did, at least, draw the line at his reckless behaviour compromising the live Slipknot experience. Looking back on the Seattle incident at the end of 1999, he would list it at the low-point of his year. 'I regret not being able to give the people of Seattle a full Slipknot show,' he said. 'That was the first time that's happened, and it'll be the last.'

GOODBYE OZZFEST

The metal event of the year ground to a celebratory halt in San Bernardino, fittingly at the Blockbuster Pavilion where it first kicked off in 1996.

Amen frontman Casey Chaos was in attendance, and witnessed Slipknot properly for the first time. 'They were like a whirlwind,' he recalls. 'People just latched onto them straight away. To me, they were the best band on that bill. It was new energy, a new vibe: nine guys in masks completely committed to going off.'

Looking back on the 26 shows they had just played to well

over half a million potential converts, Slipknot had nothing but good memories.

'We had fans in every city,' Corey told *9fingers.com*. 'We had e-mails from fans all over the country, and word started to spread even before Ozzfest started. That festival gave us the opportunity to play in front of all those kids who had heard about us. What a great way to come out – playing with some of our gods, like Black Sabbath, Slayer and Primus.'

'I can always look back and tell my children that my first major tour in support of the first album I ever did was Ozzfest,' said Shawn. 'I played with the inventors of metal and I got to see the song "Black Sabbath". I'd waited my whole life to live out a dream like that.

'It was a very virginal feeling,' he reflected. 'We were a very quiet band – we didn't party, we didn't go out, we didn't do anything. We just didn't know how to take all of it. We don't care if it's 10,000 people or one person – we're gonna kill you. The onstage part of it was awesome. It was the most natural thing for us – to just go up there and be everything you can be. I remember walking around and meeting all the bands. It's a surreal thing. There I was, in a parking lot behind an amphitheatre, talking to Bill Ward about how my drums go up and down, and he was actually interested. I learned that people are people and there are no rock stars. The real rock star is my wife. I get to see her about once a month and when I see her she's the most beautiful Playboy, rock star, movie star person I've ever seen in my life. I'm like, "Can I hang with you? Can I have your autograph?"'

Certain aspects of Ozzfest made Shawn feel uncomfortable. 'There were all these established people. You always get this vibe that you've never done what other people have done. But I don't care about that – this is my life, don't fuck with me. It ended up being a great experience.'

As for Jack Osbourne, he walked away with five video cassettes of his very own Slipknot footage, having watched Slipknot on every single date of the tour. He remains good friends with the band. 'To this day, I still call Chris and Joey,' he told me. 'Shawn just e-mailed me last night ...'

NO REST FOR THE WICKED

Unsurprisingly, given the speedy sales of their album, Slipknot's next US tour was announced a mere nine days after the last Ozzfest date. And it was big.

A three-and-a-half-month package tour on a decidedly smaller scale than the Ozzfest, it saw the 'Knot mob teaming up with their label-mates Coal Chamber, Machine Head and Amen. Coal Chamber were to headline. Due to take off in Dallas, Texas on 19 August, this enticingly heavy bundle of bands was soon dubbed the Livin' La Vida Loco tour, cross-referencing the annoyingly enjoyable Ricky Martin hit with the Chamber's most popular track 'Loco'.

Joey: 'We had been afraid that no bands would want to take us back out on the road. Loads of them were turning us down – they didn't want us opening for them. Coal Chamber were cool enough to go ahead and give us a slot on that tour. I was really excited about getting back into the club situation, because we could tear shit up even more. It was also a major goal of ours to go out and smoke a band like Coal Chamber every night.'

The tour's first three dates would pass, however, without Slipknot playing at all. The band claimed that they were being left so little room onstage that they were unable to perform.

'We're a nine-piece band with three drum-kits,' said Joey simply. 'We just couldn't fit.'

One of the dates which Slipknot cancelled was Oklahoma City – a place where they would later seem to be cursed. Realising that they would have to take some form of action, the band spoke up. Loudly.

Joey: 'We said we were gonna leave the tour, and go ahead with our own club shows. That's when things changed around, and we started getting more of what we wanted. We didn't wanna be totally picky, but if we don't have enough room to fucking perform, we can't play. Over half the crowd came to see our band. We were so pissed off by the time we started playing, that we gave some of the most visceral performances of our lives.'

RESERVOIR HOGS

The cop spoke very slowly and very clearly.

'Bud, I'll shoot you through the door.'

He meant it, too. Shawn Crahan decided very quickly to keep his hands in plain sight. He had offered to reach down and grab his driving licence, but the officer was having none of it. At the request of the other cops, the rest of Slipknot were sprawled face down on the ground of this mall parking lot in Norridge, Illinois. Crahan was sitting in one of two unmarked vans and, like his bandmates, was in full mask-and-coveralls regalia.

'When he said he'd shoot me through the door,' recalled Shawn, 'that's when I knew it wasn't funny any more. That was pretty intense.'

Slipknot were a few shows into the Loco tour. They had been running late for an in-store appearance at Norridge's Rolling Stone Records shop.

'One thing this band can't stand is to be late,' Shawn recounted, 'so we parked in the lot of a shopping mall and all got out of the van real quick. We threw these bags out on the parking lot and started getting dressed. We got in these two vans and took off. Then all I remember is this cop at my door.'

'They moved very fast,' says Joey. 'They literally came out of the woodwork. They had guns drawn and everything.'

Shawn: 'I remembered this rule from my friends down in Texas that when a cop pulls you over, you've gotta put your hands on the dash so he knows you're not gonna shoot him. I looked at the cop and said, "I'm going to reach down and get my licence."'

Which is where we came in. Thankfully, the police officers finally accepted that these masked men were not about to rob the nearby jewellery shop, as they had originally believed.

Joey: 'We had them call the record store. They eventually let us go. When we showed up, there was a huge crowd outside and it was awesome.'

The cops stood watching bemused as Slipknot spent three hours greeting over 600 fans. They even took pictures with the band, later on.

DARK SIDE OF THE LOON

The look in Shawn Crahan's eyes was scary. A faraway and somehow blank look which nevertheless exuded sheer hatred and disgust.

I was sitting backstage at the Roy Wilkins Auditorium in St Paul, Minneapolis, where no less than three US package tours had collided in one enormous metallic knees-up, all in the name of local rock radio station 93X. This indoor event had been inexplicably named the Clam Bake, even though the air betrayed not the slightest whiff of toasting clam. Marijuana, yes. Clam, no. Coal Chamber's Livin' La Vida Loco trek had found itself entwined, for one day only, with tours headlined by Fear Factory and Sevendust.

The backstage atmosphere was thick with musicians high-fiving each other and exchanging tour stories, as roadies wheeled flight cases around at high speeds, harassed by the extra-quick change-over times necessitated by this packed billing.

On the sofas before me sat Fear Factory guitarist Dino Cazares and bassist Christian Olde Wolbers, who were telling me about their recent collaboration with Cypress Hill – a partnership which was bound for the latter's *Skull & Bones* album in 2000. To the left of where we were sitting, the event's organisers had erected a make-shift dressing room, which consisted of a set of four black screens, arranged in a square. This was a place where bands could spend private time, before and after their performance.

Members of Slipknot were occupying this dark space, prior to taking the stage. Through a gap between two of the screens, you could see Shawn Crahan's profile. Sitting on a sofa with a band-mate whose identity I couldn't make out from this angle, Shawn was wearing his black make-up – Absu, as they named it, after the black metal band – and one of the band's new black boiler suits. His eyes were off somewhere else, yet there was the fear that he might suddenly turn and catch you invading that intensely personal psyche-up time. Yet you couldn't help but look.

'Sorry Dino. What was that again?'

Despite Slipknot's evident mood swings before stepping onstage, Joey would insist that the reality was not so much of a Jekyll-to-Hyde metamorphosis as you might imagine.

'We don't change at all,' he told *altrockworld.com* 'People always say, "You wear masks" and we say, "No we don't." That's the way we feel – it's the actual personality that we live every day. We just get to go onstage every night and be that. It's our medication and we're very lucky that we get to do it. Whatever you see is exactly how we are, all day long.'

If this were the case, Slipknot would surely be serving life sentences by now. As much as they might have liked to be seen as 24-7 psychos, it just wouldn't be practical, or good for their health.

The Auditorium was a partially seated venue. Its extremely wide stage had been divided into two sections – a 'main stage' which took up roughly two-thirds of the space, and a 'second stage' which occupied the rest.

Despite Slipknot's nine-man army, the band had been placed on the second stage – a measure guaranteed merely to piss them off all the more. Mingling with the crowd, I waited eagerly for my second live dose of the band.

The show was pure Armageddon, with the band reacting to their cramped conditions like sharks in a paddling pool. They were a blur, and what was happening in that small stage appeared more than a little dangerous. Shawn perched on a newly customised scissor-lift machine which took the expression 'drum-riser' quite literally. He and his metal kegs would rise up and down in the air, allowing him greater heights from which to toss microphone stands and drums.

Given the seemingly random nature of his throwing exploits, it was amazing that anyone escaped injury.

During 'Purity', Sid proved himself on more than fine form when he ran over to the Clown's hydraulic device and urinated all over it. By way of reply, the Clown leapt down and rolled around in the puddle. The duelling duo then proceeded to repeatedly punch each other in the face. Fantastic theatre – or was it? The beauty of this band was that you never knew when they were going to go too far. Would someone crack their skull? Would someone lose their mind and sincerely attack another member of the band? Would the band incite a riot? All these thoughts and more raced through my head as it nodded compulsively to the music.

'I can't remember where the whole piss thing started,' puzzled Joey. 'I think Sid might have pissed onstage two or three times before that. It became this big thing, about who was able to pull it off. Corey's been really good at doing it lately. He makes a big spectacle of it, too. He gets up on the drum riser in front of everybody in the crowd, making sure they can all see his dick. He takes a piss on Shawn or Chris' kegs before they beat them, so that piss flies up in their faces. *Very* mature behaviour!'

Such childish antics would lead detractors to dismiss Slipknot as little more than a performing circus. If you already believed those nine grown men in masks to be a touch ludicrous, then their onstage water sports only served to banish their credibility altogether.

Me? I thought it was fun. Rock 'n' roll is supposed to be primal and unlock the inner child. Urinating on each other might not have been the best way to emphasise the seriousness of Corey's lyrics, but if the alternative was Slipknot standing motionless like some grunge messiahs, then give me the yellow stuff any day.

TRIBAL GATHERING

After the social desert that was the Ozzfest, the Loco tour saw Slipknot starting to make the occasional new friend. One of these was Nadja Peulen, who was playing bass in Coal Chamber. She acted as a temporary stand-in for Rayna Foss, who had taken time out of the band to have her first child with Sevendust drummer Morgan Rose.

Nadja first met unmasked members of Slipknot at New Jersey airport on 18 August, where it transpired that both they and Coal Chamber were waiting to catch a flight to the tour's first stop-off in Dallas, Texas.

Functioning on a mere two hours' sleep, Peulen didn't immediately register that these men were in Slipknot. Nevertheless, she started chatting with Craig, Jim and Paul.

On the tour's opening night at the Deep Ellum Live venue, Nadja caught some of Slipknot's blazing performance, before heading backstage to prepare for her own set with the Chamber.

'I was surprised by how many of these guys with masks there were onstage,' she told me. 'The kids loved it – they always had a really great response from the audience. The longer we toured together, the better it got. In fact, I never heard a bad response to them, any night.'

Over the first two weeks of the tour, Nadja would exchange hellos with the 'Knotsters.

'Then we started talking more and hanging out more,' she said. 'In the beginning, I had difficulty figuring out who was in the band and who was working for them. It took me a long time to work out who was who, what they did and which mask they wore.'

Chris and Paul were spending most of their time on Machine Head's bus, attempting to drink all their booze.

Claimed Robb Flynn: 'They would come over almost every night, after their show. A couple of times, we had to kick them off! I think they got addicted to the Robb Flynn "Brown Eyes" – Absolut vodka with Coca Cola.'

Slipknot were also firming up bonds with Amen and Casey Chaos. By the time the tour reached a gallop, the two bands would feed off each other's energy and enthusiasm.

Casey Chaos: 'Every night, I watched Slipknot and went, "Holy shit!" We would go on before them and push them. By the end of our set, Corey, Shawn and the others would be going, "Fucking yes!" They were really into that vibe – I guess they felt inspired.'

Corey Taylor was definitely inspired when the tour swung into New York on 7 September, playing the Roseland venue. That was the day the frontman had those tattoos carved on either side of his neck. On one side, the Japanese character for 'father'. On the other, the character for 'death'.

'I was feeling really contemplative that day,' he admitted. 'I love New York, but for some reason I get really poetic when I'm there. I started thinking about my father and the fact that I never even knew his name. I got these tattoos to move on and it's helped.'

From a man who got his jollies from pissing on drum-kits, this was sensitive talk. In this light, it was tempting to see Slipknot as thoughtful souls whose darker, more base instincts emerged when they ran with the rest of the wolfpack. They clearly *did* change when they pulled on those masks, only to purge the personal demons which hurtled out as they stomped around a stage.

Slipknot were fortunate. They actually got paid for undergoing daily group therapy.

A DARK CLOUD

One date on the tour saw Slipknot getting involved with some offstage pugilism. A local band who wore masks, somehow adopted the bizarre notion that Slipknot had ripped them off. During Slipknot's set they allegedly started hurling dangerous projectiles towards the stage.

Joey: 'We'd never heard of them. They started throwing little metal-filled pipes. If they landed on your head they could kill you. A few of the band members got hit and they freaked out.'

Nadja Peulen was watching this sorry state of affairs.

'This local band also had banners up,' she recalls. 'It was pretty shit, because you're so vulnerable onstage. I remember a couple of the Slipknot guys jumping off the stage. It all got kind of aggressive.'

Joey: 'Some of our band quit playing and dove into the crowd with their guitars on to get ahold of those guys. Corey did a really good speech about how we were there to play for our fans, and we pulled off a really good show. After that, we got our stuff off and went looking for these guys in the crowd.'

'At that time, the whole tour became friends,' remembered Nadja warmly. 'It had already been announced that the people in this band were coming. We all walked outside, looking for those guys. It was funny, because it was a group of 20 or 30 people. I miss those days – it was cool.'

When Slipknot's posse eventually located them, tempers naturally flared.

'I remember Sonny from Amen decking one of the guys,' says Joey. 'He dropped directly in front of my feet. That was the end of it, actually – Sonny did our work for us.

'It didn't turn into too big or bad a thing, but some stuff went down. Still, we never had any trouble from them again. We've played Cleveland several times since and had some excellent shows.'

Almost inevitably, Slipknot ran into resistance on a couple of other occasions during the tour. Not that it slowed them one iota. Before one show in Texas, the band – and Corey in particular – were apparently warned to censor all profanity from their set. Corey's response was predictable.

'I said, "Fuck you, I'm going to fucking curse!"' he laughs. 'The authorities almost picked me up, because I was going at it hardcore. I asked the crowd if we were living in Nazi Germany. The fact that they have to uphold that kind of law is pathetic. It makes me sick.'

The lesson there was, of course: don't tell Slipknot what not to do, because they will assuredly do it.

Police again appeared on the scene when the band played Las Vegas.

Shawn: 'I was dumping water on the security guards. They got me pissed off that I got my keg and threw it down on the barrier. One guard was giving me attitude, so I jumped down and got in his face.'

Enter the local gendarmes, after the show.

Shawn: 'They were screaming, because they said a knife was involved. There's no way I'd pull a knife on anybody – I'd just beat your ass – but it turned out that my keg is held by this metal piece which had lost its support. My roadie had made it level with a butter knife which fell when I threw the keg. I didn't know that I'd almost got arrested until we were back on the bus, but the police were not fucking around.'

HOMETOWN HEROES

This was one hell of a return.

On the afternoon of the tour's stop-off at Des Moines' Super Toads Ents Centre, Slipknot threw a signing session at a Sam Goody store in the local mall. One thousand people showed – some of whom had been waiting five hours to see the band, and vented their frustration by tearing chunks out of corridor walls and graffiti-ing the 'Fuck it all, fuck this world, fuck everything that you stand for' chorus of 'Surfacing'.

'It's crazy, man,' Sid told *Kerrang!*'s Paul Brannigan, who was present at the event. 'It's like living in a dream, or watching a movie. This is the town I was born in, and now I'm signing autographs. It's an honour.'

The response from fans in their own town really brought Slipknot's rising profile home to the band.

'We have a lot of old-school friends here,' Shawn told fans during a live web chat. 'They welcome you as a friend, and it's cool to come back and hang out with people that you've left and been away from for ages. At the same time, it's getting pretty crazy. I have high school kids who ride by my house on their bikes and ask my two eldest kids who are playing in the yard if their dad is in Slipknot.'

The Super Toads promoter claimed that he had been turning 50 fans away an hour, and that the venue had been sold out ages ago. Couple this with the fact that the Slipknot album had now sold 100,000 copies and that the www.slipknot1.com website had received 140,000 hits in October alone, and you could smell a phenomenon brewing.

While Slipknot's blazing 45-minute set was ostensibly part of a bill headlined by Coal Chamber and featuring Powerman 5000 and Dope, it was obvious who most people had paid to see that night.

Wrote Brannigan in *Kerrang!*: 'This feels like more than just AN Other rock show. It feels *important*. Slipknot fans are not your usual "pain as fashion accessory" tattooed-and-pierced big city metal crowd, but genuine outsiders: the fat kids, the speccy kids, the brainy kids doomed to a suffocating hick town existence.'

While this did not mean to imply that all Slipknot fans were freaks, it is only natural that bands tend to attract like-minded souls. One very strong appeal of the 'Knot is that their followers can dress up in masks and become someone else – anyone else – for the night. They are getting off on exactly the same escapist fuck-everything rush that Slipknot feel. This synergy helps to make the band's show such an overpower-ingly electric affair, and one of the more life-affirming experi-ences available to humanity.

Post-show that night, Corey gasped: 'The fact that this many people still believe in us back home is awesome. Tonight was off-the-hook as usual, but this was the first Des Moines show where I couldn't see the end of the people. That was outrageous.'

As with many other members of the band, Taylor's family were present at the show. What, you might wonder, would his mom and sister make of that?

'Negative or positive, it's me,' he shrugged. 'It's a piece of me that's always been there and probably always will. I think they understand that and are happy about that.'

Slipknot were already having to find ways to cope with their relatively sudden up-swing in fortune. One method was to focus on the fans and the band's responsibilities to them.

'You can always tell a Slipknot fan,' said Corey on the bus behind the Super Toad, 'because he will go for it. He's like, "Slipknot is the shit, I don't give a fuck." That makes me feel good and makes me feel I'm doing something right. A lot of kids in America and Canada have said to me, "We need to play your album to help us make it through the day." I take that shit to heart. If you have something special, you don't ruin it with glitz and all the stupidity that ruins great bands.'

He added: 'We need to stay as strong – positively and nega-tively – as we can. The only people we give a fuck about, are the people who give a fuck about us. A lot of people would have a big head about success like this, but it's had the reverse effect on me. It humbles me and makes me go, "Thank you very much".'

The Livin' La Vida Loco tour had seen two bands dropping out along the way. Machine Head left first, followed by Amen – with the latter being ejected for alleged bad behaviour.

'It was due to the politics of the music business,' said Casey Chaos. 'Slipknot had absolutely nothing to do with it.'

Over these three months, Slipknot and Coal Chamber had strong-armed their way through the vast majority of America and Canada.

When Nadja Peulen thought over the whole trek, one particularly fun moment stuck out in her mind. 'One time, Slipknot had to go through our dressing room to go onstage. Dez was playing "Saturday Night Fever". All nine of them were standing in a row to get onstage and they were dancing to the song. It looked really funny. I wish I'd got that on camera.'

Nadja's assessment of Slipknot offstage painted an interest-ingly low-key picture of the men behind the masks. 'To me, none of them seem that crazy in private,' she said. 'I think they're really nice guys. That's obvious, otherwise I wouldn't be friends with them. But if somebody rubs them wrong, I'm sure they could get out of control.

'They've always been really nice to me and treated me really well. It's cool that we're still in touch, even though I don't have anything to offer them and I'm not "happening". Most people are fake and pretentious – they're nice to you when you have things happening, but when you're going through a harder time they're not that interested. That's a very Hollywood thing – maybe because Slipknot aren't from there, they're a little different.'

No kidding.

14 November saw the tour grind to a glorious halt in LA, at the Hollywood Palace. Slipknot celebrated onstage in a typically over-the-top style, by wrecking $8,000 worth of equipment.

Shawn told *Loud & Heavy*: 'Joey threw all his cymbals out and I broke his drum cage. Chris and I threw our drums and guitar cabinets went flying. Everything was pretty nuts and to say the least, it ruled.'

By contrast, Crahan wasn't initially sure how much he liked turning 30 years of age, as he did during the Loco tour. Then Joey reassured him.

Shawn: 'He told me I was getting older, but getting better. I thought, "Alright, man." Look at all the greats, like Jerry Only from The Misfits, Robert Plant, Kiss and Ozzy Osbourne. What have I got to complain about? I'm the luckiest guy in the world – I got eight other best friends, I got a bus and three healthy kids who will hopefully benefit from their daddy being gone. My best friend's my wife and the world's our fucking oyster. We're just trying to keep the oyster alive, instead of plucking it, picking the pearl and selling it out. We're trying to keep the actual organic substance alive and buried in the ocean.'

Just as well, considering the chaos which lurked ahead.

6
The firing line

Promoters have been talking to each other.
Now, every time we roll into town, we get a
list of what we can and can't do.
Joey Jordison, #1

We'll naturally be a target.
We'll have red dots floating around our masks.
Corey Taylor, #8

TWISTED RIOT-STARTERS

11 January 2000
Helicopters circled the Tower Theater like angry wasps. A SWAT team screeched onto the scene, modelling the regulation metal helmets and shields. Police dogs ran beside their owners. If the last millennium had ended peacefully for Slipknot, this one was literally a riot.

Problems began that night when an inspector from the Oklahoma City fire marshall's office paid a visit to the Tower Theater. A fairly old building, the venue used to be a movie theatre and still had the fixed seats to show for it.

While the venue had apparently removed the first five rows, there was still nowhere near enough room for fans to physically show their appreciation. Furthermore, there were too many of them.

Discovering that the venue was over-stuffed with Slipknot fans, the inspector fined the owner $750 and told him to make 60 people leave. This, needless to say, was asking for trouble. How did you go about telling a theatre full of psyched-up 'Knot fans that some of them had to miss out on seeing the greatest show on Earth?

Inside the Theater, Canadian metallers Kittie had managed to finish their opening set and were on the verge of celebrating the US release of their debut album *Spit* that same day.

The second band on the bill, Will Haven, were less fortunate. Recalled Kittie front-girl Morgan Lander: 'In the middle of Will Haven's set, the fire marshall came out and said, "You guys all need to take a seat, because of the fire hazard." People flipped out – going to see a band as intense as Slipknot, and sitting down, was not gonna work. The guys from Slipknot were pretty pissed off.'

Slipknot also learnt that part of the audience had been asked to leave and given refunds. This went down equally badly with the band: they cancelled the show.

Morgan: 'They could have gone on, even if people were sitting down. But they decided they would give the fans the show they wanted and deserved. They didn't think it was fair that people wouldn't get the full experience.'

'We decided that it's one for all, all for one,' Shawn told *Loud & Heavy* magazine. 'Everybody had paid for a ticket and just because some of them were standing in the hallway they got kicked out.'

Joey: 'A lot of people think we ran off with the cash, but that's not true. We just didn't wanna cheat our fans. The next thing you know, there were three helicopters over the place, 40 cop cars, arrests, fights, broken glass and all this shit. We got away from it real quick and went to the next city.'

SLIPKNOT: INSIDE THE SICKNESS BEHIND THE MASKS   159

Kittie and their crew also hot-wheeled out of town.

Morgan: 'At least no-one got hurt. If they had, the blame probably would have fallen on Slipknot.'

PURITY LOST

Slipknot's headlining quest for world domination had started innocently enough on 29 November 1999, at Chicago's House Of Blues. For the initial 10-date stretch, they would be joined by Brooklyn metalcore bruisers Biohazard and new Roadrunner signings The Step Kings.

For Joey in particular, being supported by the long-running scene veterans Biohazard felt strange. 'They had been a favourite band of mine for a long time,' he would admit. 'I'd been to their shows before, and now they were opening up for my band. Or, as I'd rather describe it, playing before us.'

On one night of the tour, Joey got to live out a dream and actually play drums with the 'Hazard boys. When the band's drummer, Danny Schuler, smashed his fingers in his garage door, Jordison was hurriedly recruited to fill in for the band at the eleventh hour.

'I learned all the parts and nailed them. That was one of the best nights of the tour – I got to play with Biohazard.'

Straight after that, however, Joey had to don his mask and make a second appearance. This demanded herculean effort from him.

'I was *feeling* it that night, man – I was tired as fuck,' he laughed. 'I was going off while playing with Biohazard, just like I do with Slipknot. The rest of the guys in my band said, "You'd better be slamming for *our* set, motherfucker!" I went at it super-hard and I got through, but I was like a corpse after that show.'

By this time, there was every indication that Slipknot were ready to buzz around America's live circuit on their own merits. The dust they had kicked up on the Ozzfest and Loco tours had become a sandstorm.

The band's *Welcome To My Neighbourhood* home video,

which was released on 9 November, had not only gone Gold very quickly, but become the biggest selling video in the US, outdoing even the likes of Madonna and Shania Twain.

They had also been threatened with a lawsuit, which is the hallmark of any proper rock band operating in America. This one was very serious, as it would force the band to pull two offending tracks from their album and re-release the whole thing.

Shawn had found a story called *Purity* on a webpage, about a girl named Purity Knight who was kidnapped and buried alive.

'It was pretty fascinating and extremely disturbing' he told *Loudside.com*. 'When I showed the story to Corey, he was lyrically inspired.'

'I still think the story's real,' said Corey. 'It fucked our whole world up when we read it. Can you imagine a girl being buried in a box and have all this lecherous bullshit drip down on her from this guy? It just hurts your head. The box alone is reason enough to be like, "I can't stand to be human."'

Unfortunately, the author of *Purity* apparently objected to this bunch of Iowan upstarts using their tale as the basis for a slice of quality nu-metal, and told them to remove it from the album. And so they did – also snipping its creepy spoken-word intro 'Frail Limb Nursery'.

Huffed Joey: 'When Anthrax wrote a song about *The Stand* by Stephen King, they didn't get sued for it, but we *did*, for some reason. This is the way of Slipknot. There's not really much to say about that situation – "Purity" is a great song and we still play it live for our fans. You can still get it out there on Napster.com and all that bullshit. It sucked, because I really liked that song.'

Shawn told *Loudside.com*: 'People want to point fingers. Whatever, dude. If you're one of those artists who isn't honoured when you influence someone to take it one step further, you can just go fuck off, you know?'

The album's re-release was great for financially solvent obsessed fans, because it gave them something new to buy.

The re-released version of the album replaced 'Purity' with 'Me Inside', and Slipknot took the opportunity to master the whole disc slightly differently. Fanatics would also notice subtle differences in the artwork, such as the tribal 'S' on the CD's spine.

'It was never meant to be a marketing scheme,' insisted Joey. 'We just had to remove those tracks, in order for our album to keep selling.'

Slipknot were now *the* band for metal fans to go and see. Their shows were uniformly packed.

Joey: 'When you get word-of-mouth like that, most of it's curiosity – not everybody necessarily likes the band. They just want to see what's up. But we gained a lot of die-hard fans out of those headlining tours.'

SLIPKNOT VS LIMP BIZKIT

'Fred, you may have a lot of money and be all over the world, but when you talk shit about Slipknot and our fans, we will kill you!' Corey Taylor stood onstage at New York's Roxy in December, and drank in the cheers which greeted his impassioned speech.

It had been addressed to Limp Bizkit's baseball-capped singer Fred Durst, who was fast becoming a rap-rock icon in the minds of many American youths. The 'Knot had heard a rumour that Durst had made the potentially fatal error of dissing them and their brethren.

Here's how Joey told it: 'Ross Robinson was at a Hollywood party that Durst was at. He alledegedly told Ross: "Dude, you'd better watch the bands you're producing. Slipknot just play for a bunch of fat, ugly kids."'

An outraged Shawn told *Loud & Heavy*: 'I represent all the fat ugly kids because I'm still one myself. We do a little ritual in Slipknot called "flip for a punch in the face". I take a coin out of my pocket, flip a coin and the loser gets a punch in the face. So Fred Durst doesn't have a choice about this: we're going to have to flip for a punch in the face. I'll tell you what –

I'll give him the benefit of the doubt and let him call the coin. We're tired of the rock 'n' roll cliché, and we're here to tell you it's bullshit.'

Durst denied he had said anything of the sort, saying: 'Slipknot fans are awesome. Who knows how these rumours arise?' During the video shoot for Limp Bizkit's 'Break Stuff' tune, he further told the attending crowds of fans that he loved Slipknot.

Robinson himself was clear that Durst did not utter the 'fat, ugly kids' slur, and wrote off the whole feud as a press invention. 'I read that stuff and went, "Fred didn't say that!"' he told me. 'The press can make things so nasty and misinterpreted. One time, somebody from *NME* told me Slipknot said I was riding on the coat-tails of their fame. I was like, "I'm sure they didn't mean it – *if* they said it!" Press gossip is all a bunch of shit. It's not what we do music for and it's not very meaningful. It's a good electrical shock if you're bored. But if that stuff gets you off, it's really time to wake up.'

In any event the next months would see him receive nightly verbal abuse from Corey, who also took to burning various Bizkit paraphernalia onstage.

'He pretty much started slagging Durst every night,' Joey laughed. 'It became his rap before we played "Surfacing", in the middle of the set.'

Truth be told, Slipknot thrived on the schism.

Joey: 'I've never met Fred Durst and I can't say I like his band. It was a good controversy, that's all I know. I liked it. It was a nice little rock 'n' roll feud. There's nothing better than a fight between two nu-metal bands – one a little bit more psycho than the other.'

SCREAM AND BLEED

While playing The Roxy, our nine heroes discovered that they were on the soundtrack to the slasher sequel *Scream 3*, alongside Creed, System Of A Down, Sevendust, Coal Chamber,

Static-X, Incubus, Orgy and more. As is so often the case with such big-time affairs, however, there was a catch – their submission was a remixed version of 'Wait And Bleed', handled by producer Terry Date.

Joey: 'Corey had done two different vocal tracks – one of which was cleaner. We mixed them together in the studio, so we would have the melody with this hard voice. The cleaner track was there for a little ambience, but much to our dismay, the label took the clean vocal track and used it for Terry Date's mix. That's one of the drawbacks of being on a label, when they do shit like that.'

In fairness, the re-jigged version is still heavier than an elephant with a sack of spanners hanging from each tusk. And bluster aside, Joey could understand why Roadrunner wanted to manufacture something for radio.

'It did help out,' he admitted. 'It probably contributed to maybe about 30 or 50,000 record sales. I don't regret it, even though I don't like the way the remix is. The album track's way better. It's just part of this ride, and part of the way things have gone. You can't make everything go your way, all the time. It did help a lot of people find a band they really liked. I prefer to look at the good things.'

Such as, for instance, their impending trip to England ...

ANARCHY IN THE UK: PART 1

While Slipknot had been splattered all over the pages of the UK's rock weekly *Kerrang!* throughout 1999, they had yet to play a single show in Britain. On the night of 13 December they finally arrived. And given the intensity of the press hype, Slipknot had a hell of a lot to live up to at London's Astoria Theatre.

'It was like starting all over again,' Joey would recall. 'We were in a brand new territory. At that time, the UK was treating us better than the US, and we'd only toured the US. We knew we had to step it up tenfold.'

Slipknot promptly became one of the few American bands

in history who cancelled US dates in favour of the UK. Normally, it was very much the other way around.

Joey: 'It was just as important to get over there as it was to do the US stuff. We needed to do it.'

The first thing which amazed the drummer about England was how long it took to get there. 'I'd never been in a plane for so many hours. I came out a new person after flying that fucking long.'

On arrival, Slipknot met their new tour manager for Europe and were escorted to their new double-decker tour bus. While this was good in theory, it meant numerous bumps on the head for the band's less vertically challenged members.

Joey: 'All the guys in my band are tall and I'm about five-foot-four. The others immediately started bitching, wondering how the hell they were going to do this. I was fine – I could walk around in the bottom *and* the top.'

The day before the Astoria show, Slipknot hit the venue for what Joey described as 'one of the most brutal, hard sound-checks we've ever had to deal with. Everyone was nervous and we had all this press that took all day long. When we were doing these photo shoots, all we wanted was to put on a hell of a show for our UK fans. That was the definition of anticipation.'

Despite the tension, Shawn for one was delighted to hit British soil. 'I was one of the guys in the band that was so optimistic about playing overseas. My father wanted me to go overseas when I was a kid, but I was too caught up in girlfriends and bullshit to listen to my father being wise and wanting the best for me. But he's even more proud of me now.

'When I went over to the UK,' he recalled, 'I wanted to experience the culture – for knowledge, and to look and touch and feel. It was great, man.'

Slipknot went on a tourist spree on the day of the show. Joey checked out Soho, finally dubbing it 'a cool place'.

Shawn went to Buckingham Palace. 'I thought those guys wore red,' he complained. 'They were wearing blue. Why not red? If you're gonna show it to me my whole life, then I get over here and it's not red ...'

You'd think that Mr Crahan, of all people, would know the benefits of changing your costume every once in a while.

RADIO GAG-GAG

'Can we cuss?'

This was virtually Shawn Crahan's first utterance as Slipknot made their debut guest appearance on the BBC's *Radio 1 Rock Show* – the UK rock fan's oasis in a sea of indie-pop airwaves. This being the Beeb, of course, the answer was no, they couldn't cuss. While the show would be aired at midnight, after the Astoria show, Shawn and Joey recorded the show at the studio on the afternoon of the gig.

Presenter Mary-Anne Hobbs found the duo in a surprisingly light-hearted mood. Indeed, all she could prise out of them for the first couple of minutes was a series of death metal grunts. The band's uncharacteristic levity was mainly down to the excitement of finally crossing the Atlantic.

Said Shawn: 'If I die tomorrow, or I have to quit because my leg got caught in my scissor-lift and they cut it off, then our music and the life that we're living right now, gave us this opportunity. We can't believe that we're over here. I would have never, ever imagined it in a million years.'

Joey and Shawn requested various suitably extreme tracks – including their own '(Sic)'. The duo also probed the outer limits of the BBC's language policy, by discussing various toilet-related matters. They revealed, for instance, that they had invented the word 'dode' for a singular piece of faeces. Shawn recounted the story of how his drum-tech Sa-Tone drank a glass of urine for a bet, then threw it up and drank it again. Joey also laid down the gauntlet to Hobbs and her producer Emma Lyne to fight naked with him – a kind offer which they politely declined.

The *Rock Show* got off lightly, compared to New York shock-jock Howard Stern, earlier in the year. As legend has it, Stern was forced to watch Sid masturbating in one corner of the room, while Shawn crapped in a bucket.

'Stern seemed more surprised than shocked,' reflected Mick. 'But I don't think he liked it.'

HELL'S KITCHEN

The Astoria show was phenomenal. Before the band even hit the stage, the air was thick with excitement. Fans had made their own masks – including one whole posse from Devon who, at a casual glance, looked like the real thing. Indeed, they so impressed Slipknot that they would later be invited to the aftershow shindig and offered merchandise in exchange for their headgear.

The band's entrance onstage was awe-inspiring. As a strobe light seemed to slow down time, the members of the band walked onstage one by one as '742617000027' droned through the hot, thick air.

'The whole thing I think is sick,' said the voice, over and over again. Then Slipknot detonated and the entire venue was swept away by the ever-astounding '(Sic)'. Earlier that day, the Astoria's friendly security team had been placing bets on whether this would be the most violent mosh-pit they had ever dealt with, and the answer was blindingly obvious.

The set only lasted 45 minutes. A master-stroke. Slipknot hit us squarely between the eyes and left us begging for more, with not one gram of fat to slow down the onslaught. Sid, in particular, inspired gasps from everyone present – including Iceland's eccentric popstress Björk. Having performed two spectacular dives from the top of the PA tower, he decided that this was no longer supplying him with enough adrenaline. Disappearing from the stage for a while, he finally resurfaced on the venue's right-hand balcony – which looked around 30 feet high. It was filled with pass-holding guests, who looked on agog as Sid went about his highly dangerous work.

Clambering over the side, he held on with one hand for a few agonising seconds, and then let go. Two thousand hearts skipped a beat and then Sid was being carried overhead back towards the stage – seemingly with all limbs in working order.

Just when you thought his insanity was sated, he appeared on the left-hand balcony and pulled exactly the same stunt. Unbelievable.

Joey: 'That was one of the first times Sid had ever done those kind of leaps. Every time he gets up there and I know he's going to jump, I still cross my fingers while I'm playing drums. The funny thing is, he'll jump down there and surf all the way around the crowd, but still get back up onstage to play his part.'

Shawn: 'I look over and see my DJ 30 foot in the fucking air and he looks at me like he doesn't care. He's like, "I'm going, and whatever happens, happens." That's the way it is in Slipknot. Sid might die, he might live but he's there and he's feeling it. This is as real as it gets.'

Joey was blown away by the reaction to his band. 'When I saw all those kids who knew all our songs, man, it was another stepping stone – another emotional high that we'd never felt before. When we got off that stage, we didn't know whether it was a good show or not.'

Shawn had been amazed to see a Clown mask in the audience. In fact, he initially thought that one of his own had been pilfered. 'I went over to him and said, "What's up? You've got my mask!" It turned out to be a different one. He loved my character The Clown so much, he went out and paid a guy to make a goddamn mask. I thought that was the coolest thing I'd ever seen. It happened first in the UK.'

Joey: 'A lot of people think every crowd's the same because music's universal, and it *is* universal. But over there in England, it's like Planet Rock. They were so nice to us. The Astoria was one of the best shows that we'd had.'

It accordingly received one of their best reviews. *Kerrang!*'s Mörat wrote: 'Slipknot are mesmerising, menacing and utterly mind-blowing ... they are the logical conclusion to the 20th century. If you feed cattle on their own shit, then you get disease. If you feed humans on war and MTV, you get Slipknot. When Charles Manson told the world that their children would rise against them, this is what he meant.'

Having conquered London, Slipknot headed off for a few select European dates. On 23 December 1999, they finally returned home and hung their masks on their Christmas trees.

'I couldn't believe what we'd just done,' says Joey. 'All of a sudden, we'd seen other parts of the world. We'd already toured America and Canada twice, but now we'd done the UK and parts of Europe. We spent Christmas collecting our thoughts about what just happened, while spending time with our families. Then it was time to set up the next year's work ...'

Slipknot did indeed start the new millennium as they meant to go on, by playing a storming show for 3,000 people at the Super Toads Ents Center on New Year's Day.

Up in Toronto, Canada, Kittie frontgirl Morgan Lander had enjoyed an extra special Christmas. Her band were about to release their debut album and she had received some very special news.

'Knowing that our band was gonna be out on a national tour with Slipknot,' she said, 'was the best present I could have had.'

POST-MILLENNIAL TENSION

The first member of Slipknot whom Kittie met, at the tour's first date in Davenport, Iowa on 7 January, was Sid Wilson.

Recalled Morgan: 'We were standing there talking. Sid came up to us with this Furby toy that was stripped of all its hair. He had rewired it, so it was making all these satanic gyrations. We were asking him about how he had manipulated this thing: he was so involved with it!'

As usual, nobody in Slipknot walked around shaking people's hands and saying, 'Hello, I'm a member of the popular beat combo Slipknot.' Kittie had to figure it out for themselves.

The next member they met was Corey.

'He started talking,' said Morgan. 'He can be really loud and obnoxious. I thought, "Who is this character?" Finally, I got the hint that he was the singer in Slipknot.'

One by one, the 'Knot boys succumbed to Kittie's charms and started hanging out with them. Everyone that is, except Mick.

'We didn't even talk to Mick that entire time!' Morgan would marvel. 'We didn't get to know him 'til the second tour. He's definitely very metal, but he's totally a nice guy. He was a guitar teacher, so he knows a lot of technical stuff, besides knowing how to shred like a motherfucker. You just have to start your conversation with him the right way – either by talking about death metal bands like Nile and Immolation, or talking technically about guitars, to get in his good books. We knew we had to get Mick on our side, because he was the only one we hadn't talked to yet. We would drop him little notes and finally won him over. He's the greatest guy – he even helps us out with technical stuff.'

On Chris, Morgan said: 'He's really quiet. He doesn't really talk a lot. He's pretty crazy, but he keeps to himself. I know he has a steady girlfriend, though: I'm sure she keeps him in check.'

Morgan describes Sid as 'pretty demented'. At the other end of the scale, she dubs Paul and Joey as 'the most normal, in terms of not carrying dead things around like Clown.'

Morgan's parents were on tour with the band. They were clearly not your average folks, however, as they didn't take out a restraining order against the Slipknot guys.

Morgan: 'Shawn would come up and say, "Momma Kittie, Momma Kittie, look at my dead thing in a jar!" But we all totally got along – my parents loved those guys. All the members of Slipknot became like my parents' children as well.'

Despite the fact that Kittie were travelling from city to city in a winnebago van, and had almost ended up in a war zone during the aforementioned Oklahoma City incident, their first major tour was a blast.

Further proof that Slipknot were not wild animals, behind the masks. Unless you happened to be a Calvin Klein model...

SLIPKNOT VS KORN: PART 1

One night in January, Slipknot's tour bus was standing at a truck stop. Various band members headed towards the magazine racks, hungry for some reading material. Having an apparent fascination with Britney Spears, Jim Root picked up the latest issue of Teen People, which bore the pint-sized pop-chick on the cover.

Joey looked on as Jim flicked through the pages. The two of them were astounded to see Korn drummer David Silveria posing with his shirt off in a super-glossy advert for Calvin Klein jeans.

'Next thing you knew,' recalled Joey, 'there was Corey with his big fucking mouth, buying the magazine. That became another nightly speech in the show.'

And how. Corey started dissing Silveria onstage every night, just as vehemently as he had Durst, if not more so. Copies of the Calvin Klein advert were ceremonially torched, for added effect. Slipknot's own dissenters would accuse them of hypocrisy on that topic, since their image arguably accounted for a large degree of their success.

Yet the band were more than capable of standing up for themselves. Corey explained to the press that Silveria's actions stirred up so much anger within the band because they had always loathed the world's commercial focus on people's physical appearances. Not to mention bands who mix rock 'n' roll with corporate sponsorship.

'Obviously the masks have a great look,' allowed the singer, speaking to the website *IGN For Men*. 'But the reason we started doing it in the first place was because we'd seen so many bands suck the money dick. They would completely cheese out, to the point where they would get onstage and be like, "Hey! Do you like the new shirt I bought on Santa Monica Boulevard today? I'm endorsed!" That's why we did the masks, the coveralls and all those things. We were like, "Fuck my face! Here's my mask – this is what the music turns me into." Music isn't a product, it's an expression. We were so tired of being let down and seeing so many other kids being let down by this shit that it was either wait or do it yourself.

'If you ever do see us doing a Gap commercial,' he added, 'shoot us in the face because we wouldn't know what the hell we were doing. We're not in this for the modelling. It's the music first and foremost.'

Shawn told *Ill Literature*: 'There's nothing that disgusts me more than seeing trendy-ass rock 'n' roll stars. Don't get me wrong – I like to wear clothes that other people wear. I am one of those fashion-monger guys that will buy something because I think it's cool. But I just don't think there's any place for it on the stage. All the music I buy is extremely brutal and underground, because those bands don't give a fuck.'

Shawn was seemingly less bothered about David Silveria posing for Calvin Klein than, say, Corey had been. 'I don't spend time in my day worrying about someone else,' he told *Ill Literature*. 'One thing I hate more than anything else is identity crisis – you are who you are, so just figure it out. Slipknot doesn't believe in trends. Think about everyone coming to a show – black, white, Chinese, skinhead, whatever – and just enjoying the music.'

First Limp Bizkit had enraged the 'Knot. Now Korn were feeling their wrath.

'We took out the two biggest nu-metal bands there are!' laughed Joey.

Slipknot clearly saw no reason to curry favour with these gargantuan acts – no matter what kind of tour support slots they could have potentially been missing out on. Korn may have helped inspire them in the beginning, but Slipknot held strict principles which had been offended.

Joey was keen, however, to tell the press that they didn't completely hate the music of Korn or even the Bizkit. 'We just hate Korn's third album (1998's *Follow The Leader*) and Limp Bizkit's second album (1999's *Significant Other*),' he pointed out. 'Their first albums, however, did greatly influence us. We do like Korn's latest album *Issues* – some of it sounds like the first one, but they could still have perfected it. We've never met either of them, but we'd like to.'

David Silveria himself would later tell fans during an Internet chat: 'I've never heard Slipknot in my life. Obviously, they've got some kind of jealousy thing going on and they need to get over it.'

STALKING JAPANESE

On 28 January, the penultimate day of Slipknot's tour with Kittie and Will Haven, a beautiful thing happened. The Recording Industry Association of America certified the *Slipknot* album as having gone Gold in America. That is to say, it had shifted half a million copies.

Four days beforehand, the 'Wait And Bleed' video had made its debut on the MTV show *120 Minutes*. This was clearly a big step forward – even if it wasn't the video Slipknot had wanted.

Joey: 'We had plans to make a real video, all concepted-out. It was gonna be really great, but the label wanted to use the live performance clip from the *Welcome To Our Neighbourhood* home video. I'd still stand by the video in itself, but we had other plans.' None of these considerations prevented the general sense of achievement from taking Slipknot's collective breath away. While they celebrated hard, there was barely any time for them to absorb all this information before they were whisked off to play their first shows in Japan and Australia.

Once again, en route to Tokyo, Joey endured the longest flight he had yet known. And once again, the results were well worth the tedium.

'When we got to our hotel,' he recalled, 'there were 25 to 30 Japanese kids who'd figured out where our hotel was. They were waiting, with pictures, when we got off the bus. It was insane. In Japan, we couldn't even walk in the street! They even knew what we looked like. They know everything. It's scary, in a way.'

Slipknot played five dates during their stay, and were amazed by the response.

Joey: 'It was a little weird. We were all the way over the other side of the fucking world, and there were these people who knew who we were! It kept getting bigger and bigger by the day. The shows were awesome.'

MEN AT WORK

Trent Reznor could not quite believe the testimony of his ears. The Nine Inch Nails mastermind was driving around the Australian outback, accompanied by his band and crew. They had taken a week out of their Antipodean tour schedule in order to explore the rain forests.

As they drove, they were listening to an interview on an Aussie rock radio station.

'I was amazed people could say "fuck" on the radio out there,' Reznor told me. 'All I heard were these huge American accents saying "fuck", every opportunity they could get. It ended up being pretty funny and I later realised it was Slipknot.'

Describing the rest of his trip, Reznor planted his tongue firmly in his cheek. 'It rained every fucking day,' he complained. 'Who'd have thought *that*?'

Oblivious to this lord of electro-rock having enjoyed a rare chuckle on their account, Slipknot were busy enjoying the many wonders of this new land.

'It was excellent,' enthused Joey. 'Unreal. Australia was brutal as fuck. We would have to fly into a city, go to the hotel, check in, go to soundcheck and then do an in-store. Every one of these in-stores – and we did one in each city – was for about three or four thousand people. They brought masks, pot plants and all kinds of shit. Then we'd go from the in-store, play the show, go back to the hotel and get to the airport at seven o'clock and fly to the next city. You can't bus around in Australia, because it's too much land. One time in Sydney, we did this in-store *after* the show. That's insane.'

Needless to say, a riot ensued. No Slipknot trek would be complete without one. ·

Joey: 'Cops arrived because kids started busting out all the windows in this mall. It was nuts. It was over-crowding – too many kids, all insane from the show. We got them all wound up and they went fucking nuts!'

Shawn would later identify the band's in-store appearance as the peak of his exhaustion that year. 'It was draining to be in the mask for so many hours,' he told *Kerrang!*. 'It was probably the low point of my career in the 'Knot. But when there's a riot and the kids go crazy, you use that energy to push yourself.'

FIRST WE TAKE MANHATTAN

For Slipknot, 25 February was one big head-fuck of a day, albeit a great one. During the afternoon in New York City, the band performed a live version of 'Wait And Bleed' on none other than *The Conan O'Brien Show*. Joey's dream, from all those light years ago in Sinclair's Garage, was coming true.

Joey: 'I remember doing soundchecks for that show. We were all slamming and playing really hard ... and there was no-one there! I'd been so excited to play that show forever. It was one of those things I'd always wanted to accomplish.'

Shawn told MTV: 'Slipknot is based on the theory of infecting as many people in the world as possible. It's world domination, and we're big fans of Conan O'Brien's show. The ongoing joke was, "We'll see what we can do. Can we get on something like *Conan O'Brien* or *Letterman*, or something like that?" And it's happened. I can't speak for everybody, but I think it's a huge victory for hard music. I love it. It's an honour.'

'The recording came out great and I met Conan himself,' buzzed Joey. 'He fucking loved us – he was watching us during soundcheck, grooving and headbanging! His favourite band's Kiss, after all!'

It transpired that Conan wasn't the band's only celebrity fan. There was also young Robert Iller from the US TV series *The Sopranos*.

Joey: 'He saw us at a New York show in December. Him and his friend came to the show with their Slipknot T-shirts on. He's a really cool metal kid. We had them sit by the stage and they were rocking out. They come to our New York shows every time we play.'

The madness of this 24 hours had yet to end, however. That night, Slipknot played the Limelight with Brit rap-metallers One Minute Silence. Half an hour before Slipknot glided out onstage, they were presented with their long-delayed US Gold discs.

Joey: 'It was very overwhelming. We'd worked so hard since we started and we could mentally see every day of that suffering, blood, sweat, tears, shows and flyers. Suddenly, it was right there in front of us – 500,000 people owned the record.'

The ever-verbose Corey announced the band's achievement from the stage, eliciting congratulatory roars from the faithful. This was also a highly amusing show, due to confusion caused by the number of fans who turned up in the newly available official jump suits and home-made masks. After members of the 'Knot went crowd-surfing, dressed-up fans followed suit and were promptly helped 'back' onstage by bamboozled security guards.

Therese McKeon, a correspondent for the trusty *slip-knotweb.com* site, was in the photo-pit. 'Some of the security guards would try to put them onstage, only to be stopped by other security guards who could tell the difference,' she said. 'The confusion was hilarious to watch.'

Just so that everybody knew Slipknot weren't going soft, what with all this Gold disc glory and mix-up tomfoolery, Corey made sure he slammed Fred Durst a good few times during the set. Slipknot's ultimate attitude towards their new Gold status was healthy, in terms of maintaining their momentum and hunger.

Joey: 'We were like, "You know what? This means nothing any more – it's time to go Platinum.'

Incredibly, this happened within two months. By now, Joey was running out of ways to say 'This rules!'

'I don't even know a hundred people, let alone a million,' he pondered. 'I can't fathom that many people owning my record.'

A note about the official jump suits, which were now on sale for $120 a pop. Joey hated them. 'They were a mistake,' he admitted. '120 bucks is too much – kids don't have that much money. First of all, they're orange. They don't even look cool. I don't know if they're still selling those things, but they shouldn't.'

Nevertheless, the coveralls were eventually dropped in price to $80 and sold a brisk trade. While you could argue that if Joey really hated the suits, he could have had them pulled from sale, sometimes the music business just isn't that simple.

ANARCHY IN THE UK: PART 2

Even before Slipknot hit the United Kingdom for their first proper tour, with One Minute Silence and Kittie in support, the warning signs were manifest.

Slipknot had become notorious.

First of all, the massive record chain store HMV backed away from a scheduled series of in-store appearances by Slipknot. In a letter to Roadrunner Records, the chain said: 'Awareness of the band is growing very rapidly and our senior management are now concerned about the security of both the fans and the stores concerned. They feel that the quantity of fans likely to turn up will be so great that we will not be able to guarantee the safety of both the band and our customers.'

'You know what?' Joey rhetorically asked *Kerrang!*, in the preceding weeks. 'They're right! That rules! HMV would probably have called the cops as soon as we arrived.'

Thankfully, the Virgin Megastore chain gladly picked up the ball and ran with it. The dates were simply transferred to the new stores.

Slipknot also met with opposition from a councillor in Wolverhampton. On hearing that the band were due to play the council-owned Civic Hall on 1 March, councillor Joan Stevenson went on the warpath. Stating that Slipknot were 'not welcome at all', she further branded them 'ridiculous, juvenile and stupid'.

'I'm sure Jim Morrison and The Doors wouldn't do what they do,' she bristled. 'I know I'm old and a fuddy-duddy, but I don't think that some of this band's actions are quite the thing we want at our Civic Hall. As a representative of some of the people of Wolverhampton, I can say that they would not find this band acceptable at all. I'm quite broad-minded, but one has to speak as one finds!'

So did Joey. Speaking out in *Kerrang!*, he joked: 'I'm going to shit in a box and send it to Wolverhampton Council! We'll see how acceptable they find *that*!'

Councillors in other boroughs of England took the news of Slipknot's imminent arrival comparatively well. Portsmouth councillor David Giles said: 'The only problem we've had recently at the Guildhall was a poetry weekend, when explicit language was used. Slipknot fans know what they're getting – and I'm sure the ticket prices will cover any cleaning up!'

Glasgow councillor Liz Cameron: 'The Barrowlands is not a public hall, so it doesn't fall within our providence. Slipknot doesn't sound like my kind of night out. I like Gaelic folk music.'

Nottingham councillor Leon Unczur: 'If they do wish to urinate on themselves, I must admit it intrigues me! If people are going to enjoy the show and no-one's hurt, I don't see a problem. I'm more worried about racism, sexism and homophobia.'

If only more public representatives thought along those lines. Unfortunately, if Wolverhampton Council were waiting for Slipknot to make a mistake, they were to have their wishes granted.

DAMAGE INC.

On 2 March, the day after Slipknot's show in Wolverhampton, they became the subjects of a damning press release.

It read: 'Wolverhampton Council can confirm that an incident occurred last night during a performance by the band SlipKnot [*sic*] at the town's Civic Hall. During the incident, which involved a member of the band, a young female who was in the audience was injured. Civic Hall security staff took her to the First Aid room where she was attended by St John's Ambulance personnel, who are always on duty at performances in the premises.

It continued: 'An ambulance was called and the police also attended. The police spoke to the young lady but we were not party to that discussion. We believe she was kept in hospital overnight for observation. Wolverhampton Council Leisure Services will be conducting an investigation into the incident, which is standard procedure in such cases.'

That same day, I spoke to an Inspector Hawkins at Wolverhampton police station. He suggested that Slipknot might be liable for prosecution.

'At 11.17pm on 1 March we had a call from the Civic Hall,' he stated, 'to the effect that a Miss Pearce suffered head injuries due to someone jumping from the balcony and landing on her.'

Hawkins added: 'The girl could take action against the assailant, who by all accounts displayed an element of recklessness. If it was an intentional leap from the balcony, the person who carried it out must look at the possible repercussions. There is the possibility of taking action, whether that be criminal or civil charges.'

On 5 March in the depths of London's Brixton Academy venue, Corey Taylor sat nursing a beer on the other side of a wooden table, at Slipknot's backstage aftershow party. He had de-masked, but there were still traces of the black 'Absu' make-up smeared around his eyes. Every now and then, a couple of fans would realise who he was and excitedly ask for his autograph, which he gladly gave.

This was the last day of the UK tour – a trek which had been sold out on every date. While Corey was delighted with the tour as a whole, he wanted to put his side about the accusations which had been thrown at the band.

'Sid was all fucked up about hurting her, and went down there himself to make sure she was fine. He gave her his grey coveralls.

Corey also claimed that the band had been threatened with legal action before. 'We got word that they'd arrest us if we were seen masturbating onstage,' he grinned. 'So, of course, we automatically started masturbating throughout the show! Tell us not to do something and we'll sure as hell do it.'

Subsequently, 19-year-old Lyndsey Pearce, the injured girl, wrote a letter to *Kerrang!*. 'I was left unconscious,' she said. 'I broke my glasses and so could see even less when I came around. And yes, I went to New Cross Hospital to get checked out. I went home feeling sick, suffering from concussion and muscular pain. But on the other hand, I had also attended the greatest gig ever!'

She added: 'Everyone treated me really well, including the medics, Slipknot's tour manager and Sid. He came to see me and was really concerned. He began to cry and I just melted. The truth is, Slipknot were everything I wanted them to be. Granted, I wasn't expecting to get knocked out. But hey – you can't have it all ways!'

In conclusion, she said: 'I think Wolves Council were unhappy with the band anyway – this incident was just the tip of the iceberg. I hope nobody gives the Council too hard a time – I guess they have a job to do, just like Slipknot.'

'We're still banned from Wolverhampton,' noted Joey in October 2000, 'and that's fine by us.'

SLIPKNOT VS KORN: PART 2

That night in Brixton Academy's aftershow bar, Joey Jordison had a big smile on his face. This was unsurprising, considering that he had just achieved another in a long series of dreams. This was the venue where his heroes Faith No More had recorded their 'You Fat Bastards' live video – the one he used to watch almost every day, on his return from high school.

He would later declare: 'When I get married and have kids, if that happens, I'll forget my wife's name, I'll forget my kids' names, but I'll never forget that Brixton show.'

The only failing of Slipknot's set during that UK tour was that they had stretched 'Scissors' to an unwieldy length. It now included what felt like a 10-minute section of pure feed-back. At the Brixton aftershow, Joey acknowledged that this was too much. The band would subsequently shave the song back down.

'I've got a great story for you,' he added. 'We've heard that Korn are threatening to pull out of the Dynamo Festival if we're on the bill.'

The Dynamo is one of Europe's most respected metal-fests, traditionally taking place in Holland's Eindhoven. It was an important event for Slipknot to play.

Korn's manager Peter Katsis would subsequently confirm that some bad blood existed. 'Slipknot don't like or respect Korn,' he said, 'and they're very vocal about it. I don't know why, considering that if it wasn't for Korn, Slipknot wouldn't be anywhere now.'

Katsis said he knew nothing of any threats. 'I haven't heard that from the band,' he said. 'If it was said, I wouldn't doubt it. I just don't know it.'

The manager admitted, however, that Korn and Slipknot were unlikely to share the Dynamo bill on 3 June. 'I don't think Slipknot will be playing, unless they get real,' he said. 'If they don't like Korn, why would they want to share a bill with us?'

All of this was clearly giving Dynamo organiser Rob Trommelen something of a headache, given that both bands were presently booked to play the event.

'I'm trying to find a solution,' he said. 'I've got two stages and there's a 10-minute walk between them. Hopefully that will be enough! They're great bands and we want the kids to enjoy both.'

What a nice man.

EUROSHOCK

17 March was the last night of Slipknot's first European tour. The problem being: it wasn't meant to be. The juggernaut came to an abrupt halt in Madrid, 12 dates earlier than expected, and the band flew home.

Since the London show, the tour had continued to thrive, as the band played to audiences of between two and four thousand people per night. Shawn, as always, was enjoying the experience of seeing new countries.

'The one thing I fell in love with more than anything is: you can look funny, you can talk funny, you can eat funny shit, but no matter where you are in the world, music is the universal language. We come together to speak it, and I love that. I love breaking down the international barriers and sticking to what's real.'

'That was the most brutal tour we've ever been on,' said Joey. 'We did a massive in-store every day – even in France and Spain. We were so on fire!'

Morgan Lander of Kittie recalled an escalation in backstage bad behaviour during those dates – including one quite literally shocking bout of fun with an electric cattle-prod.

'They had a competition to see who could shock the most people with this thing,' she said. 'They had a video camera going, and I'm sure if they release a new home video, you'll see one of the people in the band getting shocked by the cattle-prod and going into convulsions.

'There was a lot more destruction going on,' she continued. 'Thrashing around in the dressing room, the throwing of food – that kind of thing. As we got to know Slipknot more, things became more and more immature and childish. They definitely know how to have fun. They're enjoying their fame, their stardom and their ability to do what they really want.'

When the tour met that premature end, it was because one of the band members had what Joey describes as 'a family problem'. 'I didn't like it,' said the drummer, 'because no-one likes to tour more than me, but I understood, too. We had other German dates lined up, so we ended up doing them all at once, later that summer.'

At the Euro shows which Slipknot *did* manage to play as scheduled, it was clear that their profile was rising swiftly, even in the staunchly traditional German market.

Joey told me: 'Me and Chris got completely wasted on five hundred dollars' worth of alcohol in a hotel room in Hamburg, then set the place on fire. When the police and fire trucks came, we didn't get arrested. That could be a sign that we're getting pretty big.'

SEX, FEAR, DRUGS AND VIOLENCE

As you will have gathered, Slipknot approach on-the-road hijinks in a manner unlike any other band.

While they are not rock 'n' roll in the traditional sense of snorting cocaine from groupies' backsides, they are more than capable of acting like overgrown kids, throwing stomach-churning dares at each other. They will cause damage, but it is generally to disposable items, themselves or each other. Theirs is a self-contained chaos. The fact that they are generally amiable characters is attested by the many friendships they have made with females in various bands.

When I once asked Shawn and Joey about the sado-masochistic, sexual side of the masks they wear, they looked openly relieved.

'Finally,' sighed Shawn, 'someone's asked us!' He went on to explain that 'most of the masks are bondage hoods which we've made into personalities that people live on the inside. Some of the band are into the restraint and the pain of it. I can't tell you how much pain is involved with what we do, but we dig it.'

Talking about the masks in detail, Shawn became almost

misty-eyed with sentimentality. 'There's nothing like a red-ball gag,' he said. 'Every time I look over at Chris, I see something different every day. The black hood cuts his circulation and every time he puts it on he's like, "I'm going into my special place" and he means it. Then he puts that nose-thing on – it's a very phallic symbol and he likes to play with it.'

Shawn further noted: 'Everyone in this band has a very perverted side to us, but we know where to draw the line. We don't put it in anyone's face to the extent where it would be deemed disgusting.' The link between music and sex is obvious to Shawn – even in terms of Slipknot's noise.

'That's why a lot of people fuck with music on,' he reasoned. 'One time before a show, Mick got so excited that he felt the need to jack off in front of the rest of the band. Seconds before we played, I looked over and he had his full-on dick in his hand, going at it because he was so excited to play.'

'He didn't bust a load, though,' pointed out Joey. 'He was just building up tension.'

Fair enough.

Shawn would seem to have some kind of scatological fetish going on. Gentler readers – or those who are eating – might like to skip a page at this juncture.

'I'll usually eat a lot, the night before a show, because I like not taking a dump,' he confessed. 'It makes me feel fucked-up. It excites me, but I always joke that I'm gonna shit my pants onstage. And believe me, if I did do it, the whole place would know about it. I would make a spectacle of it, and so would everybody else.'

The band stress that while some of them have violent tendencies, they don't support violence itself.

'We don't want anybody to get hurt,' said Shawn. 'We're sick, we're demented, we're perverted and we live the way we want to live every day because life is short. This band feels right because we're not hurting anybody. We take our aggressions, and the fans' aggressions and make something else out of them, so no-one's out killing or raping.'

Other bands never ceased to be amazed by Slipknot's no-drugs policy within their tribe.

Shawn: 'Because we get so mental onstage, people wanna know what we're on. But we're on the truth: live music. We're all on the same page. Drugs ruin the greatest of bands. Screw that!'

'Drugs never felt right for me,' echoed Joey. 'It feels like I'm being poisoned inside. I'm fucked up as it is: I don't need drugs.'

The unspoken rules which regulated Slipknot were partly driven by fear of letting the other members down.

'When you're from Des Moines and you make something work like this,' said Shawn, 'there's a certain fear involved. We're from nothing and now we're something, so to have that taken away from you would be scary. Getting kicked out of the band for doing drugs, for not doing your job or because you fucked your knee up, is unthinkable.'

'You can't let anyone down, because we're all in this together,' said Joey. 'If anyone starts letting the tribe down, they're out.'

'That fear,' continued Shawn, 'is insane. It's like prison.'

In the first interview I did with them at Ozzfest '99, Slipknot claimed to have individual replacements lined up for themselves. There was a great appeal to this idea – it made you picture a production line of 'Knot clones, like the robot soldiers in *Star Wars I: The Phantom Menace*. Whether it was actually true seemed irrelevant.

'The insanity of Slipknot is that we're constantly preparing for everything,' claimed Shawn. 'Joey's got substitutes for himself. Isn't that sick? Think about that for a while! Hey, we wear masks. Don't fuck up.'

Shawn went on to note, however, that any misbehaving members of the band would be granted a second chance. Within reason. He said: 'If someone walks in here on an eight-ball of heroin and punches one of my bro's, they're gone. I don't give a fuck who it is. But if someone's got a problem and they really need help, then we're family. We'd try and conquer it, but you wouldn't get two chances.

'It's a sick way of living,' he concluded. 'But y'know what? We love it.'

WHITE NOISE

On 7 April 2000, with their personal issues resolved, Slipknot returned to the road for some Canadian dates, again taking Kittie along for the ride. For Morgan Lander and co, this was finally a chance to play some big shows in their native land.

Morgan: 'Everyone was like, "Wow, you girls must really have made it!" A lot of my friends got to meet the band.'

Morgan also recalls one typically twisted way in which Slipknot would pass time on the road. 'They had this interesting electronic drum machine toy thing, which they were using to play the same jazz tune over and over again. It was loud, obnoxious and really annoying.'

From the fan's perspective, there were two notable things about this cluster of dates. Firstly, it saw the debut of the band's new white coveralls. In truth, these weren't as effective as their predecessors, but gave people a surprise.

'Everyone was so used to the red, black, grey or green,' said Joey of the band's fiendish reasoning. 'Nobody expected white! The girls like it, because when they get wet you can see all the way through them and we don't wear anything underneath. We didn't get any more groupies though – chicks don't know who we are!'

Secondly, a date at Montreal's Metropolis venue on 8 April saw Corey implement one of Joey's ideas for crowd participation. The process involved getting everybody in the audience to sit down and then spring up in unison when commanded to 'Jump the fuck up!'.

After those Canadian dates, Kittie would bump into members of Slipknot once in a while.

Morgan: 'When we're in the same area as them, a couple of the guys will show up to support us, watch the show and say hi. They look out for us. It's nice to have nine scary guys on your side.'

COREY'S TRIBE

Corey didn't only use his 'Jump the fuck up!' phrase during Slipknot shows. When the band swung into Phoenix, Arizona on 27 April, the singer was enlisted by metal godfather Max Cavalera to contribute to the second album by his post-Sepultura band Soulfly.

'We stole him from Slipknot's soundcheck!' said Cavalera at the time. 'He already had lyrics written because I'd sent him a tape. The song was originally called "Getdafuckup", but Corey thought it sounded more like "Jumpdafuckup", so that became the new title. It's about helping a friend who's going through stuff in life and kicking the motherfucker in the ass. It's really cool and I think people will be surprised.'

Unlike the disappointing shelving of that Sticky Fingaz track, 'Jumpdafuckup' did indeed make it on to the *Primitive* album, which would be released in late September.

Corey engaged in more extra-curricular activity when he contributed a vocal to the album *Strait Up: A Tribute To Lynn Strait*. The titular Strait fronted up-and-coming LA punkers Snot, until he died in a car crash on 11 December 1998. Corey joined a stellar cast of nu-metal vocalists such as Limp Bizkit's Fred Durst, Korn's Jonathan Davis and Coal Chamber's Dez Fafara, all of whom teamed up with the surviving Snot members for various songs on the album. Finally released in November 2000, *Strait Up...* would be a long time in the making, but worth the wait.

THE SIGN

In a band? Clearly, you're nobody in America unless your wares send born-again banner-wavers ballistic.

On 30 April 2000, at San Francisco's Warfield venue, Slipknot were picketed. Outside the Warfield stood a gentle-man solemnly holding a board which proclaimed something to the effect of 'Listen To Slipknot And You Will Burn In Hell'. Needless to say, Slipknot took this as a compliment.

'That ruled!' glowed Joey a few days later. 'It shows we're making a difference. We tried to con the banner out of the guy, so we could put it on our stage ...'

SLIPKNOT VS KORN: PART 3

The long-running feud between these nu-metal Goliaths came to an unexpected end in May, when Korn frontman Jonathan Davis spoke out in *Kerrang!*.

'There *is* bad blood between Slipknot and David Silveria,' he says. 'But that's it. Slipknot just had a problem with David doing those adverts – but so did everybody else in Korn! I think they're right. I have nothing against Slipknot – it's between them and David. I just thought those pictures didn't suit us and weren't in good taste – they embarrassed us. More power to Slipknot, man. It's obvious that we've influenced them a lot, but they're awesome. I'm glad that something that heavy is getting respect.'

Davis added that he had been incredulous when he heard that Korn and Slipknot would no longer play the Dynamo again.

'I found out what was going on and said, "Fuck that!"' he admitted. 'Now Slipknot are back on Dynamo with us. There's no beef between us and Slipknot.'

Come 3 June, not only did Korn and Slipknot both play Dynamo, but they finally met up. No punches were thrown.

Joey: 'They basically said we were right about this David thing, and that bands like us should stick together. There was definitely some truth to that. The feud was ended and done that day. I didn't have a drink with them, but I think [Korn bassist] Fieldy was way ahead of me as it was. He was wasted!'

KING HELL

When Slayer guitarist Kerry King looked down at his dog, part of him truly resented her.

Tonight, on 12 May, Slipknot were playing LA's Hollywood Palladium. This pesky creature had chosen this day, of all days, to have puppies. Kerry wouldn't be leaving the house. This celebrated guitar mauler, who had spent the past two decades in a seminal guitar tag-team with fellow riffer Jeff Hanneman, hadn't always been a Slipknot fan. Quite the opposite. When he first heard about them, during the 1999 Ozzfest, he had been less than impressed.

'I was totally sceptical, but I didn't listen,' King told me. 'I just said, "Masks, jump suits, who cares?" Everyone on Ozzfest was saying, "Slipknot this, Slipknot that" and I told them, "Fuck off. Who brainwashed you guys?" I probably even met the band on Ozzfest but it didn't register, because the name Slipknot didn't mean anything to me.'

A couple of months later, when people were still telling King how wonderful the masked marauders were, he finally caved in and picked up a copy of *Slipknot*.

'I put it on the stereo,' he laughed, 'and went, "Oh! *That's* why!"' When the Palladium date came up, King thought he was finally going to see the band. Cue puppies.

'I was pissed off,' he said, 'because I was really into the band by then – I was ready to shoot that dog in the fucking head!'

Recalled Joey of that night's Palladium show: 'It was crazy. Everyone was trying to get backstage and it made me mental. Every band in LA was there, and every manager. A typical LA show, but great.'

King discovered that Slipknot were playing the slightly smaller Glass House venue in Pomona, an hour-or-so's drive away on the following night. Standing among the crowd, the guitarist finally got his first dose of the sickness.

'They had their noisy-ass intro on and they just walked out all slow and drone-like through a strobe light,' he recalled. 'It was spooky as hell. When it went off, it was huge. Absolute fuckin' chaos.'

Right there and then, Kerry King became a Slipknot fan. Which was ironic, considering that to the band members, he was God. King and Slipknot were destined to spend more time together. After all, both Slayer and our heroes had been confirmed for a new US festival tour that summer, intriguingly named Tattoo The Earth...

7
Tattooed and torn

Over and over and under my skin/
All this momentum is doing me in.
Corey Taylor, #6, 'Surfacing'

September 2000
217 shows. 116 stitches. 45 broken ribs.

Those last two statistics were shared between nine men. Still, something had to give. The world had long been waiting for confirmation that Slipknot were human. Even though this band made self-abuse their business, and injuries had become an inevitable by-product of the ritual, it still came as a surprise when a Roadrunner Records press release stated that one of the band had collapsed from exhaustion in the departure lounge at Los Angeles' LAX Airport.

At least, when you were in Slipknot, collapsing in public wouldn't be nearly as embarrassing as it might be for, say, Guns N' Roses frontman Axl Rose.

The Roadrunner press release stated that Slipknot's autumn US tour had been cancelled, in order to allow the band a well-earned rest in Des Moines before returning for a short run of US dates starting 27 October.

What exactly had happened, though? And to whom?

The label claimed they were unable to be more specific on the matter.

'It's hardly surprising,' said their UK spokesperson of the LAX incident. 'They've been on the road since last June. When they came over here to play Reading and Leeds, they were starting to get really burnt out. And let's face it, we all want another record.'

Slipknot's side of the story wouldn't surface until later on, when Joey spoke to me. But this had been one busy summer, which saw the band pushing themselves to the limits and beyond. And almost blowing themselves to pieces in the process ...

NOTHING LASTS FOREVER

June 2000

'We won't be around as long as Kiss. This band has only about three more albums in it.'

Before Tattoo The Earth had even begun, Joey was casting doubts over his band's longevity. Speaking to *Kerrang!*, he was breaking the hearts of fans who wanted their idols to be around forever.

'This band is too fucking extreme, dude,' he explained. 'It's too over-the-top. When things get too big – which they already kind of are – we'll stop. The mission will have been accomplished. Nothing's worse than making a parody or a mockery of yourself. You end up staying for the money or for self-satisfaction. I love this band completely, but that's the way it's gotta be.'

Jordison also revealed that he was not only playing with The Rejects again, but planning an album with them. He reeled off a list of song-titles including 'Mommy's In Rehab', 'Let's Fuck', 'Either Way I'm Fucked' and 'Drugs, Cunts & Rock 'N' Roll'. Frankly, you couldn't help but suspect he was making some of these up. Joey was also planning two other side projects with some newfound friends. One unnamed project, he said, would see him teaming up with System Of A Down guitarist Daron Malakian and Ryan Martinie from Mudvayne - – the latter being nu-metal newcomers who had been championed by Shawn Crahan. Their debut album *LD:50* would appear later in the year, bearing the Clown's credit as Executive Producer. It was a well-intentioned, but fairly run-of-the-mill affair. The band's demonic make-up ensured, however, that nu-metal fans gave them more than a cursory glance.

As for the System Of A Down man's involvement, Joey said: 'Me and Daron hit it off really well and we talked about playing together. The music of this band will be a little bit pop, with pure grindcore and ambient tones.'

For the third, similarly nameless band on Joey's agenda, he wanted to join forces with New York's Dan Lilker – a man who spent the '80s playing bass with thrashers Nuclear Assault, and the '90s playing even more extreme noisecore with grind merchants Brutal Truth.

'Me and Dan's band will be full-on, straight-ahead grindcore,' predicted Joey. 'Nothing too thought-out or special – just fucking complete mayhem.'

While Joey wanted all three of these projects to record and tour, the reality was naturally set to veer from this game plan. The summer was certainly all mapped out for Slipknot, as their seemingly tireless assault on America continued, hitting new territories every week.

Joey told MTV: 'We were destined to go to places where other bands would not go. We play in a lot of places where a lot of bands don't go. Those kids take that to the grave and it really means a lot to them when you go to a place where the population of the town is 2,000 people and 70 kids show up. It's still a show, and those kids buy your record. Therefore they deserve to see the band, just like a kid in New York or LA or Chicago gets to.'

Naturally, Slipknot's own remote upbringings played a part in cultivating their remarkable work ethic.

'Ozzy was one of the biggest metal artists, besides Kiss, who would really be able to come through Des Moines,' Joey told *MTV*. 'Half of those shows would get cancelled, but the underground bands never come through. That's why we want to go through all those markets and cities, and make sure that happens for those kids.'

Slipknot's efforts would see them rewarded with fierce loyalty. Given the intensity of their show, however, and the number of shows they were playing, you'd be forgiven for wondering if cracks ever showed. Did none of these nine men ever suffer a migraine before going onstage, and not feel vaguely like bringing the noise?

Joey once admitted: 'Sometimes, even we get into a rut where we're like, "Okay, we've gotta play *another* show..." But after about 10 seconds of being onstage, I know what I'm doing and why I'm doing it.

'I caught the 'flu twice in a two-month period,' he continued. 'My body was shutting down and telling me I couldn't do this anymore. We did five or six shows in a row when I had the 'flu. We had doctors come in and I could not move my body at all. I still went up and played, because those kids had been waiting two months for us to come down. I did that for a week-and-a-half with the goddamn 'flu! I lost 10 pounds and I'm a skinny fucker.'

NEW TATTOO

Kicking off on 15 July at the Portland Meadows venue, Tattoo The Earth was a fresh addition to America's growing fleet of travelling rock festivals. As the name suggested, it intended to marry the long-booming body modification business with some of the finest names in extreme metal.

Several celebrity tattooists were drafted in for the ride, including Paul Booth, Hanky Panky, Sean Vasquez and Filip Leu. The musical side of things proved altogether trickier for the organisers to co-ordinate. Slipknot had been locked in to headline, with Slayer in the slot directly before them. Two of the bill's other major bands, however, left at the eleventh hour: Soulfly defected to the Ozzfest, while Coal Chamber bailed out to concentrate on writing their third album. Two of the smaller bands, Cold and PUYA, also departed before the tour even began.

Brazilian thrashers Sepultura and the rather incongruous rock 'n' rollers Nashville Pussy were brought in to bolster the bill, which also featured the likes of Amen, (hed)PE, Hatebreed, Nothingface and One Minute Silence.

Joey was unequivocal as to why Slipknot decided to go with Tattoo The Earth, rather than headline the Second Stage at Ozzfest 2000. 'Slipknot thrives on the unconventional. We wanted things to be rough around the edges and go with a heavier bill. By doing our own tour on a lower budget and bringing out heavier bands, it remained a little bit more true to our integrity. I don't wanna go big and corporate – I wanna keep it underground, so all of our fans can still come to a show. It's a big chaos tour that doesn't conform to anything. The Ozzfest is fucking cool, but we did it last year. It would have been nice to do it again, but we want to cover as much ground as we can.'

Tattoo The Earth would see Slipknot upping the ante in terms of stageshow, incorporating a sizeable lighting rig and pyrotechnics for the first time – despite what the band had previously said on the subject.

'We've always tried to stay away from the strippers and big fancy explosions,' Shawn had once stated. 'That's not saying that, in the future, we won't push the envelope wherever we're going. We'll always push it to the next level.'

Clearly, with Slipknot it should always be a case of never say never. Which made you wonder whether a hundred 'We'll never take the masks off' quotes might one day come back to haunt them.

For some reason, Slipknot were unable to use their pyro on the first Tattoo date in Portland, Oregon. Furthermore, as this was a show in honour of a local radio station, born-again grunge stars Stone Temple Pilots were added to the bill as headliners. None of which deterred Slipknot as they stepped out in front of 16,000 people.

'It was some of the best fun we've ever had in our career,' said Shawn after the opening night. 'We were unable to do anything we had planned, but we just went out there, looked the revolution in the eye and had a great time. We don't need to rely on a bunch of props. We have a mediocre production going on, but it's big for us. We're *trying*, man.'

The Portland show also saw the debut of Shawn's new mask, which saw the original design being given a brilliantly evil overhaul.

Asked what would become of the first clown mask, Shawn said: 'You cannot retire him. He'll know when to show up. What I will tell you is: he's done 16 years and he wanted to be at home right now. I got the new guy. It'll be an occasion when the old guy shows up again.'

Despite Slipknot's unflappable nature, the tour seemed to be full of bands who were discontent with how the festival was being run. After the first two dates, the LA industrial-metallers Spineshank left the bill, apparently citing the event's lack of organisation.

Slayer's Kerry King tried not to let the goings-on bother him too much. 'Us and Slipknot were taken care of every day because the organisers knew that if one of us left the tour would be over! I think that a lot of the smaller bands weren't taken care of, but there was nothing we could do about that – it was a big new festival.'

'It was totally fucked up at the start,' conceded Joey, 'but it ended up working out pretty damn well. There were problems here and there but the kids really liked it.'

When Slipknot's pyro finally kicked in, it was worth waiting for. Not least for the way in which it boosted the onstage danger factor.

Said Shawn at the time: 'If you love the Clown, you'll understand that I am still walking that fine line of eternity. There's a fluorescent piece of tape that goes along the centre of the stage and when the pyro goes off you need to be behind it. You'll notice that I'm four feet in front of it. This is complete danger at all times – just the way I like it. It's not the best on my ears, but I'll deal with that the way I have to. The first couple of shows in which we had pyro, I got motion sickness. It blew up my blood cells – it was like being in a fucking war. It's interesting, but it's taken our heads to a new level. We're starting to invent some new ways of thinking and that's exciting.

'The firsts are always the ones that are very, very scary, but they're also the ones that are rewarding, because they're true. We're not out here to be some overblown rock band – we're doing it to be Slipknot. We're stepping up our show at every possible opportunity.'

Kerry King: 'Their pyro guy was hilarious – he was insane! I remember them lighting one of the fucking monitors on fire one night. That wasn't supposed to happen, but it was pretty cool!'

Slipknot had always been wildly ambitious about their stageshow, having been inspired by the sky's-the-limit attitude of Kiss' OTT theatrics.

'We're probably not gonna be happy in this band until we're all flying onstage,' Shawn told me at the previous year's Ozzfest. 'Then when we fly, we'd better fly for the whole set. Then when we fly for the whole set, we'd better climb to the top and jump off!'

For now, Slipknot would make do with explosions. Once the teething troubles were banished, they began to relish the Tattoo experience.

'So far everything's been ground-roots,' said Shawn at the time. 'I'm all about potential. I don't let water or Mother Nature or crowd attendants or anything bring me down, because every day is a day of new potential for tomorrow. It feels really good. We're really lucky to have the slot that we have. I've been watching all the other bands and talking to everybody and it seems everyone's getting along. It's a great line-up.

'What I love about this tour is that no-one knows whether it's gonna work or not,' he continued. 'I love that challenge. I wanna take something that's incomplete and make it complete.

It's not a Space Shuttle tour with all these fancy things – it's just a bunch of bands, playing out in fields.'

It was clearly more than that to the growing legions of 'Knot maniacs. Joey, for one, was starting to find the adoration and its attendant pressures unnerving.

Said the drummer at the time: 'Right now, I'm more scared about my life and my band than I ever have been before. I couldn't give a fuck about pressure. I would not change a thing and I'm very grateful for everything. But even wearing a mask, I can't get outside the bus without being mobbed. That's fine – I'll gladly sign any autographs. But rumours are starting to spread about us and you hear all this shit. People back home start hearing stuff that isn't true and it's just scary.'

For a long time now, there had been innumerable Slipknot fan websites, and they were still popping up like rabbits. While these were mostly excellent displays of devotion, going so far as to present the guitar tablature for Slipknot's music, or MP3 downloads of rare tracks, they were inevitably stuffed to the gills with hearsay and such ludicrous rumours as Craig's mask having been stolen.

Joey: 'We've never lost any of our masks. I've given a few of mine away, to hardcore fans who have been hospitalised with leukaemia and stuff like that.'

SHOW NO MERCY

If Slipknot had felt strange about headlining over Biohazard, then playing above Slayer on this bill felt downright wrong.

'I don't understand going on after Slayer and I won't *ever* understand that.' admitted Shawn. 'Thankfully, Slayer and us are friends. We're hanging out and talking. It's an extreme honour to look at your mentors and be able to have a conversation about a basketball game or Australia.

'Kids change, generations change and it'll be the same with us one day. We're just trying to have as much fun and give as much as we can.'

Ask Kerry King for his feelings about playing under Slipknot and, as always, you'd get an honest reply.

'I understand music,' he said. 'It don't matter how many records we've put out – we've never gone Platinum anywhere, with anything. Slipknot's record is Platinum, they're hip, they're hot and people want to see them. So it would have been anti-climactic, at that point, without us having any new records out, to play after them. Businesswise, it wouldn't make any sense. I can understand that.'

Even though Slipknot had superseded Slayer in some ways, King was one of their few real supporters among his own generation. You got the distinct impression that many long-standing rock and metal outfits had their noses put out of joint by the sudden success of these nine juvenile upstarts. Such stars would ridicule the band's masks and dismiss them as a bunch of chancers. In some circles, 'Slipknot' almost became a by-word for 'fake'. Slipknot were too busy getting off on Slayer's nightly performance to give this much thought.

'It's totally cool to be able to watch Slayer and then go on and do our thing,' said Corey. 'I remember growing up and listening to *Reign In Blood*, so it's amazing.'

The frontman was equally excited when Tattoo The Earth crossed paths with Metallica's summer tour at New Jersey's Giants Stadium on 20 July. This date saw Slipknot gracing an altogether bigger stage.

Raved Corey afterwards: 'We're out here having a great time with a bunch of our friends and destroying shit wherever we go. Giants Stadium was really cool. There were so many people out there, it was insane!'

Joey added, however, that Metallica had laid down the law to Slipknot. 'Metallica told us that if we do any pissing or shit-ting onstage, they will sever our ties with them forever,' he claimed, before settling down behind the kit.

Presumably, the 'Knot kept their bowels and bladders in check that afternoon.

THE BOOZE BROTHERS

By now, Kerry King was bonding with various members of Slipknot, via the ever-popular medium of alcohol.

Joey: 'There was probably more alcohol abuse than we'd ever endured before. Me and Kerry literally hung out every day, after the show. If we weren't hanging out, we were watching each other's bands play. Kerry's as cool as fuck.'

'We took our shot parade over to Slipknot's bus all the time,' laughed King, 'and made them do peppermint schnapps with us. It's 100 per cent proof: a bad boy!'

The prime drink offenders were Joey, Kerry, Paul Gray and Slayer drummer Paul Bostaph.

King: 'We were the liquor patrol. We'd try to hook up on days off. I'm sure the peppermint schnapps led to some silly behaviour, but the problem with that stuff is, you don't remember! I didn't really talk to Chris that much or the nail-headed guy. I didn't talk to Sid much either, but he was always around doing something! Clown was always off doing his own thing, but he came up and watched us quite a bit. Joey always wanted me standing behind his drums while he played.'

Joey cited Amen's Casey Chaos as another bad influence on his liver. 'Casey doesn't help,' he said. 'When Casey and me are around, it becomes bad. Debauchery happens. He's like my evil twin.'

'I hear I'm to blame,' Chaos would chuckle. 'But whenever everybody wants to start drinking, I'm the guy who always says, "Let's do it!" I go from one extreme to another: let's not drink or let's get fucking annihilated!'

Casey claimed that he was the man who nightly ensured that Joey returned to the Slipknot bus in one piece.

'Every night, Joey would come to the bus and go, "Let's drink, motherfucker!". I'd end up having to cradle him like a baby and carry him to his bus, three out of seven nights. I'd just put him back in his bunk!'

This tour was important for Amen, as they had started to accrue a reputation for causing trouble. As a clause in their

Tattoo The Earth contract threatened to have them thrown off if they misbehaved, this kind of harmless, insular drunkenness was probably a good idea.

Casey: 'We were able to show we were good monkeys who could jump through hoops. We proved we wouldn't be banned from every tour we play!'

After the booze-free Ozzfest of the previous year, you would wonder how Joey managed to keep the pace this summer. 'I just learnt how to drink and not feel it the next day,' he insisted. 'I became able to moderate myself.'

While onlookers might have worried that Slipknot had become complacent and lost their abstinence-boosted edge, Joey insisted that their indulgence on this jaunt was simply down to the social environment.

'It was our last tour and all our friends were there – Slayer, (hed)PE, Mudvyane, Amen. It was a big travelling party, the whole time. At Ozzfest we didn't drink much because we wanted to be responsible, but we didn't know anybody anyway. This time, a whole year later, we had plenty of friends.'

Shawn bonded especially well with Brian 'Yap' Barry, the amiably fast-talking Irish frontman of Brit metallers One Minute Silence.

'Yap is probably the greatest friend that I made this year,' Shawn would declare, 'and I have a lot to learn from the whole band. They are some of the most real people that I have ever met in my entire life and they work so hard, but are so humble. They don't act like rock stars.'

Even so, Slipknot did not get on well with everyone they met on the Tattoo tour.

THIS IS A WAR

The story has yet to be told from Shawn Crahan's point of view, for legal reasons. But it goes something like this: On 28 July at the Tattoo tour's Somerset, Wisconsin date, the Clown, his drum-tech Sa-Tone and One Minute Silence's Yap were riding around backstage on a motorised golf cart.

The event's security took exception to this behaviour, believing the trio to be endangering people in the area. When Crahan refused to stop the vehicle, they allegedly pulled him from the cart while it was still moving, then maced him. Some reports claim he was also placed in handcuffs.

The band Hatebreed ran over to help their friends and also became involved in the fracas. The incident shook the whole tour, and rumours spread that Slipknot would cancel their appearance. While they didn't, Hatebreed did pull out, claiming that they were acting in support of their friends.

Security chief Lt Pat Lais told *MTV News* that Crahan had responded to requests to stop the cart with 'obscene gestures' and had thrown the first punch. He added that as the arrested parties were being led to the venue's front gate, further skirmishes took place – some of them involving audience members. Both parties filed police reports, but no further action was taken. Crahan wisely played down the event.

'I'm not really talking about it yet,' he said. 'Everybody will understand real soon. I'm logically thinking things through.'

While Joey and Paul got drunk and schmoozed with their friends, Shawn seemed to be gradually becoming more intense. Part of this was a burning desire to keep Slipknot fired up and together.

'When people come onto our bus and see me, they leave,' he said during Tattoo The Earth. 'I got that aura about me now. People are freaked out about me. Now that things are rolling better, I'm more vocal and visible. Now, a lot of the hard work is done and I wanna get psyched. I want everything to run like a Special Forces unit, like a tribe.'

He added: 'This tour is trying to kill every one of us. I wouldn't necessarily say we've had problems, because I don't believe in problems: I believe that you create them. The world's trying to keep us down from what we do best. That's been a test and we don't like to take tests. We've done all the studying we're gonna do and now we're just trying to convey ideas.

'On this tour, we wake up and ask ourselves whether everything's alright and everybody's still alive. We've had some real tragic things happen to the band recently. Real close people have had some terrible news. We're pushing forward – we'll pick up the pieces as we go and use it as a learning experience.'

One of Shawn's preoccupations was with changing people's attitudes to life. Making a dent in their fans' philosophy, as well as their ear drums.

Having said that, he had the utmost faith in people who loved the 'Knot. On 27 July, when the tour hit Des Moines' Water Works Park, the police made their presence felt. The band's reputation had once again preceded them. Yet the fans behaved.

'The police made everyone uncomfortable,' said Shawn. 'But out of 7,000 people, there were only three arrests. I think they were either drug or alcohol-related. I would call that a success, because I heard of no incidents of extreme violence or anything like that. The whole town showed up – it was great.'

Crahan was trying not to think too hard about his band's spiralling fame. If he was prone to exaggerating the adversity which Slipknot met, then he downplayed their commercial achievements. He said: 'I still don't know how big we are. We're not selling multi-millions, but we're kinda doing what I always wanted to do. I don't wanna be credited for producing alternative music for four or five years – I wanna create a way of life. That way of life is to stick a middle-finger in the air and tell everybody to suck ass. I'm not here to make you happy – I'm here to live my life. I'm here to do what I have to do to get by, and that's all that should fucking matter.'

LAST STAND

After 18 dates, Tattoo The Earth wound itself up at Phoenix, Arizona's Manzanita Raceway on 13 August. In a once-in-a-lifetime display of band-splicing, Slipknot were joined onstage by Kerry King, who lent a third guitar to 'Spit It Out'.

'I don't get nervous to go onstage anymore, unless I'm on someone else's stage,' said King. 'I don't care if I fuck up my show, because I can normally hide the mistake. But I get some butterflies, going on someone else's stage. If I fuck up, I fuck up *their* show.'

These butterflies probably contributed to Kerry's guest contribution starting badly – at least as far as he was concerned. 'I didn't catch the drum roll right and I didn't start right,' he would admit. 'But I don't think they even had me up in the mix yet. Once I got in, it was fine.'

King was particularly impressed with his stage-eye view of Corey's now-notorious 'Jump the fuck up!' routine. 'That's one of the most awesome things I've ever seen,' he said. 'When that part came along I took my guitar off and started screaming at the crowd.'

After the show, there was no official end-of-tour party.

King: 'We tried to party real bad. But then you get bus drivers wanting to get to the next tour and people having plans you didn't know of. It's like, "Thanks for telling me!" As it turned out though, the promoter had a bar, so we showed up there and drank forever.'

While the band's barflies knocked back the firewater, Shawn Crahan reflected on Slipknot's achievement that summer. His right leg bore a tattoo of his band's logo, which had been inked by nine people, including Sid.

'Now, I believe we're road warriors,' he said. 'I know when to do my laundry, I know when to take a shower and when to take a shit. These are important things.'

If Shawn was yelling at the world to bring it on, and becoming angrier at admittedly non-specific targets, then Joey was continuing to shrink away from the band's status and everything that went with it.

During the tour, Joey had expressed serious reservations as to the size and extreme behaviour of his band. Talking to *Kerrang!*, he recalled an onstage incident in which he claimed someone almost died.

'It was very fucking close,' he said. 'I was playing my drums and thinking, "Oh my God, we're going too far!" I'll tell you this much: I've never been as scared as I am right now in my life. Seriously, this band is getting too out-of-control. I'm usually the one who wants to play the most shows that we can, and right now I'm thinking that we need to go home and let this thing seriously sit on ice. It's not getting any smaller and it's scaring me.'

Needless to say, Slipknot weren't about to be put on hold just yet. There was more work to do.

MADE IN ENGLAND

Slipknot were overtaking increasingly popular bands on the ladder of success. Come late August, at the Leeds and Reading festivals in England, they played above Rage Against The Machine on the Main Stage bill.

Joey: 'Reading was a great show. Playing after Rage Against The Machine was not easy. Especially in the UK, because they're so fucking huge. I wanted us to play *before* them! But it was another one of those challenges: rise to it, overcome it, do the best you can and see what comes of it. What came of it, was that it was one of the best shows we've ever played.'

At Reading, we were very much witnessing the changing of the guard. In all honesty, Rage seemed tired and outdated on that Sunday afternoon. Indeed, a few months later, frontman Zack de la Rocha would leave the band.

When Slipknot took to the stage, on the other hand, it was as though we'd been transported to another universe. The Clown, for one, looked fantastic, having customised his mask yet again, removing the hair for an even more malevolent effect.

'Playing Reading was definitely a highlight for me,' he would rave. 'It was a lot of fun because it was a big show and if it never happens again I was still a part of it. It was also pretty special because we played with Rage there, shortly before Zack left. I feel pretty honoured to have done that.'

On 29 August Slipknot attended their first ever ceremony, in the shape of the seventh annual *Kerrang!* Awards. The only event of its type, the Awards that year took place at the Hammersmith Palais. It saw the arrival of guests including Marilyn Manson, Blink 182, Amen, Ross Robinson, actress Britt Ekland and ... nine men in masks and boiler suits.

I was appointed to look after the band, and had arranged dressing rooms for them. They arrived in a black van with opaque windows, which was parked a few steps away from the Palais. Nearby, a bystander held a camcorder by his side. One of the band's assistants asked me to get him to switch it off, so that Slipknot could leave their vehicle.

'We don't do video,' he explained.

Exactly why was unclear, seeing as the band were masked. Still, I did as the assistant asked, discovering as I had suspected that this camcorder-clutching heretic had no interest in Slipknot whatsoever.

When the band finally emerged from the vehicle in their black coveralls, it was surreal to see them set against the back-drop of a London street. I led them in through the venue's front doors. The caterpillar chain thus formed, immediately caught the attention of the guests who were already inside, cradling their champagne flutes.

As I guided the band, along with their two road managers, their make-up girl (employed, curiously, to apply the Absu to their faces and keep it topped up) and their guest Nadja Peulen upstairs, it became apparent to me for the first time how genuinely unpredictable Sid was.

As we walked through an empty upstairs restaurant area, the DJ violently yanked a whole row of chairs backwards, one by one, eliciting indignant yells from the venue's security staff. There was no audience for this random act of vandalism, and Sid did it for no apparent reason.

When we reached the dressing room, Joey grabbed Sid by the arms and hissed: 'Just calm the fuck down, okay?'

Sid, being the scary character that he was, said nothing in reply. A few members pulled their masks up onto their foreheads and breathed. In all honesty, they looked subdued. Part of this was down to fatigue, and part of it was due to the magnitude of the event bewildering them.

'That Awards ceremony had an atmosphere I'd never been in before – it was weird,' Joey later told me. 'It was uncomfortable, in a way, because we didn't know what to expect. I knew, from the minute we sat down at the table, that something was gonna happen.'

Ah yes, the Slipknot table. It was positioned right by the foot of the stage, so that the band would have easy access to the three awards they were about to win. No sooner had they taken their seats, however, than Sid ignited something in front of him, bringing about a modestly sized fire on the table.

The interesting scenario was as follows: when Slipknot normally pulled on their masks, they were about to go onstage and tear shit up. Here, they were at an awards ceremony. A *rock* awards ceremony, granted, but a relatively stylish and semi-formal affair nonetheless.

Joey: 'There was an uncomfortable feeling of not knowing what was going to happen – whether we were gonna win anything. We didn't know what the outcome would be, so it was really weird.'

As it turned out, Slipknot bagged *Best Album*, *Best International Live Act* and last but not least *Best Band In The World*. Each time they went up to the stage, there was more chaos. The first time they left their table, the band smashed their glasses on it.

Anticipating serious trouble and/or damage, one of the venue's security guards asked me to stop the band from causing further breakages. Which would have been like asking the Pope to advertise rubbers.

'If anyone like Sid or Shawn had heard that, it would have got worse,' laughed Joey on reflection. '*Other* band's tables would have got smashed.'

The second time Slipknot won an award, they threw their own chairs up in the air, on top of the table. The third and final time, they flipped the entire thing over. It was an incredible spectacle – like watching their stage show take place *in* the audience.

Nadja Peulen, who had been sitting with the band at their table, was bemused by these sudden destructive spurts. 'Earlier that day I felt a little sick and almost didn't go to the ceremony,' she said. 'When I finally got there I really wanted to eat, but that wasn't possible because the table was gone. I had to go search for my purse, underneath the debris!

'I didn't know what they were gonna do,' she added. 'I figured we were gonna sit there, take these awards and then leave. I had no idea that they were going to be so intense. Before I got up to present one of their awards, I told Paul to make sure they didn't kick my ass when they accepted it.'

Slipknot's destructive behaviour was hugely entertaining and lent the ceremony a real edge. Yet it illustrated that they could be in danger of becoming trapped by their own stage personas. Because they were wearing the masks, they felt unable to simply step up and gratefully collect their awards – a brief speech from Corey excepted, in which he stated that he wished his grandmother had been present.

Many of the rock luminaries in the room seemed to think that Slipknot should grow up. At one point, people started throwing food at the band – which hardly demonstrated their *own* maturity. Motörhead's mainman Lemmy Kilmister, for one, would comment that he hadn't been too impressed with Slipknot's antics that night. Marilyn Manson, on the other hand, saw the band's behaviour as the entertaining fun that it was. He also claimed to feel a kinship with them, on account of their lack of admiration for Limp Bizkit.

Asked after the event what his plans for the evening were, Manson was characteristically deadpan. 'Well, I think these guys from Slipknot are going to set fire to my hotel,' he said. 'So I'm not sure.'

In a press room upstairs after Slipknot won *Best Band In The World* – and were handed Gold discs for the UK performance of *Slipknot* – they posed for pictures with their awards. They were joined for a few snaps by Ross Robinson. As they stood in front of that white screen with their producer, the gathering seemed to sum up their achievements in such a short space of time.

Joey: 'That's how that whole cycle ended. We went to the *Kerrang!* Awards, won three golden K!'s and came home. *Kerrang!* was the first magazine that gave us any press, and it ended with them giving us the award for *Best Band In The World*. How much cooler can that get?!'

That night, Joey and Shawn went to the Awards' aftershow party for a while, but the day had proved too much for them. After profusely thanking several people for their support, they headed off – Joey bizarrely complaining that he felt like there were snakes in his arms.

Nadja Peulen: 'We all went back to the hotel, and they were all really happy about receiving the awards. They were so excited, I don't think they gave all the damage a second thought.'

The following day on 30 August, the majority of Slipknot flew back home. As they were passing through LAX airport, the alleged incident happened, in which one of them supposedly collapsed. So, what was the story?

'Here's the story: that never *happened*,' Joey would insist. 'It was bullshit. We cancelled the next American tour outright, by a band vote, to write our new record. If we'd done another tour, we wouldn't have been able to write any new material and we would've been back home at Christmas. We wouldn't have written any new material at Christmas, either, because we wanted to do the family thing. So we would've finally started the album in January, which would have meant putting it out in late 2001. That's just too long!'

'Shawn was just sick on the way home,' said Ross Robinson. 'He picked up 'flu or something and the press took it to a new level. It was cheap fucking bullshit – you would never see a member of Slipknot collapse. They're too hardcore, man!'

The press were hardly to blame, seeing as their stories were simply derived from the Roadrunner press release. The truth may never be known. A few members of the band opted to stay in LA for a few days, namely Joey, Paul and Jim. I bumped into them at the Ozzfest in San Bernardino, which was once again the last night of the festival's summer jaunt.

The after-show party was thrown in association with the glossy porn company Vivid – hence the TV screens showing hardcore sex. That night, Joey seemed to have formed himself a mantra, which involved listing the journalists who had first supported the band, at various stages of their career. This wasn't even vaguely sycophantic – it was just his way of remembering where he had come from and keeping his feet on the ground.

The next night, I ran into Joey, Paul, Jim and Ross Robinson in the cosily small Whisky bar of West Hollywood's Sunset Marquis hotel. They had been drinking for a while, but thankfully no chairs were flying around the place and their table remained upright. The 'Knot men looked understandably exhausted, although Paul still mustered enough energy to chide me for not recognising him without his mask.

The following morning, they would be heading home to Des Moines. And as Joey Jordison walked out of the Marquis' foyer into the night, you could see that he couldn't wait to get home.

Upon his arrival in LA, Shawn Crahan had decided to drive back to Des Moines: driving, in a car he had bought from a friend. For him, it was a way of completing the cycle which had started with the band's road-trip to LA, before recording the *Slipknot* album.

'I left my wife and kids to make an album and be the best band in the world,' he said, 'and came back from Europe with an award stating that the fans thought we were the best band in the world. I drove all the way home to complete the cycle. I had a lot of revelations during that journey and reflected on all of it. The four European tours, without depending on radio or TV; meeting people who were forced to pay attention to the

'Knot and just depending on the kids, the way it always should be. The last two years turned out slightly different to how I planned, but they've been pretty exciting.'

Even more exciting for Slipknot, however, was the thought of what was coming next.

8
Future war

Sometimes we think that we're gonna be the first people to cross the genres of human and super-human. We've got to live up to this fucking monster we created and it's bigger than we are.
Shawn Crahan, # 6

KILL EVERYBODY ... AGAIN

What would Slipknot do now? And what *should* they do? As the band finally settled back down in Des Moines, the second cycle of their career began. Unfortunately, Slipknot's success meant that the pressures on them would be quadrupled. Every fan wanted them to come back as quickly as possible with an even better album, and every doubter wanted them to fall flat on their masks. Either way, these were the kind of expectations which could bring a band to its knees.

Joey continually made matters worse by insisting that the band's next album – rumoured to be called *Nine Men, One Mission* – would be 'ten times' better than the last. For him, the secret behind maintaining the band's momentum would be simple: do not stop.

'When we got back home, we had a couple of days off, then me and Paul started working on new material. I don't take breaks. I wanna keep writing music and working every night. I still live in the same house I've always lived at. I'm here to make music and that's it.'

For almost the past 12 months, Slipknot had been talking about their second album. During that debut US headlining trek with Biohazard, they started pre-production work on five new tracks.

'I can't wait for our fans to hear it – they're gonna shit themselves a brick!' enthused Joey. 'It's so fucking hardcore. Everyone will give us respect for this album. Even if you don't like it, you'll give us respect for being that insane.'

In November 1999, Joey revealed that the band had named a new song after one of their T-shirt back-print designs: 'People = Shit'. 'This song will completely smash you over the head,' he said. 'Imagine if The Cure became Satanic murderers and killed a small village – that's what it sounds like.'

Joey was keen to stress that the second album would be the antithesis of the commercial follow-up which bands some-times delivered. 'The album will start with intense grindcore blast-beats with four layers of black metal screams. Don't expect it to sound like Korn or Limp Bizkit!'

Whenever the band talked about Album Number Two, they made it sound like the apocalypse. As a result, they would have a lot to live up to. So what kind of pitfalls lay ahead? And which were Slipknot most likely to fall foul of?

KORN FOLLY

In summer 1996, Korn were up at Indigo Ranch, recording *Life Is Peachy*, the successor to their self-titled debut album with Ross Robinson. It had only been just over a year since that first disc emerged, and scheduling meant that the band had to work fast on this one, in order to make the October release date.

I visited the studio, for a *Kerrang!* feature. While Jonathan

Davis seemed relatively untouched by his band's ascendance from the underground, you couldn't say the same for some of his bandmates.

At one point while Davis was playing me some of the new songs in the studio's living room, drummer David Silveria walked in and abruptly turned the stereo off.

'What are you doing, man?' frowned Jonathan.

'We need to talk about this thing,' shrugged Silveria, leading an embarrassed Davis off into another room, without acknowledging my presence.

Korn hardly made things easy for *Kerrang!* photographer Dave Willis, either. Certain members of the band insisted on having their pictures taken, hip-hop style, in front of their expensive new cars. Towards the end of this short session, they became impatient, finally announcing that Willis had five pictures left to take. As he snapped, they counted down the number aloud.

While *Life Is Peachy* had its fair share of good songs, it had clearly been rushed, and wasn't a patch on the original. Korn had lost focus, and would later admit that the album was a mistake. They subsequently regained their edge and made some fine records, but that disappointing second album might have killed lesser bands.

As a consequence, Ross Robinson was terrified of the same syndrome befalling Slipknot. In early October 2000, he predicted how Slipknot might be feeling by the time he got his hands back on them. 'They'll be completely debauched-out Beavises,' he said, 'totally confused with worldly riches and fame, too fast, too soon.'

Robinson flatly refused to allow a band so precious as Slipknot to lose their innate fire. 'I swear to God, man,' he told me, 'I'm gonna take those guys and put them under my wing so hard. I'm not gonna let nobody fuck with them. The second Korn record sucks compared to the first one, mainly because they became really big and got given all this free shit. The fame and the money was starting to roll in, and this is exactly the same scenario with Slipknot. Only, Slipknot is bigger than Korn was, at the point of making their second record. So they're in deeper hell.

'Two or three want to get married, or something,' he added. 'They're buying cars and this and that. They don't know what's going on. It needs to have a nucleus again. They're having their first time-off and they're innocent. They're perfect kids that need to be protected. I've been there – I had to do a record like that and it didn't turn out so well.'

Robinson had faith, however, that he and Slipknot would create another stormer. He laughed: 'I'm going to make sure it's *only* the best record ever made, of all time!'

Once again, this was Joey-esque hyperbole which raised expectations frighteningly high.

'I know what to do,' insisted Robinson. 'I know how to inspire them and make sure they bring it back. I'll be their best friend, their guru, whatever. I'll be there for them and make sure that their management company knows how to treat them. I'll really have to do a lot of soul-searching with each guy and make sure they know that the only thing important in their lives is this fucking record. Nothing else really exists.'

At that point, Ross hadn't heard any of the new songs. He did know, however, that the band planned at least one track in the general vein of 'Tattered And Torn'.

'They have a couple of those type of things, that I want to record,' he said. 'Really experimental, fucked-up, trippy songs. Those are my favourites.

'They've had this last month to hang out and write. Joey and Paul have written seven songs so far and they've got four more. Then there's some really great older material that I want to work with. It's basically their first day back to school, after vacation. I'll be like a teacher, asking to see their homework!'

On 13 October, which appropriately enough was a Friday, Robinson went to see Slipknot rehearse their new material, at home in Des Moines. Besides hearing the new songs, Robinson made a half-hour spiritual speech for the assembled band members.

Joey: 'It was great. Ross basically said, "Look what's happened in the last year and look at what you guys need to do now." He told us to remember where it all came from. He got everyone really in touch with each other and made us get the hunger back. We worked mainly on my parts and sections of the songs. Just him being there was great – he was on fire like he always is. When I look at him, I realise how he hasn't lost touch with himself, and how he knows what we're about.

'He makes that kind of speech every day, before we play,' Joey added. 'He will go around and ask each one of us what the band means to us. He makes sure we communicate to one another what's bothering us, if there is anything.'

Robinson also voiced his concerns about history repeating itself.

Joey: 'He reminded us about *Life Is Peachy* and said, "I'm not gonna let that happen to you guys." I don't believe it will.'

The drummer told me that the band currently had eight songs completed. He made it clear that, as far as he was concerned, the next album wouldn't shock fans in a negative way.

'A lot of bands try and go to new meadows and branch out to a new crowd,' he added. 'I don't. I want to make sure that everyone who bought our last album is happy with this next one. This is new blood, new tears. A new chapter of the same type of music, but one-upped a little bit. The first album barely touched on what we can do. This is the next step.'

Said Shawn of the new album: 'It's gonna be off the fucking hook. Nobody has any idea of what we really are yet. We came out pretty blatant and easy, because the whole world is so conditioned. People grow up with a set of beliefs that they didn't even invent. You have no idea what's coming from Slipknot. Take everything and times it by ten.'

That scary multiple again. However, when Ross Robinson returned to LA, having spent a few days in Des Moines with the band, he was able to echo their gleeful predictions.

'This album will absolutely incite the full-on destroying thing inside of you to rip!' he said, nonsensically but with passion. 'It's all built perfectly. There's some good black metal influence on it. One of the songs is really weird – the chorus is full-on blast beats and the rest of it rips your head off. It's totally different from what they've been doing.'

Ross had nothing but praise for Corey's latest batch of lyrics. 'He's growing up a lot – he's becoming a man and his new lyrics reflect that. While they're rehearsing the song, he goes around the practice room throwing shit, as if he's on stage. I watch him and I laugh – he's totally freaking out and they're just working on a song!'

There had naturally been a certain tension in the room before Slipknot showed teacher their work.

'When you're writing you're extremely vulnerable,' Ross acknowledged. 'They totally respect my opinion and what I hear. But it's all good – every riff and drum-beat is from the heart. Last time, I put in input, but this time I don't need to contribute so much. I might change a little thing here and there or suggest something, but not things that change the whole song.

'They've grown into their own thing,' he confidently announced. 'The bird has been set free.'

Nevertheless, did Robinson still worry about them?

'Of *course*,' he laughed. 'I'm worried about the fact that they didn't have health insurance until about three months ago. Can you *believe* that shit? There's so many of them, I guess they just fell through the cracks.'

LOSING IT

While Slipknot have always pledged to keep all 18 of their feet firmly on the ground, misplacing the plot has also been one of their greatest fears.

In November 1999, after showing *Kerrang!* writer Paul Brannigan around Des Moines, Shawn Crahan told him: 'We're trying to stay grounded because the band is so much bigger than any one of us. It's easy to lose it in this life. On the road I see how people get fucked up, because you're playing in front of thousands of kids who worship you every night. Everyone's kissing your ass and sucking your dick. But this band will always rise to the occasion – we won't get sucked into shit like that.

'If in five years I've changed at all,' he concluded, 'I'll get on my knees and you can belt me in my fucking nose as hard as you want. You can hold me to that.'

This was a noble sentiment. The problem with it, of course, would be that if Shawn *did* change, Brannigan wouldn't get near him. He would instead be talking to a personal bodyguard.

'We come from a place where, when you get something, you really appreciate it,' insisted Joey. 'This is our gift and we can't take it for granted. Don't abuse your gift. It's not something that can be fucked with. I want it to last as long as possible, because I know it won't last. We'll go on to do other things after a while: they may suck, they may be good. Who knows? None of it will be Slipknot and none of it will have the substance of what we've already created. But we'll always remember where we came from and how hard it was to get here. That's why we'll always kick 100 per cent of your ass every night. If you keep a baboon in a cage for 24 years, the beast has got some shit to work out when it's released.'

Knowing Slipknot's general aversion to narcotics made it seem unlikely that drugs would creep into the picture.

'Out on the road,' said Joey, 'I've been seeing how people get dragged into that lifestyle so easy. You're living on a bus going from town to town, playing for thousands of kids who worship you. You're signing autographs, doing in-stores, women are throwing themselves at you. The thing is: we can still remember being down in the basement, or playing in all those different bands, 10 years ago. We remember the work ethic.'

Predictably, Shawn finds something perversely appealing in the idea of losing his mind. That's if he ever had it in the first place. 'There's nothing wrong with losing it,' he once said. 'I want to legally lose my mind, because then I can *really* do some shit up there onstage. I think we're grounded. When we went to LA to mix the album, I'd never seen so many people who didn't know who the fuck they were or what they wanted to do. I go to New York and they're all cattle. Bullshit, dude. I'm me and I don't feel like I'm gonna change, but never say never.'

In August 2000, Slipknot admitted that they would have to take steps to retain their down and dirty hunger.

'There is one word that can kill us,' Shawn told *Kerrang!*, 'and that word is "comfortable". My parents have told me that if we wanted the same basement where we wrote "Spit It Out" and "Wait And Bleed", they would move out and let us have it to write this next album. Corey has already talked to his bosses at the porn store. He's going to go back there and work, and write his lyrics just as he did before.'

'What more inspiration do you need,' noted Corey, 'than a fucking porn shop with a load of freaks rolling around!'

Losing what made them so special in the first place was clearly Slipknot's chief concern. Being from Smalltown USA had lent them a naive purity which other bands couldn't buy. The music business, with all its attendant vices and ego-stroking bullshit, represented a very real threat to their precious core. To their credit, the band recognised this and were genuinely trying to learn from the mistakes of their forerunners.

Corey verbalised the importance of maintaining a level head with hip-hop speak.

Said producer Sean McMahon in November 2000: 'The thing I hear Corey talking about is "keeping it real". He lives in a very modest apartment in the 'hood, for goodness' sake! I'm like, "Corey, you could go out and buy a house! Why are you living where you are?" And he says, "I'm keeping it real".'

MESSRS SELF-DESTRUCT

There was always the chance that Slipknot might turn on each other. Internal bust-ups were hardly rare in the rock world, where in the worst cases, even attempting to decide on the contents of a dressing room rider could cause ructions.

Slayer's Kerry King: 'The only problem I would predict for Slipknot, longevity-wise, is that there's nine of them. It don't matter how good the friendships are: it's hard enough keeping *four* guys together: they've got *nine* motherfuckers!'

Towards the end of 2000, there was confusion when a new video for 'Wait And Bleed' – which featured puppets of the band – was seemingly completed and then snatched back from MTV's eager hands. Industry rumbles suggested that this eleventh-hour change of heart was down to dissent among the band as to the promo clip's suitability. If this was the case, then Slipknot's apparent all-for-one philosophy had already started to show wear.

If anyone had words of wisdom about keeping a band on the same page, it was Kiss bassist Gene Simmons. 'Hopefully Slipknot will understand that, at the end of the day, it's never gonna be about one guy,' he told me. 'Any good commando team have to figure out the give and take – you can't always be the guy that runs with the ball. Slipknot are a wolfpack, and those things only work if they work together. The easiest thing to do is take the smallest disagreements – "You like blue, I like red" – and break the band up. Girls will break a band up, or money. There's always going to be something to argue about, and the smart ones realise that what does not kill you makes you stronger. The alternative is learning how to correctly pronounce, "Do you want fries with that?"'

Simmons' advice was simple. 'Argue as much as you want, but stay in the band. Everybody always thinks they can have another band that's gonna succeed, but they're wrong. Usually, you only have one time up to bat. Of course, musicians are delusional. We actually believe what we read.'

Joey insisted that Slipknot handled their inter-band disputes well. 'No matter how mad a band member can get at a situation, all the positive stuff comes in and it's gone. A band member can't stay mad at another band member – it just can't happen. No matter how much a guy can be a dick or be in a mood, I can't stay mad at him the next day. Or even a couple of hours later.'

If one or more members ever *did* head off into the sunset, you'd wonder how Slipknot might proceed.

Joey: 'We would continue, even though it wouldn't necessarily be the same thing. If you have someone who is no longer on the same team as you anymore, you still have a responsibility to the fans who love your music and want to buy your music. We'd have to tackle that situation when it came, but right now, I see no reason for that to happen.'

Shawn: 'It wouldn't be the same if someone left. We've been through a lot of blood, a lot of piss, a lot of poop together. If anybody goes, I'm going to be very, very upset.'

Kerry King was brutally frank about Slipknot's prospects for continuation, should they lose the odd member. 'There's so many of them, that I think you could drop a couple and it'd still be the same band. Unless it's a guitar player, don't replace them. Say you lose one of the percussion guys – don't need 'em! They're just up there for more chaos – which is cool. But don't bring some Joe Schmoe into the fold, just because you wanna have that extra guy up there.

'They all seem cool, though,' he noted. 'No-one was venting on the road – not about band stuff, anyway.'

Slipknot have also addressed the even more disturbing possibility that one of them could die in a freak stage accident.

'We would go on,' said Shawn. 'But if someone dies from something falling on him from the rafters, I'll be pretty torn-up. I'm going to be a loose cannon.'

Amen's Casey Chaos was a man only too familiar with peril. Ask him about the possibility of one or more Slipknot members coming to grief and he laughed maniacally. 'With those nuts together, of *course* there's a chance of them getting fucked up! Anyone around Sid at any time risks serious danger. Even Joey, when you get a few drinks in him – as little as he is, he's very compact. Very bomb-like!'

GOD MONEY

As Gene Simmons pointed out, the almighty dollar could always be relied upon to ruin a band – either by causing disputes or by motivating musicians in the wrong direction.

While Slipknot may have bought themselves the odd new car with their hard-earned cash – in Joey's case, a Mercedes – they claimed not to suffer from excessive greed.

Shawn: 'Money can fuck people up. My worries about money are not so much what I'm gonna get, as what I'm gonna do with it. I want to put my kids through college and give them everything I didn't have. I've never been materialistic and there's no-one in the band who's ever been materialistic. Most of my guys are happy that we have fucking insurance now, with our publishing company. It's a normal thing, but we're freaking out. It's big.

'At one point, our manager was wondering whether he should take some of the money and buy everybody an acre in Des Moines, in this suburb that's way out. I asked him why he would do that. He said, "Because I want you guys to have something." He wants to get all the acres next to each other. If we don't wanna live on our own acre, maybe we could build something in the middle of all of it, for us, in the name of Slipknot. That almost brought me to tears, because it summed up our thinking. It's not about getting money and buying a fancy car one day. We want to continue our lives safely, with a roof over our heads.'

'We care little about the money,' insisted Joey. 'We don't really make that goddamn much, since there's nine people in the band. We have a crew of 25 people just to make sure our shit sounds right, because we're playing these big shows now.'

On the other hand, Slipknot aren't about to work for peanuts. In the summer of 2000, Shawn pointed out that his band shouldn't feel guilty about earning cash.

'People want to crucify me because I go up onstage, kill myself and make money?' he said. 'I'm *glad* that my kids finally have a dental plan. With all the money I make, my wife and I are going to take all the retired elephants from the circus and zoos and get them back to where they come from, to let them die in peace. That's where *my* money's going.'

A remarkable statement from a man who was renowned for causing mayhem. Slipknot's claim to live a continuously apocalyptic lifestyle was clearly in tatters. Yet they became all the more admirable as people as a result.

Noted SR Studios owner Mike Lawyer: 'Slipknot have chosen to still live in Des Moines, when they could live anywhere they want. That was a decision they made a long time ago. I kept expecting everyone to move to LA or New York or something. But they haven't – Corey's engaged to a woman from Des Moines he's known forever.

'Part of the pull is, they're on the road so much,' he believed. 'At one point, Joey and Shawn wanted to record everything in Des Moines. Ross Robinson said he'd fly anywhere they wanted to go, because they wanted to be able to go home to their families at night.'

UNMASKED?

If Slipknot had a dollar for every time someone asked them if they will ever take off the masks, they would have an amount in the region of $834.

On the 1999 Ozzfest, Shawn told me: 'We don't wanna bite ourselves in the ass by saying never. We're big into the middle finger – we spit and we're mean. But if I got mad enough onstage and someone thought I was hiding behind the mask, I'd take it off right then and let them know that I'm not hiding behind shit.'

'There's no real reason to take the masks off,' seconded Joey. 'When we walk around without them, kids find us. We pay them respect, because they're the reason we're on the bus.'

'I don't think the masks coming off are in our future,' he decided. 'If the band got overwhelmingly big to where it was starting to alienate the old fans, we'd probably hang the masks up before we became parodies of ourselves.'

A year later, the duo were even more set against the idea of mask removal – probably as a result of everyone continually asking them.

'The masks won't come off with the Clown in the band,' Shawn told *Kerrang!*. 'I started the motherfucker and I could quit now, because I have nothing to prove to anyone. I will never let anyone kill what we represent. To change it up and take off our masks would mean that I would have become comfortable. If I get comfortable I want to die, because I don't need to be comfortable until I'm dead.'

Said Joey: 'Kids don't want to see us any other way. I won't say that you'll never see any of the band members without masks, because we might do other projects. There'll be bands after this one. But for Slipknot, shows without masks aren't on the cards.'

THE BACKLASH

In the world of rock, fans often weren't as delighted as they should be that their favourite band is suddenly also everyone else's favourite band. As outfits gained new fans, they risked forfeiting some of the older, more hardcore devotees.

'Sometimes if a band gets a lot of MTV play,' Joey told *altrockworld.com*, 'the next thing you know people are automatically not liking that band, because some schmuck down the street, who has no clue what heavy music is, is listening to it now. The part that will pave the way for us will be the next album coming out, twice as heavy as this one. Our true fans will understand and they'll stick with us.'

One example of a band who made the big crossover is Metallica, whose relatively accessible *Black* album led to cries of 'Sell out!' in 1991.

Gene Simmons: 'Metallica are just one of the great bands who have learnt that it's not enough to shake your head. Give me a statue that explodes, give me explosions, give me something, because I'm paying 50 fucking dollars for a ticket. Metallica learnt that lesson, then lost "credibility" with the hardcore fans. There's a price to say – you either stay down there with the coolest of the cool, and the masses don't come to you. Or, if you want to go to the masses, you've got to sprinkle some sugar on top, I'm sorry to tell you. You'll lose those original core fans, but you'll have the masses – you can't have it all.'

Sooner or later, Slipknot would have to address this issue. What they appeared to be hoping, was that they could become stadium-sized while not compromising at all. This would make them the first ever extreme band to achieve such a feat.

Considering the commercial allowances which the band had already made – selling the jump suits, allowing the cleaner version of 'Wait And Bleed' to radio – it appeared that further concessions surely lay ahead. If Slipknot wanted to become stadium-sized, like Metallica, they would have to record their equivalent of the *Black* album. Which is hard to imagine, but not impossible. They would probably also have to stop the onstage urination and indecent exposure. Which might be a little easier – if only to save on the dry-cleaning bills.

Slipknot had unlimited ambition, populist instincts and the will to build upon their stage-show. Whether they could make that jump to mainstream success and alienate their younger fans, while simultaneously drawing in older ones – who currently viewed them as a transient fad – remained to be seen.

Most importantly, there was also the question of whether this was what they even wanted.

STAGEFRIGHT

On 24 October, Slipknot headed back out onto the road for a string of US shows – one of which saw them hit New York's Hammerstein Ballroom on Halloween. The first show took place in Grand Rapids, Michigan. Amen also played, giving rise to drunken backstage shenanigans once again.

'We had a drinking competition,' related Casey Chaos. 'It was all of Slipknot against me. I told Joe, "Here's 300 bucks. If you're standing by the end of the night, you keep it." Sure enough, Joey passed out first. I put him on a food catering cart and rolled him back to his bus, past screaming fans. The next thing you know, he came running back to the bus and said, "Here's your money – you won, I lost!"'

On the dates that followed, Shawn introduced a number of severed, skinned cow's heads to the stageshow – at least until they rotted to such an extent that they would have been dangerous to keep around.

The Clown posed with the heads for *Kerrang!*'s Christmas cover – placing the bovine craniums on the floor in a circle around him, with Santa hats on and some tinsel. The resulting shots were so bizarre, and potentially controversial, that the photographer asked us not to credit him in the magazine.

The pictures saw Shawn further modifying his mask by installing a mohican made out of nails. The macabre starkness of the whole scene seemed to herald both The Clown's new hardline approach to life and the tone of the band's forthcoming album. We couldn't wait.

ATTACK OF THE SIDE PROJECTS

In November 2000, it came to light that almost half of the people in Slipknot were working on their own projects.

Joey was working with The Rejects again, recording an album at SR Studios with Sean McMahon.

'There's always five more songs they wanna record,' laughed McMahon. 'It's a misnomer to say I produced it – I'm definitely down there as a co-producer. At this stage in the game, these guys clearly know what they're doing and I'm just happy to have some input.'

'It's a hysterical album,' said Mike Lawyer. 'It's almost comedy. Don't think there's anything on it which could be played on the radio without being bleeped or edited.'

That month, The Rejects played two shows at Hairy Mary's, the former Safari. In the tradition of those early Slipknot dates, one was an afternoon show for under 21s. According to Mike Lawyer, these sets were fun 'free-for-alls' which saw various members of Slipknot making guest appearances onstage. Unmasked.

'The thing is,' said Lawyer, 'around here, everyone knows what the band look like. If you want to see Slipknot unmasked, go to Hairy Mary's. Half of them will probably be drinking at the bar.'

The other two projects of which Joey had spoken that summer, had not yet come to fruition.

'I've been too busy with Slipknot,' he said. 'Dan Lilker has pursued the idea with me, and I feel bad because we haven't been able to do anything.'

Towards the end of 2000, Sid signed a new record deal with 1500 Records, under the name DJ Starscream. Needless to say, the label plastered everything with the word 'Slipknot', nevertheless. Sid started work on his own album, which was expected to fully indulge his leanings towards mad jungle and techno.

'I keep asking about Sid's project,' said Mike Lawyer, 'and I don't even know where it's being recorded! He's not recording here or at any other studio in Des Moines, so he's probably recording in his own home.'

Even more intriguingly, since June, Corey had been working on his first solo album. When Slipknot's first cycle ended, post-*Kerrang!* Awards, he began recording at SR Studios with McMahon. The project had its origins in a screenplay which Corey wrote.

McMahon: 'He started developing a number of songs which he had in mind for the soundtrack of that movie, if it were made. We demoed these songs – he really wanted to present the screenplay and some of the song ideas to a film company.

'He may very well end up doing the movie,' continued the producer, 'but this turned more into an album project.'

Taylor was playing with guitarist Josh Rand – his old Stone Sour associate – and Danny Spain, the former Atomic Opera drummer who by that time played in Anders Colsefni's band Painface.

'At this point, we're mixing every Monday,' said McMahon in November 2000. 'There are eight songs that are straight-up rock. It's a pretty cool batch of tunes. One of them, that I'm most excited about is a song called "Deadweight". It's essentially a two-movement piece. The second half of the song is kinda like the Des Moines All-Stars. Corey brought in people including Anders and The Rejects' singer Dizzy.'

McMahon also enthused about a ballad named 'All I Know', and some of Corey's spoken-word rants in the vein of Alan Ginsberg or Williams Boroughs. The producer added that the rest of Slipknot had been 'very supportive' of Corey's album, which then bore the title *Super-Ego: Click Here To Enter*.

Judged Mike Lawyer in January 2001: 'The album's just phenomenal – much more commercial than Slipknot, with hints of '80s pop-metal. Some of the tracks are radio-friendly, but it still has the edge and the sound. Corey's trying to get that finished before they go back on tour.'

The most secret of all the 'Knot projects belonged to Shawn Crahan, who was insistent that his side endeavour be kept away from prying ears. Shawn had apparently started the project before most of the other band members.

'He's just been so busy with Slipknot and business stuff,' said Lawyer in early 2001. 'His project's been temporarily shelved. To me, it sounds like Nine Inch Nails with a little bit of A Perfect Circle.'

Early January also saw Slipknot being nominated for their first Grammy Award in America: 'Best Metal Performance' for 'Wait And Bleed'.

Corey's statement on the matter again reflected Slipknot's current determination to keep it real. It was also a shade eccentric. 'In the fifth century BC there was a Samurai warrior who had an interesting way of celebrating his birthday. Every year, he had what he called his "Resurrection Day", where he would give himself a new name, possibly to become another person. He did this every year, taking a new name and living his life as if that would be the last year he was alive, which in theory was correct.

'The parable here is that you never know what is going to happen as your life goes on. This year, Slipknot is nominated for a Grammy, which I consider a great honour. But you never know what's going to happen next year. My heart is thrilled that we've even been considered for this. At the same time, my brain tells me to be happy, but never *ever* be content. For content is the death of dreams. And we've got a lot of dreaming left in us.' In the end, Slipknot lost the award to The Deftones.

Around the same time, Marilyn Manson commissioned Joey to remix his 'Fight Song' track. This job became the priority at SR Studios, leading to the further delay of Shawn's project among others.

'None of these projects may come to fruition,' warned McMahon. 'Who can say? They've got a lot on their plate and I believe that, right now, their main focus is on developing material for the next Slipknot album.'

'We're just glad to be a part of it all,' said Lawyer. 'A couple of their solo projects here, if they're marketed right, could be very successful – especially Corey's.'

WAR ENSEMBLE

In December 2000, Slipknot were preparing to enter an LA studio with Ross Robinson on 3 January – which was destined to end up being 17 January. They would have two months to record the new album, as their new live schedule was due to start in March.

'The album is on fire, the imagery is on fire and the band's all ready to go out on tour,' said Shawn. 'We've been home for two months and it's been really nice to be grounded and do nothing, but we're ready to go. You know, we've been playing songs like "(Sic)" for three years but we've got new material now. The show will be an hour-and-a-half and it's going to be crazier.'

When not rehearsing with Slipknot or working on his own music, Shawn had been working on a new house in Des Moines with his wife.

'We're still fixing it up,' he said in mid-December. 'My wife and I like to construct but it takes time and I'm leaving in less than 30 days to start the album. We have a dining room now where we can sit as a family and eat dinner together – I can't remember the last time we did that religiously. I can sit down and look at my kids and ask them what they've learnt at school – no TV or anything, just a family sitting down and talking together.'

Those decent family values once again. Mere weeks beforehand, Shawn Crahan had gleefully sported a nail mohican while surrounded by dead cow flesh. These conflicting messages to the world might potentially have confused the hell out of fans. They certainly led the more traditional metal follower to accuse Slipknot of merely switching on their aggression for the press when it suited them.

The truth was simple enough. Nu-metal had brought with it a new openness in bands, which it in a sense adopted from grunge. So many traditional metal stars had been one-dimensional macho caricatures, who never let you behind their facade as they tethered screaming ladies to onstage medieval torture racks or licked their guitar necks. Ironically, given that they wore masks, Slipknot were far more willing to let you in on the widescreen picture of their lives. Joey was such an intense character that he didn't believe himself to change when he pulled on his mask. And maybe he didn't, but he was still happy to admit that he still lived with his mother. Other members like Shawn or Corey blatantly lived two lives and didn't care who knew it.

To accuse Slipknot of being deceitfully two-faced was to mistake their candour for an unintentional flash of their secret real identities. The fact was, nu-metal's figureheads were now allowed to have loved ones and talk about things which upset them, without their fans branding them pussies.

Coal Chamber's frontman Dez Fafara, for instance, spoke incredibly touchingly about his mother's cancer in late 2000. Celebrities like Dez, Korn's Jonathan Davis and Slipknot were *bona fide* 3D people, whom fans could readily identify with. They were larger-than-life and oozed star quality, but they made sense. Their sensitive sides may not have been apparent at all during shows, but sensitivity did not make for good catharsis. As Ozzy Osbourne once sagely observed, you couldn't be called Black Sabbath and sing about flowers.

The most enduring traditional metal names realised early on that you had to separate your stage self from the real you. Alice Cooper was eventually forced to draw the line between his bloodthirsty character and his real identity, Vincent Furnier. He would even refer to the two as though they were different people. Shawn's cosy family life didn't make his anger any less valid. Hence he felt perfectly at ease detailing the process of taking his kids to school, while his wife lay ill in bed.

'You have to get up at six,' he said, 'dress two kids, take them all the way across town to one school, then wait an hour and wake up the youngest and get her ready for a whole different school. Four hours later, I'm back to pick them up. So while I'm out being a fucking stupid rock star, my wife is normally taking care of the real important things.'

Sean McMahon offered an interesting perspective on Shawn Crahan's present state of mind. 'The Clown is a changed guy,' he said. 'He's kinda mellowed out quite a bit. He still has issues, but he used to be a *very* angry person. He, out of anybody in the band, has been least affected by their success – much to his credit, he's keeping a real level head about it all.'

Shawn still had anger to burn, however, when you got him started on the right subjects. The Clown's vitriol practically squirted out of *Kerrang!*'s Christmas issue.

'I'm personally taking a stand against everyone and every-thing,' he raged. 'It's not about rock 'n' roll any more – I only care about the world we live in. If we all hate the things we're hearing and seeing, then why aren't they changing? If that means me beating everyone in the face with a baseball bat from now on, that's what I'm going to do. Everybody has got an opinion, but no-one likes to talk to my face. I bite, I punch, but I listen too.'

The way Shawn talked, together with the fact that his listening pleasures of choice had lately been the noisy likes of

Today Is The Day, Neurosis and Merzbow, you could tell that Phase Two of Slipknot was definitely going to be more intense than the first. One worrying, if unlikely, possibility was that the band would overstate their anti-commercial point and unleash an album of white noise, sacrificing their identity.

'This next cycle is probably going to be the death of me,' said Shawn. 'We're *here* now. I'm not going to co-operate, I am not going to try and beat you over the head to get your attention – either you're with us or you aren't, and if you aren't I'm not going to be around you. I'm done with all the games, I'm done with all the people taking stabs at Slipknot. All I've got to say to everybody is that Slipknot is the greatest band that there has ever been in the entire world, in terms of our philosophy, our well-being, the way we present our life, the way we live our life and the way we project our life to the kids. We're extremely responsible and everybody else can fuck off. It's not the way it used to be. It's going to be *on*!'

It was initially hard to tell exactly who Shawn was railing against, as Slipknot had scarcely received many critical knocks at that point. A fair proportion of his rage seemed reserved for those who saw Slipknot as a joke and the music industry in general, suggesting that Crahan had experienced more than his fair share of behind-the-scenes schism.

'The whole industry can suck my ass. I don't have one specific guy that I'm against – I just take a look around and see all the shit that people are doing and the things they are allowing and I think people should be ashamed of themselves. I'm embarrassed by bands, by albums, interviews and total unoriginality. We're all conditioned to begin with and it's pretty hard to stay original – the only original thing about our lives is that you and I live them differently. We both live under the sun, we both live on the earth, we obey certain laws but the key is while we're all living our lives in this way we should be living them as originally as possible. Instead, it's the same shit every day, the same fucking bands. I don't feel anybody is stepping up, so fuck them all.'

In the next breath, this ever unpredictable character was

enthusing about having met The Eurythmics' guitarist Dave Stewart, at a German festival that summer. 'They were on the main stage with Sting and Santana,' he recalled. 'I was told Dave Stewart's son was a big fan of Slipknot, so I ended up getting invited to go meet him. Dave was a very, very cool dude – he knew our songs and he invited us to go watch his show. I watched the entire thing and saw that band move 70,000 people. I saw it from a different perspective. Never in a million years would I have thought that I would have met someone like that. Most people don't want to meet us, but he was acting like a human being. Musicians are just artists – people who try to change the world with their words and sounds.'

Shawn and his wife had been invited to see in the year 2001 with One Minute Silence's Yap, at his father's house in Dublin.

'I'm not sure whether we can make it,' said Shawn, regretfully. 'It was a special invite for me and my wife and we may yet end up doing it.'

They didn't, but it had been a nice thought.

LIFE EXPECTANCY

One of the things that made Slipknot so edgy and volatile is the realisation that they could fold at any time. Eventually, of course, they would and should. To paraphrase a Nine Inch Nails song: this wasn't meant to last. This was for right now.

After all, the idea of Slipknot hurling their zimmer frames around a stage was preposterous.

'It's an old Neil Young-ism,' offered Sean McMahon, 'but it's better to burn out than fade away. Knowing Slipknot, and from my talks with them, they would rather go out having peaked. Here in the Mid-West we've got Lynyrd Skynyrd and all these bands from the '70s and the '80s that are still going around, playing these bars. Those kind of guys should've given it up 20 years ago, but they're still trying to make a comeback.

'I really don't see Slipknot in that position,' he asserted. 'I could see them very easily succeeding in solo careers or some different permutation. But I don't know how long they'll be able to take this. I'll be real curious to see how the band evolves during album two. I'll also be curious to see if their stage personae are going to change.'

Whether Slipknot lasted another day or another decade, you can almost guarantee that they would be rivetingly chaotic while there was breath left in them.

'I think Slipknot's gonna be around for a long time,' reckoned Amen's Casey Chaos. 'They just blew up very quickly. Of all the bands coming out of America in the last couple of years, they'll have the same lifespan as Bizkit and Korn.'

They insist that they will know when it is time for them to stop.

'The honest-to-God truth,' said Shawn, 'is that my wife and kids will tell me. I won't listen to anyone else. My wife has got bigger balls than mine, and mine are like cow-balls. She will pull me aside, and she is my angel. I love her more than I love myself.'

'When I look out into the abyss,' Joey reiterated, 'into that sea of kids, and I think, "This ain't working," I'll know it's time to stop. I once said that after the third or fourth album I didn't see any more progress for this band, because we're so extreme. Kids were fucking pissed off at me, asking how I could possibly do that to them. I just don't wanna be one of those bands whose stuff becomes expected and stale after a while. We have to break new ground every time. I love every one of those Slipknot fans, and I'll do anything I can for them. I won't let them down with a record. But if I look out at a crowd during a gig, and I see that it's not working, that's when I'm out.'

Shawn: 'If you know Slipknot well enough to know anything about us, you'll understand that we *have* to take this a step further. This can last for a long time.'

As Corey said about the Grammy nomination, Slipknot have a lot of dreaming left to do. What they do is hard work, and potentially life-threatening. But they're having whole truck-loads of fun.

'Every day, we reinvent ourselves onstage,' said Shawn Crahan. 'Every day, I'm proud to be in the greatest band in the world. Whenever I think the band is burnt out we go again, we go harder, and new shit is invented. We're not a gimmick, we're not a theatrical presence: we're the real deal.'

THE JOY OF SLIPKNOT

One day, when Corey Taylor was a kid, he told his mother that he wanted to become Spiderman. Mrs Taylor dutifully complied with her son's demands.

He would recall: 'My mom painted my face up and made me a home-made Spiderman outfit. When she'd finished, I was the *shit*. I was running around, feeling like God.

'I got a taste of that,' he said. 'And, now, I get to do it for a living.'

Afterword by
Gene Simmons

Masks are wonderful. Women wear them all the time – it's called make-up.

When I think of Slipknot, I think of Greek tragedy. Those plays dealt with the human condition: anger and jealousy and other primal emotions. The actors used masks: sorrow was represented by one kind of mask and evil by another.

If you wear masks in the way Slipknot do – or make-up in the way that we do in Kiss – you're not hiding anything: you're just expressing yourself differently. Knights in shining armour hid themselves, because you couldn't see who or what they were. But masks can express certain feelings – from clowns to warpaint to Kabukis.

Slipknot would appear to be the new Kiss, and that's fine by me. I tip my hat to anybody who gets up onstage and does more than just strum guitars. Oasis do a fine job of strumming guitars, but unless you think Liam or Noel are wonderful to look at, there's not much going on. For something to work across the globe, it's got to be about more than 'Here's the next song from my album.' I also respect the way that Slipknot have treated their masks as self-expression. Wearing masks can be too simple. If you're going to hide your face, why not your entire body?

Those faceless, early San Francisco bands had big psychedelic lightshows, but you never knew what they looked like. Why did they even have to appear? They might as well have just turned on the sound system and played their recorded music. It can go to ridiculous extremes. But if what you're expressing is also expressed by the music, then I think it connects. If you're gonna go out there looking like Slipknot and play Strauss waltzes, it might take me a while to understand what's happening. It's certainly better to sound like Slipknot if you're gonna *look* like Slipknot. Then it's consistent and I get it: it's a fully realised dream.

To me, Slipknot are fun. Everybody thinks it's all about aggro. I think that great aggression onstage, without anybody getting hurt, is a lot of fun. The rappers who do it offstage need to get slapped around a little bit: no good comes to those guys when they take their business offstage.

If you're doing what we, Slipknot and a few other bands do, you've got to be comfortable in your own skin. Offstage, we don't have to be what we are onstage. There is certainly room for Jekyll and Hyde. Although they're opposites, they're both equally valid: one does not negate the other. You can be Slipknot onstage, but offstage it's okay to have milk and cookies. You don't have to be that person 24 hours a day.

It's very much like a boxer before he gets into the ring. Right before the fight, he might be offstage watching cartoons or whatever. But when the adrenaline kicks in, he's a different person. Physically, you can measure it: the chest cavity is larger, the heart is larger, more blood is pumping through your veins. And guess what, there's a different chemical going through you: testosterone. You're literally changing. So it's okay to be the caterpillar and it's okay to be the butterfly. But if you're trying to be either all the time, something is fake. Slipknot's kind of onstage aggression is great, like a gorilla pounding its chest and roaring – but only if it's real and coming out of some deep primal thing inside them. If you're running onstage with the pig mask but what you're *really* thinking is: 'I can't wait to go back to the hotel and watch cartoons', it may not be the right headspace. You probably need to run around the block a couple of times. Sometimes when actors need to get into a scene, they'll slap themselves in the face, so that it hurts. You've got to be in the moment.

The teamwork of Slipknot is appealing. If we have to go back to pre-historic times, I've always preferred The Beatles to The Stones. Of course, I love The Stones, but it's all about Mick Jagger. If he has an off-night, they're dead. But if John Lennon had an off-night, you could go to Paul, or George, or Ringo. I like four-wheel drive vehicles, because the ball gets tossed around and it's not all about one guy. With Slipknot, you've got a nine-wheeler and it breaks the mould.

In October 1983, our original members Ace Frehley and Peter Criss left Kiss and we washed off our make-up. We would remain bare-faced until 1996 when the guitarist and drummer returned.

Once Ace and Peter left it didn't feel right. Initially, we did try make-up with one or two new members, but then it sort of became: 'Who's the next guy gonna be: *Snake- Boy*?' It just didn't quite have the right feeling. At the end of the day, it proves that you can't just splash make-up on your face and be convincing. It has to reflect who you are. Girls understand this more than guys, because they keep fiddling with make-up until they get the kind of make-up they feel comfortable with. There's tons of different types of make-up – there's the girl-next-door make-up and of course the whore make-up, who all of us want to bring home.

With Kiss, we thought we were always gonna be all about make-up, then at some point we decided to take it off and put it back on again. The question is: what happens to Slipknot if they decide to take the masks off? Does that mean the end of the band, or does it simply mean metamorphosis? Does it mean the caterpillar becomes the butterfly – Dr Jekyll becomes Mr Hyde – but it's still innately the same thing?

Evolution should be a part of a band, if you're going to stand the test of time. Slipknot have to live out their lives, figure it out for themselves and be comfortable with it. If they feel they've taken it as far as they can, they should decide to say, 'Thank you very much, goodbye.' The ethical band – and I think Slipknot will turn out to be an ethical band – will themselves decide how long they want to go on. In Kiss, at the end of the day, we've made peace with ourselves. We've taken it as far as we can. It's almost 30 years and 80-plus million records later. That's enough.

We in Kiss don't determine who the baton is passed onto. If the people say that Slipknot will get the baton, that's who gets it. That's rightfully the way it should be. Because remember, musicians don't know anything. We barely know how to tie our shoelaces, much less how the world should work. The great unwashed masses do have a kind of a wisdom about them. They know what's what. And if they want to pass the baton onto Slipknot, then so shall it be. I've already had mine – what have *I* got to complain about?

Gene Simmons, Kiss
Los Angeles
December 2000